F
C85   Crawford, Oliver.
            The execution.

DATE	ISSUED TO

F
C85   Crawford, Oliver.
            The execution.

Temple Israel Library
Minneapolis, Minn.

Please sign your full name on the above card.

Return books promptly to the Library or Temple Office.

Fines will be charged for overdue books or for damage or loss of same.

THE
EXECUTION

THE EXECUTION

OLIVER CRAWFORD

St. Martin's Press
New York

Library of Congress Cataloging in Publication Data

Crawford, Oliver.
  The execution.

  I. Title.
PZ4.C8993Ex   [PS3553.R294]   813'.5'4   77-9225

ISBN 0-312-27422-X

For Bert

Because she is—this is.

**I am indebted to Dino Fulgoni,
Head, Trials Division, Bureau
of Central Operations, Los Angeles
County District Attorney's Office,
for his invaluable contribution.**

Certain events depicted herein are factual but the characters and events derived from them are solely the products of the author's imagination.

BOOK ONE

WINDS, FLOWERS, JOKERS, CRACKS, BAMS, DOTS and DRAGONS

1

"Oh, my God!" she screamed inwardly, "it *can't* be him!"

The unuttered denial was a reflex reaction to what had been instant recognition. Yet straining every fiber of her being to deny that it could not be *him* confirmed that it was.

His sudden appearance was dizzying. Their eyes met and she was as certain that he recognized *her*. But his gaze was unseeing and moved elsewhere to be swallowed in the babble of the lunchtime crowd. She shuddered involuntarily and braced against the cashier's counter, fearful she would faint. But the tremor abated quickly in the split second of it, and no one, not the cashier, not those seated nearby, or the two others before her waiting to be seated, noticed.

Foolish woman, she thought. If she *knew* it was him, he could *not* possibly recall her. A one-time meeting eons ago. She had retained the bitter memory of the ten most brutal minutes of her life precisely because it had been dismissed as so little to his own.

Steadied now, food suddenly anathema, she moved out into the brightness of a crisp autumn day to her car parked just outside the restaurant entrance. She whipped out of the lot and sped down the road. Only later, after nearly sideswiping an oncoming vehicle onto the shoulder of his lane, did she realize that she was driving out of control. She slowed and came to a halt before a public phone at a service station.

Her impulse was to call the others but halfway out of the car she thought better of it and eased back onto the cushioned seat to compose herself. She lit a cigarette and reined herself in with the first deep inhalation.

An attendant in soiled coveralls suddenly startled her, peering in through the open window, asking with masked concern, "Are you all right, lady?"

She smiled wanly. "I'm fine, thank you."

"Sure?"

"Yes. I felt a bit faint but it's passed."

"There's a ladies room if you care to——"

"Thank you. You're very kind. I'm fine."

"Okay. Must be the smog," he said and returned to the pumps.

"I'm fine," she thought ironically. "I was fine until minutes ago. Now everything is changed."

The day had begun typically. Up at the usual hour and the ritual breakfast of coffee and buttered toast with Gil, grunting themselves awake through second cups. Then going their separate ways, he to his job and she to the small boutique she ran on Ventura Boulevard just off Laurel Canyon in the Valley.

She dawdled over bills until Valerie, her young assistant, arrived. Then she left for Malibu Beach to meet with the artist whose metalwork creations had been recently displayed at the outdoor arts and crafts festival held twice yearly on the streets of Westwood, the home of the University of California Los Angeles campus. She had admired his wizardry in fashioning such intractable articles as wire hangers, assorted hardware and automobile parts into graceful compositions and had offered to showcase them at the boutique. An agreement was reached, and she was returning to fulfill it.

She drove leisurely through winding Topanga Canyon Road and, spur of the moment, decided to stop at Papa Grossman's restaurant midway between Malibu and the Valley. At ease with herself and the world in general, she thought nothing more than to have a light lunch and continue on.

Then *him*.

And knew with virtual certainty that this day would alter forever all the days to come, for it brought back the terror of those other days, long submerged, almost forgotten, now inadvertently resurgent with ice cold recall.

Breathing evenly now, could she be all that certain it was him? It had been so many years and life experiences ago. Should she tell Gil? Tell the others? What's the point? It's over and done.

Or is it ever?

The women would not meet until Wednesday. From now till then there would be time to think about it. If she still believed that she had seen Wilhelm Gehbert in the person of Papa Grossman, she would confide in them, and if they were curious, take it from there.

On the other hand, was she being unduly melodramatic? Very likely it had been a throwback recall, a trick of the mind and eye, triggered by a gesture, a look, whatever, having no substance whatsoever in the present. Upon reflection, perhaps she had not seen at all what she thought she had.

She did not for one second believe that.

She stubbed out the cigarette and drove out of the station.

Five women.

They played Mah-Jong every Wednesday night. The game was in its twentieth year. Also, they had been raped by the same man. The forced invasion of their bodies by this man (and others) was perhaps the least of indignities endured and survived. The clitoris of three had been amputated.

They were younger then; the youngest fifteen, another eighteen, two were twenty, the eldest twenty-two, mothers and grandmothers now. They had been five of many thousands, and they did not know each other at the time. It was not until a later time far from the original scene that they met. Their collective trauma served as introduction, but it was their love for the brightly colored tiles that united them. Thirty years later their weekly Mah-Jong game would become the operational base to avenge themselves upon their tormentor.

Three of the women were Jewesses; Freda Friedkin, Hannah Epstein and Sophie Langbein; Gertrude Simon was half-Jewish, but she had been as zealously victimized as if full-blooded for the sin of her mother's unfortunate birth. It did not help that her father was only a notch up on the vaunted Third Reich racial scale, being a member of another persecuted minority, Jehovah's Witnesses. Elsa Spahn was the lone Aryan and a Catholic, the resident gentile, affectiontely dubbed the token *goy*.

8

Elsa's sudden statement uttered in the midst of discarding a tile impacted like grease spattering on a griddle.

She had said, "I saw Gehbert."

It was simply stated. But she had undergone five days of turmoil preceding the statement. This was her week to hostess the game, and if she was ever to say anything it was now.

"It was Gehbert," said Elsa, her voice whispery and slightly accented. She was the youngest, diminutive, and looked to be the frailest, which was deceptive. She was sturdy as an oak.

Silence.

Then Hannah Epstein, tending to stoicism and arthritis, broke it, her voice betraying no emotion.

"Wilhelm Gehbert?"

Elsa nodded.

Then Sophie Langbein, fat Sophie, soft-spoken, ventured incredulously:

"The *doctor?*"

"That's not his name now," said Elsa. "He's Papa Grossman. He runs or owns a small tucked-away restaurant under that name in Topanga Canyon."

"How do you know Grossman is Gehbert?" From Gertrude Simon who squinted a great deal. She was fighting cataracts, worse in one eye than in the other. There was nothing she could do about the condition until the film matured, and then they would be removed.

"If you saw him you'd know. You'd just know, wouldn't you?"

"But that was over thirty years ago," said Sophie.

"I know. Still."

It hung between them.

Elsa said, "You want to hear?"

They wanted to hear.

"I was driving in from Malibu over Topagna Canyon and stopped for lunch at a place called Papa Grossman's. I'd never been there before."

"I think my sister-in-law told me about it," Hannah chimed. "Good food. Go on."

"Yes. Very woodsy, gingham cloths, sawdust on the floor, atmospheric. Gemutlich. *He* was there."

"What does the bastard look like now?" asked Freda, speaking for the first time. She was the eldest and most cosmeticized of the group.

"The same. I mean, a man doesn't change that much. Loses hair, puts on weight. But the expression. The same watery blue eyes. That doesn't change."

Freda again. "A prick like that lives forever." Among themselves the women privately referred to her as Foul Mouth Freda Friedkin. She did not seem to mind.

"And gets away with murder," Gertrude amened. "And worse."

Hannah, "Did you talk to him?"

"Oh no," said Elsa. "I almost fainted. But the moment I saw him I *knew*." She got up and helped herself to a cup of coffee.

"If it is him," Sophie said tentatively, "then..." But she did not know what then.

"Suppose it is him," said Hannah, "is it something we want to think about?"

"Hannah dear, does it ever go away?" Gertrude said poignantly.

"I only mention it. Such a shock."

"If I told Leon he'd strangle the no-good—" Hannah struggled for an apt word to complete the thought.

"Son of a bitch," Freda offered succinctly.

Leon was Hannah's husband and after all these years, three children and four grandchildren later, including Hannah's assorted aches and pains, was still an intensely jealous man; of past lovers, fancied and real, guiltily possessive of her because he'd escaped her camp experiences. His devotion was occasionally irksome, but she considered herself a fortunate woman for it. He was also a half head shorter.

"What do we do? Follow up or forget?" asked Freda.

"Who forgets?" From Gertrude.

Freda continued, "We've got to make sure. I think we all ought to look at him."

"Why?" From Sophie. "I mean, what's the good?"

"You don't have to do it."

"But what good will it do now?"

"Don't go."

"I'll go," she said surprisingly. "But then I think we should go separately."

Freda completed the thought. "Good idea. That way we won't influence each other."

Gilbert Spahn came out of the bedroom, Elsa's husband. He yawned and stretched.

"Oh, shut your big mouth," said Freda.

Gil grinned. "I wish you gals would play on a football night. There's crap on TV on Wednesday nights."

"Go to a movie," said Hannah.

"Crap at the movies. Any good jokes, Freda?"

"Sure," Freda said, "two queers had a fight at a bar so they went out into the alley and exchanged blows."

He laughed. No one else did, but he assumed they had heard it before.

"Guess I'll go for a walk."

"Be careful," said Elsa.

"Don't get mugged," said Gertrude.

"Don't get raped," said Freda.

He crossed into the vestibule, opened a closet door, put on a jacket and went out. The women regarded the tiles unseeingly. Then Freda spoke.

"Is it agreed? We all look. We should all agree that Gehbert is Grossman, or Grossman Gehbert. If even one of us doesn't agree that it is the fucker, then we'll forget it."

"Forget what?" asked Sophie, chewing into her lip.

Freda shrugged. Nobody answered.

"Let's get started," said Hannah.

The tiles were mixed and stacked along the racks. The game resumed.

"One crack."

"West."

"Two dot."

"Call."

Finally Elsa said, "But suppose that we all agree. Grossman is Gehbert. So? What then?"

"What then?" Gertrude repeated dumbly.

"Yes. What do we do then?"

They did not know. They honest to God did not know.

The decision by the five women to kill the Butcher of Birkenau would come later.

3

It was Gertrude's turn to hostess the game on the following Wednesday.

By then three of the four women had visited Papa Grossman. Sophie had gone with her husband, who enjoyed German cooking, Hannah with her husband, who did not, and Gertrude, whose husband speared everything on his plate that did not move.

Before the game Elsa asked if the others had been there. Freda said not yet, she hadn't seen the fucker. Freda was a widow, manless, and was fearful of going out at night without an escort. She had to plan her evenings in advance. Nothing more was said and would hold until next week.

On Monday following, Freda cornered her granddaughter, and together they went. Vicki was pert and ingenuous. She adored her grandmother, so different from those of her friends. *Their* grandmothers appeared ancient, waddling sideways down steps and clutching handrails in the manner of old people. In the manner of young people thirty-five was old, and past fifty was another country.

Her grandmother was an exception. Vicki did not know her age (fifty? fifty-five?), but it did not matter. She looked years younger, with a vitality that belied chronology. Importantly, they communicated. Grandma was well groomed, another seeming characteristic of old age being carelessness of dress; her wit and

13

laughter quick albeit boisterous. Grandma swore like a soldier in heat, although whenever the family gathered, she was admirably circumspect. Occasionally, however, when walls were thought to be better insulated and the little ones out of earshot, Grandma's propensity for profanity would assert itself. It was a source of embarrassment to her mother, Freda's stepdaughter, whose own language was only sporadically blue, that Grandma's vocabulary was not more benign as befitting a grandmother.

Vicki, a good student in her first year in college who neither sniffed, smoked nor drank and still a virtuous eighteen and given to careful language, nonetheless felt that this was an endearing and young quality in her grandmother. They exchanged confidences, for her own mother was often too harrassed with daily chores and a younger sister and a brother to give her the attentive ear of a loving heart.

Vicki was on a nostalgia kick harking back to the black and white glamor of Bogart and Tara, preferring the adventuresome search for a Maltese bird, a jailbreak and Mom to Dustin Hoffman, who was a bit too relevant. Yesterday enabled her to endure today. She was, however, aware that her grandmother's yesterday was far removed from celluloid adventure; that Grandma had undergone great tragedy in Nazi Germany.

As a child, affectionately hoisted to Grandma's lap, she had caught tantalizing glimpses of Grandma's right wrist. A number was tattooed on the underside. It was usually covered by a long sleeve or heavy jewelry. Its imprint was recorded as indelibly on the mind of the young girl as it was stitched onto the skin of the older woman.

B 366753.

She longed to learn more about the horror of the brand, although it was obvious why the number had been affixed. She assumed her grandmother was sensitive on the matter since, despite the warmth between them, she did not ever introduce the subject. Since Grandma did not bring it up, she did not, but she hoped that one day Grandma would bring herself to talk about it.

For now Vicki was content. She was not boy-crazy, although

well liked by both sexes. Home was placid, and these excursions with her grandmother—for they often sought out places together—were a welcome relief from her studies in child care. It was fun to be with Grandma, but ever since entering the restaurant she appeared to be abstracted.

"Any special reason why we've come here, Grandma?"

Papa Grossman's was pleasant and spacious. Its dark wood beams contrasted white plaster walls punctuated by lead-beaded bottle-bottomed windows in the Alpine tradition so dearly beloved by the denizens of sunny Southern California. It was nestled in an unobtrusive shopping center and was the flagship attraction among the several small shops in a green pocket of eucalyptus and pine.

The center's dimensions were reasonably harmonious. Which is to say it did not appear to be gouged out of the land but rather gently set upon it. Included were a pharmacy, a papa-and-mama food store, a cleaning establishment and a hardware store. The parking lot was blacktop, long since grayed and fissured and perpetually layered with pine needles and eucalyptus leaves. The center had been constructed just prior to the Korean War and with the patina of age exuded a certain tacky charm.

One beat a path to Papa Grossman by way of a winding road off the Valley side. With little or no advertising, mostly word of mouth, it had over the years built a steady patronage. It maintained the esteemed hallmarks of a good restaurant: food tastily prepared and ungrudgingly served, augmented by an artistic wine cellar in a relaxed environment for prices that made sense. It took a bit of doing to get to it, some areas and inhabitants of Topanga Canyon still retaining the last remnants of its original wild life state, but most agreed it was worth the trip.

"I mean it's real nice," added Vicki when her grandmother did not reply. "I mean Black Forest cliché, right?"

Freda nodded, ah yes, real nice, but she had been as removed from the Black Forest as a Brooklyn inhabitant from the Gullahs of West Virginia, and thought:

Ah liebschen, why indeed are we here? You are such a lovely

product of your time, a love-child, sheltered and cocooned, and despite the horrendous time that is now, growing into unsullied young womanhood. But if you cannot understand the vagaries of your age, how can you be expected to understand the nightmare insanities that were mine.

She loved this child. All the more perhaps because she had never borne one. Could not. The child she might have had, denied to her by a ravaged and desiccated womb.

She focused inwardly and back in time... in a previous life *they* had come, heavy cleated and madly arrogant... first Papa taken... then Mama and Ernst torn away... never to be heard from again... madness, pain, incomprehensible... weeping until the dryless ducts burned... numbered and drained of the life-force, she should have perished with them, yearned for the release, even courted it... but deeply within some stubbornly resistant spark with an undaunted will of its own, nurtured by a capricious fate, would not yield... By what rhyme or reason that only she of all those near and dear had endured, she could not fathom then or fathom now.

Perhaps the answer was here, thirty-two years later, over sauerbraten and May wine.

"Are you expecting someone, Grandma?"

"What?"

"You keep looking around."

"Oh," Freda said.

She had hoped not to be obvious in her curiosity. She was certain that anticipation would color the expectation, and forewarned, she had placed herself on guard against it. It seemed to her too remote; of another time and another place, over a great void of what was then, for any part of it to be again.

Four people entered. Two men, two women. One of the men, by an odd turn of the head, gave her a sudden pang.

Nate.

Then he turned full face in her direction, turned again and the illusion evaporated.

Dear, loving and gentle Nate.

When they met, he was twenty years her senior and three years a widower whose wife had succumbed to cancer. There were two children, Jeanette and Robert, only fifteen and sixteen years younger respectively than herself. When she'd married Nate and officially assumed surrogate motherhood, they were already grown and more like a younger sister and brother.

She recalled the period prior to meeting him. Strangely, she could remember with clarity the inhumane acts perpetrated upon her and others: the whippings, the rapes, and starvation and experiments. But her delivery from Birkenau was hazy. Enslavement was a comparatively short period of her life, but the experience was so oppressively total that it had overwhelmed any previous period and the immediate one following her liberation. It was as if living in a dark room, forever it seemed, that when thrust into the sunlight of release, a vertigo so dazzling ensued it reduced her to a state akin to somnambulism. It would take years for the bends of the mind and spirit to ebb.

Through a cascade of bewildering events; release and wanderings, an infamous number replaced by a restored name. There was hope again and renewal, and smiles again. Yes, smiles and helping hands and hearts, from Jews and non-Jews alike; a war over and the world to be better for it (hah!); a relative located in Los Angeles, who sent for her, and across a bobbing ocean to the fabled city of a fabled land, to a new life with a discovered portion of family on her mother's side.

"Look! Rachel's daughter. A scarecrow. She'll fatten. A beauty under those skin and bones. You'll see. A millionaire she'll marry!"

A millionaire she did not marry, but true to prophecy, the pendulous flaps that were her breasts rounded and the flesh firmed and Freda Baum, daughter of Rachel, did indeed flower into a beautiful woman. Outwardly she was provocatively but innocently sexual, exuding a come-hither quality that drew many men. She did not reciprocate, in fact, could not bear their touch.

She was certain, she believed, to remain a spinster, and it did not disturb her.

Until Nate Friedkin.

He was not moneyed but his coin was in the human spirit. A giving man, a supporter of causes, white and black, Jewish and non-Jewish, whether in Germany or Georgia. That is, as much as a furniture salesman can give and still support a family.

He was a cousin thrice removed, and they met at a family picnic. He was the son of Russian immigrant parents, who'd bootstrapped himself out of a Chicago slum to the managership of a furniture store.

Gently, never pressing, aware of the difference in their ages, he prevailed upon her, with deep religious conviction, to live for the future. It was God's will that she had survived. So where was God while the chambers hissed? By what reasoning in the Grand Design of All Things the inclusion of cockroaches, crab grass and cancer?

He was displeased by her blasphemy but did not remonstrate. He would prove to her by word and deed that not all men were consumed by male fires and bestialities. Slowly, with kindness and understanding, she came to depend upon him. He was family and friend and ultimately husband and timid lover.

There was no passion between them. He understood and was undemanding. He would not come to her until she beckoned.

A week after they were married she did so, earnestly hoping to puncture her mental hymen. He was as good as his word, gentle and caressing, but merely adequate as a lover, fumbling like a schoolboy. She did not let on. She was grateful that there were only infrequent couplings and would simulate the throes. It served for her and pleased him. In his later years, as his mild drive diminished, there was no sexual demand. She did not miss the contact. In twenty years of marriage she did not experience a single orgasm.

He provided well, and she cared for his children, kept his

house neat, cooked the meals and kept herself well groomed so that he was proud of her, his one vanity—this old buck with the voluptuously young wife.

They saved enough to buy the furniture store, a sometime *schlock* operation; but in keeping with his essence, it was upgraded into a fine quality operation. With Jeanette and Bob grown and married, she became involved with its routine and learned how to keep its books.

An irritating factor between them, it had to be admitted, was her profanity. She could not remember when she'd first embarked upon colorful invective but, living as she did for the moment, it was the language of the moment, and it came as easy to her as inhalation. She knew Nate did not like it. He was a controlled man and vented himself with nothing more profane than an occasional Victorian "damn." If it seemed to her that her husband was out of step with his time, which was an appealing aspect to him, she tried earnestly not to displease him and would tamp its offensiveness in mixed company, so that molehill remained a molehill.

As he lived so he died. Quietly and without warning in his sleep, the way he hoped it would be, to spare her the agony of a lingering illness.

Thank you, Nate, thank you for the healing years. For restoring my faith in humanity, an oasis of a man in a parched and damned world. I could not buy your belief in a just and humane God, but a good word could be made for Him for having brought us together. And further I thank you. We did not have children, but it was a joy to know and raise your seed out of another woman and to have brought into my life a Vicki.

And now there was melodrama. Papa Grossman appeared out of the kitchen.

He nodded amiably to the customers, some who seemed to know him, chatting, pulling up a chair. Monday was the least trafficked of the nights, there being about twenty people at various tables. From the distance he looked almost comedic in his mushroom cap and stiff white jacket. Freda's immediate impression was that it would be impossible to attribute villainy to anyone in chef's garb. She looked away and concentrated fiercely on the sauerbraten.

Then he was close and he spoke.

"Enjoying yourself, ladies?" His voice was mildly accented and bland in origin and modulated.

"Yummy," Vicki nodded vigorously.

"Good," he replied, pleased.

Freda looked up. Eyes met eyes. His were the color of faded denim in a face remarkably unlined. Other than the soulful eyes the rest of his features were unspecific. Surprisingly he was not fleshy, as are many cooks. His sideburns were thick and speckled with gray. He was neat, exuding no kitchen odors, slightly under six feet tall she judged, and carried himself well.

Whoever he was, time, as with her, was not a spoiler.

Their glance held. She smiled below her eyes, twitching a cryptic Mona Lisa grimace. Then he nodded with a barely perceptible movement of his head and returned to the kitchen.

"Grandma—?"

Eyes... her father's, mother's, brother's... those of the countless doomed... a collage of cue ball eyes popping out of their sockets in skeletal faces...

"Grandma. Is anything wrong?"

"What?"

"You look like you've seen a ghost."

Freda drew a deep breath to compose herself. The flush left her face, and striation eased from her lips. She reached for her wine glass and sipped and felt her pulse returning to normal. Then she reached over and patted Vicki on the back of the hand.

"I'm fine," she said. "For a moment there... something crossed my mind... not important." Then sprightly, "What would you like for dessert?"

On Wednesday night they convened at Hannah's.

The bridge table was perched squatly in the living room; the tiles, dragons, flowers, winds, bams, cracks and dots, numbered one through nine, were mounded in the center, and the game card for each player rested before the preset racks. There was also a hostess spread of coffee (or tea or Sanka or soft drinks), two kinds of cheeses, two kinds of crackers, small thin-sliced sandwich rye, and Danish, principally to accommodate Gertrude's sweet tooth.

The five women milled loosely in pregame chitchat—about their husbands' jobs, the latest trivia about children and grandchildren and the assault on their purses at the supermarket. Although they played religiously one night a week for twenty years, they were not truly intimate, not even on the basis of their pre-Mah-Jong traumas. Until the Grossman|Gehbert business, they never discussed their early lives. It had been a door closed. The same with discussing the present in depth. It was a tacit rule: THOU SHALL NOT BURDEN OTHERS WITH THY TROUBLES. I HAVE COME TO PLAY.

Actually, they knew a great deal about each other without exchanging confidences, gleaned from this tidbit or that, however superficial, by weekly proximity and coffee osmosis. Whose husband was doing well or poorly, and with the advance of years an expanding litany of aches and pains, and whose kids

21

were good and kind and whose were shitty. Between them there were nine children and sixteen grandchildren.

Three resided in homes (Elsa, Gertrude, Sophie) and two lived in apartments (Freda, Hannah) of a general middle class mien. Their husbands' occupations comprised a CPA (Elsa's), a *schmateh* (ladies' ready-to-wear) salesman (Sophie's), metal salvage worker (Gertrude's) and a pharmacist for a drug chain (Hannah's).

Freda was widowed. The furniture store left by her husband was now run by his son and his daughter's husband. It provided an ample living for both families and a monthly stipend for Freda, who occasionally assisted with the bookkeeping. With the modest sum plus a small estate left to her by Nate, she was reasonably comfortable in a second floor apartment in an older building located in the West Wilshire section.

It would have been cheaper to live with the son or daughter, or to rotate them. But despite avowals of their love, she knew their invitations to share bed and board with them were half-heartedly extended. Also, however dutifully affectionate her grandchildren were, they were not only zestful but occasionally obnoxious. Living with a child meant doubling with a grandchild. Not for this loving grandmother. Distance lent enchantment and gratitude for periodic baby-sitting service, and she was content to keep it that way. She respected her independence as did her son and daughter, with whom she got on quite well.

Hannah produced two dice. As the hostess for the evening, she automatically assumed the favored east position to break the wall and take the first tiles as the other four women rolled for the three seats remaining. The combination adding up to the lowest total stayed out while the game was finished, and east relinquished the chair to the waiting player. That was Gertrude, who solaced herself during an impatient wait by munching on the danish.

Freda's total was the highest, and she was the last to draw tiles. She shuffled them into a single row lined on the rack and studied them.

"A crappy hand," she said, and then added, "I went to Papa Grossman's."

The others looked up, suspending the play.

"That means we've all seen him, doesn't it?" said Hannah. "So what do we all think?" She turned to Elsa. "Elsa?"

"You know what I think."

Gertrude flicked a crumb from the corner of her mouth. "I agree. Grossman is Gehbert."

"Or Gehbert is Grossman," said Sophie.

"Same thing," said Hannah, "I think so too."

"Think? Aren't you sure?" asked Elsa.

"I mean, yes. I suppose so."

"Can't you be surer than that?"

"I guess as sure as I can be."

Elsa turned to Freda. "Well, Freda?"

Freda spoke with a measured cadence. "I am absolutely certain that Papa Grossman is none other than that piece of syphilitic afterbirth, Doctor Wilhelm Gehbert. I could vomit just thinking that he is still alive and well and living in scenic Topanga Canyon."

There was a moment's silence. Only the muted sounds of the radio turned to a station that featured semiclassical music and oldies filled the room.

"That's it," said Elsa.

"What's it?" said Hannah.

"We're agreed who he is. So the question is, What are we going to do about it?"

"Do?" said Hannah. "Do?" As if challenged, feistily.

"Hold it," said Freda. "As much as I believe that Grossman is Gehbert we must satisfy outselves beyond a shadow of a doubt that that is the case."

"I don't understand," said Gertrude. "We're all agreed and you just said ——"

"I know," said Freda, "I am playing devil's advocate. Consider this: one always reads about—it is said that for each one of us there is somewhere in the world—a twin. If there is even the barest possibility that that is or could or might be the case——"

"You believe that?" asked Elsa, her delicate features reflecting agitation. "Do you?"

"No, dear Elsa, I do not," said Freda. "But I think that every possibility should be explored to rule out any mistaken identity whatsoever."

"Right," said Hannah, nodding. "Right."

It was very quiet. The radio wailed a heartbreak ode to unrequited love. Then Freda spoke again, hushed.

"Another possibility. Consider this as well. If, for the moment, we abandon the twin theory—suppose Wilhelm Gehbert is dead?"

They started to babble through each other, but Gertrude raised her hand in the manner of a teacher gesturing for order in gentle admonishment. "Girls."

"Consider," Freda continued. "Any time through the years Gehbert had died. And the man we are all so certain—yes, I believe—to be Gehbert is *not* Gehbert."

"I've read stories," Sophie spoke up. "Nazis masquerading as other people. Even as rabbis. Even to live in Israel. So he does not have to be dead, and Grossman is really Grossman."

"You are confusing me," said Elsa feeling that something was getting away. "First, we are convinced he is Gehbert, and now you say——"

"That's right," said Freda. She rose from her chair and paced the room like a courtroom attorney. "We know what we feel. But is it enough? Consider further, these possibilities. Grossman *is* Grossman, an unfortunate look-alike whom we believe after *thirty-two years* to be Gehbert. But Gehbert is dead after all these years, dead under his own name, or dead under someone else's name, or somewhere still alive under his own name or alive under another. Or in any case, dead or alive, he cannot be located. And in the extreme, Grossman is not Gehbert."

"What are you saying?" said Gertrude, "that our memory plays us tricks?"

"A distinct possibility. Our senses betray us."

"Each one of us?"

"I did not go to Papa Grossman's with predisposition," Elsa was softspoken. "Yet I was overwhelmed. I saw what I saw."

"Yes," Gertrude agreed. "I too went and as agreed there had to be no margin for doubt. Otherwise I would not believe. That was the case. I went. I saw. I believe."

"That is still subjective," Freda said. "For the moment I am going past my feelings. But can what I have said be ignored?"

Elsa was shaken. "I do not know what to think."

"All right," Sophie said solemnly. "What Freda poses makes sense. What we feel and think and *know* is not the final word. It would be disastrous to attribute guilt to an innocent man. So," she worked her lower lip furiously, "we must find out what is known about Wilhelm Gehbert to this moment."

"Thank you, Sophie," said Freda. She closed her eyes and pinched the bridge of her nose and wiped away an imaginary fleck from the corner of an eye.

"Well," said Gertrude, "I suppose if I wanted to know about Martin Bormann, the latest on him, it could be learned."

"Yes," said Freda opening her eyes. "I suppose so. I imagine the information is available."

"But if we learn that we are wrong," there was a quaver in Elsa's voice, "then that is the end of it, right?"

"The end of it, of course."

"Hold on," said Hannah. "Let's go back. It is confirmed. Grossman is Gehbert. What then?"

"Turn him in," said Elsa.

"To who?"

"The government."

"Which one?"

Sophie, who had been thoughtful through most of this, said, "Ours? The United States?"

Freda made a mirthless sound. "Why should the United States care about crimes that happened on foreign soil over thirty years ago?"

"The United Nations, you think?" Even as she said it

Hannah knew that was naive.

"The United Nations!" Freda could not conceal her contempt. "After Arafat?"

"Germany," Hannah persisted. "They are still trying war criminals, no?"

"Extradition," offered Gertrude hopefully.

Sophie shook her head. "Extradition is requested, not offered."

"There may be a statute of limitations," said Freda.

"On murder?" From Elsa.

"*We* say murder. But can he officially be charged with murder? The legalistics would be fierce."

"Murder, murder," Sophie said softly in a singsong wail.

"It wouldn't be simple everyday murder. This is so-sorry-it-happened-please-don't-remind-us-go-away kind of murder. Even Willie Brandt, a good man, an anti-Nazi, said that it was time to forget."

There was a chorus of "no's!" and Hannah cleared with, "Couldn't we contact Simon Wiesenthal?" She was referring to the man who had become the symbol of hope for a haunted generation in the apprehension of Nazi criminals and was best known for his discovery of Adolph Eichmann's South American hideout.

"Yes," Freda agreed, "And hope that he can tell us something. But I have heard that it could take months. If he can or does answer at all, depending how important Gehbert ranked in his crimes."

"That would be true of any inquiry we made," said Gertrude. "Including the Yad Vashem," a reference to a memorial of the Jewish victims of Naziism and a documentation center on Naziism in Israel.

"Even so," said Hannah, "I must believe, after all is said and done, that he would be tried. Surely in Israel."

"Perhaps. But Gehbert is no showpiece like Eichmann. His trial was to remind the world of the horror and tragedy of the

Holocaust. And the truth is the world does not give an owl's fart for Jews, dead or alive. Preferably dead."

"Ridiculous," Gertrude suddenly said. "For over thirty years we did not concern ourselves with Wilhelm Gehbert. Now we are impatient to verify him."

"I suppose you're right," Elsa said unhappily.

"Shut that damn thing off!" Sophie suddenly cried.

The radio was playing "The Blue Danube." The others were arrested by her outburst.

"'The Blue Danube.'" Sophie's voice broke. "I can still see the lines, marched off by it to the crematoria. It played and played, the lines were endless. God! It was ghoulish." She composed herself, then added, "Not the least of the tragedies. A beautiful song forever ruined."

"No," Hannah said stoutly. "Strauss has endured. Hitler cannot prevail. Not now, not in my living room."

Sophie did not persist, but her hands shook and she stilled them by reaching for a cracker. The last haunting strains played out and were followed by a raucous commercial, welcome in relief. The women seemed spent.

"Bullshit!" Freda exploded. "One believes or one does not believe. The man is Gehbert. Allowing for thirty-two years he can be none other. Older, heavier, whatever. It *is* him."

"Fine," said Hannah, "as far as it is humanly possible to determine that—after thirty-two years—in my case, thirty-one, yes. We are five—young girls—who pass through Birkenau within two years of each other, 1943 and 1944. We are five of many thousands. We do not meet, we do not know each other, and we are spared. We come to America. To Los Angeles. We are many hundreds, and now we meet at the '38 Club. Our experiences bring us there, but we do not talk about them. Instead we find we enjoy Mah-Jong. We form a group. Once a week for twenty years we play. We are mothers now, and grandmothers. The past is the past, we think. Then! We see a man we are convinced is—is Die Bestie—!"

She faltered slightly and continued. "Yes, it is outrageous, but not any less now than then. It is true. It is him."

A silence followed, and then Freda said, "So?"

Then Elsa said, "How old would you say Gehbert is?"

"What difference does that make?"

"How old?"

"He was then—what?" Gertrude puckered her lips. "Thirty? Thirty-one or -two? I guess he'd be in his early sixties."

"Sweet singing Jesus," said Freda. "By the time he'd be identified, caught, turned over and tried, the bastard could die of old age."

Gertrude shook her head ironically. "Or we."

"Unless—" Elsa started to say, stammered and stopped.

The seed, deeply imbedded, thrust and nurtured forward, transmitted to the others, unstated but palpable between them. Silence was fertilizer and irrigation. Even the usually uninhibited Freda was quiescent.

There was no sound in the room save the radio exuding something soft and schmaltzy.

Hannah sighed. "Let's play."

The large parlor was dark as her mood. Elsa peered through the glass doors overlooking the patio to the kidney shaped swimming pool. It lay unshimmering, turquoise translucent, like a giant jewel in a bed of velvet-green lawn. Rimmed at the far edges with palms, cypress and fruit trees. Looked beyond the gaunt shapes devoured by the maw of a moonless night, unseeing.

It was five minutes to midnight, and she could feel the dread of the next twenty-four hours. She abhorred liquor but tonight, and early into the morning, she would drink. She had started and was on her way to becoming drunk, calculatingly, stuporously drunk, until oblivion would overtake her where she fell. But there would be no relief. Anguished memory would sear, she knew, even in her deepest sleep.

Tomorrow was her birthday.

Until her eleventh birthday every birthday as far back as she could remember had been a convivial family affair. But the heinous events of *that* night of that day had turned joyous celebration into everlasting torment. Every birthday since had been an annual descent into hell.

It had caused her first menstrual flow and doubt of God. Until that night God had been as loving and meaningful as Mama, Papa, her sister Helga, a year older, and her beloved uncle Karl, Mama's brother. Uncle Karl was a priest. Tall, over six feet,

29

trim of body, with his thick hands constantly in motion whenever he spoke in a richly resonant voice, his kindly hazel eyes twinkling in their nest of crow's feet, even as he sermonized, patient and compassionate, personifying to her all that was good and truly loving. He was always available to her, for he never regarded her with the patronizing patience exhibited by so many elders no matter how silly her questions might appear to be.

She loved the trappings of the church, its theatrics, the priestly robes, the incense, the rituals and incantations, the cool, reverential hush of the fifteenth-century cathedral where the family worshipped and Uncle Karl held sway. And the dust motes in the sunlight streaming through the stained glass windows, how she loved those. She could imagine God's gentle breath upon them, dancing them this way and that. All of it so richly textured, so beautiful, and so rewarding in the sure comfort that life was in order from conception to heavenly consignment.

One simply believed. There were other beliefs, she knew and she could not understand this. If there was the one true faith how could there be others, as sincerely worshipped? But then perhaps they were all lacking an Uncle Karl who made it all sound so real and down to earth. He had pointed out that the beauty of God's garden was in its profusion of flowers.

Even now she believed. Believed because Uncle Karl believed. That great and good man died for life. His untimely death gave credence to it. She could not think otherwise, or his faith would be a lie, and that would be the most intolerable terror of all. No, no longer the rigid, mind-vacating belief on demand but rather the searching one of spirit, even if only residual, that had guided her through the torturous shoals of a stygian period.

Harking back, she recalled that Uncle Karl's visits were more frequent, his voice more subdued but no less passionate on subjects she did not comprehend and would not until *that* night. Words like "Jew"—"gestapo"—"concentration camps..." Mama and Papa had, with misguided love, performed a disservice in sheltering her from an existence outside the home and church. Or was theirs a losing wisdom to isolate her in order for her to cherish the fleeting serenity of a childhood before it succumbed to the inevitable reality?

The family had gathered that afternoon along with Uncle Karl in their small flat on the second floor at 44 Ottostrasse above Herman's Bootery, Fine Footwear for the Family. There was chilled buttermilk and Mama had made apple dumplings and her favorite confection, sour milk cherry tarts. Twelve candles, one for good luck, nested on a sideboard.

She had not gone out all day, aglow with anticipation. There were alien noises emanating from the street, thickening groups of people scurrying, the distant breaking of glass, muted, but mounting in intensity as the afternoon wore on. The radio was strangely silent. Instead, Helga played classical music and Caruso records on the victrola, and Mama bustled in the kitchen. What questions she might have put were forestalled by their busywork and evaporated in the excitement of the birthday event.

They ate and presented her with gifts, Uncle Karl bringing a book of English verse, and there was much teasing and toasting to her future. In her childish glee, she was to recall later, she could not sense the camouflaged strain.

Then abruptly there was a fierce pounding on the door and someone asked for Uncle Karl; she could not see who. They spoke in low muffled tones, and Uncle Karl's face went hard and dark as she had never seen it before; and then they left with him. The party was suddenly over. She retreated to the room shared with Helga to put the gifts away, but with a sense of foreboding.

The radio replaced the victrola in the living room, and she could barely hear the muffled tones of an exhorative speaker in a gutterally rousing speech she could not make out, intermittently punctuated by martial music she instinctively disliked. She was frightened. Then it became eerily quiet, and she ventured back to find Mama, Papa and Helga sitting starkly silent in the soundless room. Mama reached out and caressed her to her bosom, and she could feel her tremor. From the expression on their faces she could see and feel that something alien had entered their lives. She was distressed for what the day had promised but was now becoming, not yet knowing but sensing that a dark magnitude loomed, and that it posed a palpable threat to irrevocably alter the life she had known, as outside the breaking of glass increased in tempo and the crowd noises swelled.

Memory overwhelmed and she began to tremble, then suddenly strong arms circled her from behind. Her husband had quietly returned.

"Happy birthday, darling," Gil Spahn murmured, without irony.

She turned and buried her face in the annealing strength of his chest as if to burrow deep into it could blot out the surging harshness of anguished recall.

"A birthday shouldn't have tears."

She looked up gratefully into the strong evenly featured face barely visible in the dim spill of the night light on the patio.

"I didn't realize that I was crying."

This birthday thing, he thought, involving a dire event and a relative, combined with the traumas endured under a heartless regime, had to leave scars, but in all other areas, including her inability to have children, she wore well. Elsa did not drink or smoke and was extremely loyal and devoted to him and the least he could do was to *try* to understand this weird annual rite of drunken recall.

He nuzzled her and thought further, she's mine. Ever since I walked into the USO and made a pass at her which she quite rightly rebuffed. She was dispensing coffee and doughnuts to libidinous GI's bored with the letdown of Occupation after the war. Well, he'd wanted to occupy. No dice. She was so pitifully thin, but none of the other locals were prize packages. Unhappily, most of the available WAAC's were preempted by officers. Still there was something about her, not a physical beauty, that was tamped down, but an indefinable something-or-other that shone through ravagement to set her apart from the others.

But at the time he'd been on the universal quest of the Army of Occupation. Piece. Here's another chick that would be grateful, he was sure, for any attention that great American lover, Technical Corporal Gilbert Spahn of Boston, Massachusetts, would bestow, a few bars of chocolate and a carton of cigarettes to grease the way to a roll in the ruins.

He was later to admit, and they would both laugh about it, he was pretty crude. His German was as gross as his proposition. With a hauntingly hurt look in her eyes, she merely stared at him for an interminable length of time, and the look, out of the young-old face penetrated and impaled, and damn if he didn't become embarrassed by his own vulgarity. Then she simply turned and wordlessly walked away and out of his life. Or so he thought.

But the look lingered with him and he felt self-demeaned. What kind of man was he? Barely twenty at the time, he was aware of his own good looks, enhanced by the uniform and a victor's attitude to a subject populace. Geez, he was shitty. If he'd wanted to get laid, the ruined city was one vast womb to sink himself in. She was thin, pinched, typically the kraut, arrogant even in defeat. Whatever her sad story was, who needed that?

So he went back, once, twice, three times, each time she was not there, made inquiry but no one knew where she was, and he despaired. He stayed away for weeks, but then went back for a last time, no longer hopeful of ever seeing her again, and lo! There she was. By now she knew of his queries, had filled out winningly, smiled winsomely and accepted his apology. Language melted, they melted into each other's arms and he proposed and surprisingly, she did not accept.

He was stunned. He loved her, she loved him, so why not? Her objections were not strenuous, but the reasons were formidable. His family for one, for she had none, the United States Army would obstruct for another, dissimilar background, life experiences, et cetera. He dismissed them all, and his youthful ardor was such that he threatened to kill himself if she continued to reject him. She did not, of course, believe him, this crazy American, refusing to accept her "no" stated in at least four languages. But he was so funny-serious, and it had been so long since there had been laughter in her life she finally yielded.

His commanding officer refused to grant permission to marry, yet another sturdy American youth snared by a predatory fraulein, but through the intervention of a Catholic chaplain, the marriage was arranged. Much of Berlin was a shambles, but they found a small ragtag apartment, shared with another couple. It could have been a bombed-out stable for all that it mattered. For three months until his discharge it was Eden.

Home was Boston. Gil's parents welcomed Elsa warmly as did his two younger sisters. Whatever fears they had conjured in anticipation of Gilbert's bride, and they ran to the Wagnerian stereotype, every fräulein a busty and thick-waisted Brunnhilde, their doubts were pleasantly dissipated. By now Elsa had filled out, which is to say, that she was diminutively compact, attractive, deferential and properly grateful for transplant to the land of the free and home of the brave. Above all, she was Catholic.

They moved in with his parents. The elder Spahn was a certified public accountant, and Gil, like-minded, joined with him after completion of courses interrupted by the war to form "Spahn and Son." Elsa knew a serenity she had not experienced since before the war. The elder Spahns hoped for an early and first grandchild. After gentle but repeated proddings as to when their wish might be fulfilled, Elsa felt that she could no longer dissemble. They had to be told. She could not conceive. Too many insertions of instruments, blunt and sharp, had rendered her barren. A coolness grew between them. It was not overt. They sympathized for the appalling indignities heaped upon her but, Elsa perceived, found it repugnant that she had been a victim, as if to a degree it had somehow been her fault to have been unfortunately careless to have become one. Gil's two sisters had married within the year and within a month of each other had become pregnant.

Gil's relationship to his father had also become strained. Although Gil was a partner in the firm, senior continued to treat him as if he were still the obsequious fuzzy-cheeked son who had been drafted four years earlier. Despite maturing overseas experiences and a marriage, little boy obeisance was still expected. Elsa and he moved into an apartment, but the situation did not improve, exacerbated when a sister's husband, also an accountant, was admitted to the firm. When Spahn & Son became Spahn & Company, Gil declared independence. He and Elsa bid polite farewells and joined the postwar hegira to Los Angeles.

It was a good move. They prospered. Gil was now comptroller for a large liquor distributing firm. Elsa also worked, various jobs from saleslady at the Broadway Department Store, private tutoring in German and French, the meantime her English becoming increasingly fluent, a receptionist, a fling at real estate selling and finally to ownership of a plant boutique on Ventura Boulevard off Laurel Canyon Drive in the Valley. It kept her occupied, and augmented Gil's income, enabling them to live well in a comfortable sprawling ranch house in Toluca Lake. Elsa felt no compulsion to adopt children, and Gil concurred. They accepted Sartre's credo that hell is other people and it is already here on earth. The ferment of the sixties through the Vietnam War with so many of their friends complaining of the loss of control over their children to the burgeoning drug scene and open sexuality, convinced them that their decision not to adopt was a correct one. Gil played golf, occasional poker, and Elsa avidly Mah-Jonged weekly. They were theatre and concert subscribers, gave generously to charities on a nonsectarian basis, entertained often but selectively, mostly small affairs from a wide circle of friends, ate at the best restaurants, enjoyed consistently good health and led, they felt, the good life, consciously selfish in some respects, but unapologetic for they were hurting no one. Middle of the road Democrat and staunchly Catholic, they could, nonetheless, disapprove of the Church's position on the abortion issue without erosion of faith. For Elsa Spahn, Birkenau had happened in another life.

Save once a year on her birthday.

Debit that from the pluses and it worried the shit out of Gil. In all other respects, 364 days out of the year, Elsa was normal (whatever that was) average (or that) a resolute compact woman whose petiteness belied her energy and drive, still attractive to him (and to some of his less-inhibited friends) for all that she was pushing fifty, still titillating between the sheets despite her camp experiences.

She was not, he knew, a secret drinker, too forthright for deception, least of all to herself. Although she had been doing this for years and he had come to reluctantly accept it—scratch that—live with it, it always astonished him that his wife, so otherwise controlled all the other days of the year could yield to such abject self-pity on her natal day.

That first time—when?—ten, twelve years ago—Gil was shocked when he'd found her insensate on the kitchen floor in the Burbank house before they moved to Toluca. He'd picked her up and carried her to bed and stayed home the next day, certain that when she wakened she'd be sick as a dog. But when she arose at her usual time she was recuperatively amazing. She was bright as a bird, offered no explanation, and he did not press for one.

The following year it happened again. And the year after that. By now she talked openly about it, but he could not understand a compulsion she could not explain even to herself. He suggested that she consult a psychiatrist.

"Why?" she countered. "To learn it isn't my mother I hate but Schickelgruber?"

Since it didn't change anything between them he dropped the subject. By tacit agreement he'd taken to leaving the house around eight, go to a movie or arrange a poker game where he would invariably lose, knowing that when he returned what he could expect to find.

But tonight—morning now—he'd gone to a double feature, enjoyed the first picture, walked out on the second, stopped at a bar, had two drinks, spurned the open invitation of a homosexual, and rejected the subtle eye of a spectacularly endowed redhead whose much older escort was deep in his cups. Finally he went home to find Elsa wavering in the quiet gloom, softly silhouetted against the glass doors overlooking the patio, her slight body sheathed in a clingy housecoat.

As he came behind her he noticed the half-empty bottle of

vodka on the coffee table, the bottle of mix, and melted ice cubes in a silver bucket. The truth was it didn't take all that much for Elsa to become drunk. Being a nondrinker, the effect was in the potency of emotion.

"Don't mean to cry," she blurted.

"Do no good, baby."

"Happy birthday, Elsa," she said sardonically.

"All day," he said, "where'll we go for dinner? Tail O' the Cock? Scandia's?"

"Kristellnacht," she muttered.

Yes, Kristellnacht. By now he knew its litany of woe and could recite word for word with her. It was amazing how many people did not know of Kristellnacht as they did the Reichstag Fire, including Jews.

"Kristellnacht," she repeated. "Birthday—Uncle Karl——"

"I think you've had enough, Elsa—"

"On November 7, 1938," she was undeterred, and the words cascaded with bitter clarity, "a German diplomat was assassinated in Paris——"

"Yes," he sighed.

"By Herschel Greunspan, a seventeen year-old Polish Jew—"

"It's in the books, baby," he beseeched, "you ought to lie down."

In a sudden move she spun from him and lurched to the sofa where she sat tightly, drawing her legs together, propping her elbows on her knees and cupping her face in her hands as if to anchor her skull. She rambled on in a bleeding but surprisingly lucid recapitulation of the night that marked the point of no return for a nation.

"He shot the wrong man."

She dribbled vodka into her glass, almost to half, added mix, sipped, continued to speak, the words peaking and dipping in uneven cadence until she became inaudible, but he knew them all, the litany ritually unchanged from year to year.

"—unhinged by the death of his father...casualty...concentration camp...determined...arouse conscience of the world...instead mistakenly shot...third legation secretary...irony...Ernest Von Rath...man of isolated good will...opposed anti-Semitism...himself under surveillance...gestapo..."

Silence...through which she tilted the glass to her lips but his mind, Pavlovian-triggered, filled the void: the world did not heed, but it was the pretext for Richard Heydrich, the head of the SS Security Service, to order all synagogues in Germany and Austria to be burned and destroyed on the night of November ninth. What hope lingered for even the most myopic Jew that the festering madness would abate was irrevocably buried under ashes and shards. The streets resounded and were blanketed with broken glass from the smashed shop windows of Jewish establishments, hence the name—it was "the night of the broken glass." Kristellnacht.

Until then millions of Jews lived under the all-pervading Nazi power in agony. Tortured by anxiety, insecure in the present, unable to anticipate the future, torn between hope and despair, they were helpless in the face of a tremendous machine always ready to crunch them.

"We maintained the fiction," Elsa said, and realized that she had been speaking, his thoughts matching her words almost verbatim, "that the Jews were being brutalized by a few thousand Storm Troopers...We good Germans...looked the other way..."

"Elsa——"

"It was so vast...the pogrom...over a million ordinary citizens...unleashed like mad dogs..."

"I know," he interposed with textbook rote, and he did not mean to be sardonic, "Rushed to carry out the order with lynch fervor in a paroxysm of plunder, rapine and slaughter. Come to bed, Elsa."

She rolled on, her voice thickening, slurring a word, stumbling over another, but into a second wind of such remembered intensity that the words spewed out in volcanic clarity. "Herman Kohlbert owned the shoe store above which we lived, came up, knocked on the door and spoke to my dear Uncle Karl. Then they went out. Uncle Karl came back with an old Jew, I remember his beard was bloodied, and went out again. He did that all night—going out and coming back with more Jews. Mama begged him to stop, he'd be killed himself but he wouldn't stop. The room filled with Jews, beaten and bloody, men and women, and still he went out. Poor Mama and Papa were already into it without leaving, doing what they could. And I remember—there was hardly a sound. All those people in all of the rooms, over a hundred, packed like sardines, did not make a sound. They made absolutely *no* sound—as if they knew they were already dead. I hid under the bed and threw up my lovely cherry tarts, why I can't abide them today. Then I felt pain and sticky between my legs, blood oozing out and I was so scared, afraid that I was being punished and going to die because of all the people in the house— and I lay there in my vomit—unable to move and said a thousand "Hail Mary's" and waited for God to strike me dead—until I fell asleep in my own stink."

The room became quiet again and his mind raced like a runaway horse, unable to set aside all that he had learned from her... knew the statistics of that infamous night, for he'd heard them often enough, drummed in, had read about them... in the major cities alone, the streets buried under the crystal shards of $3 million worth of broken glass; 190 synagogues and 173 Jewish-occupied apartment houses burned to the ground; over 7,500 Jewish shops, stores and factories looted and destroyed; 218 Jews killed—including 56 women and children—thousands beaten and maimed; 20,000 Jews arrested for "provocative acts" in disturbance of the peace, 10,000 sent within the week to the Buchenwald camp where, ultimately, more than half perished.

The pogrom was staggering, but beyond numbers, he'd discerned another corpse. Fires were ignited all over Germany, but one ceased to burn. The conscience of the German people. Doused by those who defiled or who were accessories by apathy, no man or woman alive could any longer have remained unaware of the evil that was rampant among them; underscoring that virtually midway into the twentieth century it was proclaimed for the first time in all of the recorded history of the world that the destruction of a race—genocide—was a fit, viable and altogether proper function of a modern, civilized nation ... knew too, since it is also recorded, that in all of the land seven ministers called for justice from their pulpits ... knew of the wrath that bore down on Elsa's family. They paid dearly for effrontery. Her mother and father were separated from their daughters and never heard from again, the two girls spared by the intervention of the Church, sent to a work camp for rehabilitation.

Despite steeling himself against the yearly recounting that freshly renewed and sustained the bloody twisted horror of the crooked cross, he could feel the gorge rise in his throat ... Elsa's voice permeated:

"Uncle Karl never came back——"

"For God's sake, Elsa, stop torturing yourself."

Her voice had thickened again. "—the next morning found dead where he'd been thrown through Herman's window—a piece of glass in his neck."

God damn it, shut up! he heard himself inwardly scream but only an empathetic inaudible cry issued, strangled, from his throat ... I know, I know, I've known for almost thirty years that Uncle Karl did not come back ... know that Helga, fearful for their lives and hopeful of uniting with their parents, kept her counsel and seemed outwardly to conform. Not so Elsa. Uncle Karl dead, parents gone, she did not delude herself. Catholics were being persecuted as vigorously as Jews. She could not, as Helga did, discipline herself. She was informed on for "prejudicial remarks" in the intemperate tradition of a beloved uncle. At fifteen this steely wisp of a girl was dispatched to Birkenau as a clear and present danger to the state ... Helga, she was later to learn, died of typhus at Treblinka.

Birkenau ... a madman, Colonel Wilhelm Gehbert, a doctor, so-called ... Elsa's first sexual encounter, a brutal affair with him, never repeated, he preferred only a one-time use and with an inexhaustible supply of luckless females, could indulge his sadism with impunity... the unspeakable medical experiments that she had somehow miraculously survived...

And recalled their first meeting at the USO a bare two months after her liberation by the Allied Forces. God, he'd been so callow and unthinking to have made that pass at her... It's a wonder that she could take a prick, even his, after all she'd been through.

His reverie was burst by silence. Elsa had ceased babbling. She lay back upright on the sofa, her head tilted upward, eyes shut, mouth inelegantly open. He went to her and lifted her and gently carried her to bed.

Next year, same time, same place.

Freda was appointed to be a Committee of One to pursue the matter of Grossman/Gehbert with the '38 Club.

The '38 Club had been founded just prior to the entry of the United States into World War II to deal with the mounting refugee flow of the victims of Nazi persecution. Although its membership was largely Jewish, non-Jews were welcomed and served as well.

It was located in a modest two-story building on Beverly Boulevard just east of La Cienega. The lower floor was comprised of shops and offices, unrelated to the organization. The upper floor was completely occupied by the club's offices and large recreation room that doubled as auditorium and social center. Its activities included the placement of refugees, uniting families and locating friends, job assistance and placement, financial aid, medical and psychiatric counseling and English classes. It worked closely with other agencies in kindred areas, the International Red Cross, Council of Churches and Synagogues, ORT, Jewish Federation Council and various government agencies, here and abroad and was a funnel for the West German Federal Compensation Law for Victims of National Socialistic Persecution.

It was called the '38 Club, derived from its official title: The November 9, 1938 Club, Inc., a nonprofit organization, to memorialize Kristallnacht. The early days of the '38 Club were bustling, but with the inexorable attrition of time, membership was dwindling and much of its agenda was now social.

It was here that the five women had met; five out of the many thousands that filtered through its doors. It was over a period of years, seeing each other, occasionally meeting and serving on functions, that they became friendly, but no more so than with others who had been drawn together by a shared bond of butchery. But then, by way of a Mah-Jong tournament notice tacked onto the bulletin board, they were joined.

All were excellent players, less combative in approach than defensive in their play. Joy was the keynote to their game. Meeting weekly for twenty years over the tiles, consuming gallons of coffee and pounds of snacks in the interim, they had never, by tacit and unvoiced understanding, ever discussed their early years.

Until Grossman/Gehbert.

Esther Wexler, the director of the club, was not sanguine when apprised of the purpose of Freda's visit.

"Yes, Freda. We can write to Wiesenthal and Yad Vashem. But anyone can. You can as an individual."

"They must get thousands of inquiries. An individual one could get lost."

"It's possible, but they are conscientious."

"Your stationery would be impressive."

"All right. You can make the inquiry through the club but don't be surprised if nothing comes of it. The war is over thirty years. Time obliterates much. It would help if you had a picture of this Grossman."

"So would a confession," Freda replied dourly.

For three weeks nothing was heard from Wiesenthal or Yad Vashem.

The women, by implied agreement, did not confide in their families, discussions between them on the matter was minimal and they continued to play each Wednesday. The games were less ebullient than usual. They were concerned for Grossman/Gehbert's longevity.

Freda recognized the dark humor of the situation and maintained buoyancy by refurbishing an old joke.

"Two Israelis were dispatched on a mission to kill Arafat," she said. "He passed a certain spot at a precise time every day. When he revealed himself they were to blast the bastard with machine guns. If unsuccessful—to throw grenades—failing that—to shoot with pistols—failing that—to leap upon him and stab him—and as a last resort, to beat him to death. They were at the designated place, well hidden, long before his arrival. Minutes ticked away. Arafat doesn't show. He is late. Five minutes—ten—fifteen minutes. Finally, one Israeli turns worriedly to the other: 'Do you think something happened to him?'"

It merely elicited wan smiles, not the usual rollicking response to a Freda Friedkin joke.

"Oh, fuck you gals," she said. "Who designed this hand? Attila the Hun?"

Elsa had in the interim, without announcement, gone to Papa Grossman's to recheck his presence and continuing health, and to verify her initial reaction to him. It was a Saturday night, a full house, and he was nowhere about, which was worrisome. But a question casually put to the cashier rested her mind. Papa Grossman had gone skiing and would be back in three days.

She went back the following Saturday, and he was there in the mushroom cap and gleaming white coat, smiling and nodding to customers in his usual fashion. Elsa's husband, unsuspicious, averred that he was getting tired of German food and that next week he'd like to try Chinese.

She was satisfied that her initial reaction was the rightful one and so informed the group attesting to the apparent sturdy state of his good health.

"The gangrenous cock," Freda muttered. "One bam."

In the fourth week, within three days of each other, separate and unrelated letters were received from Yad Vashem and Wiesenthal. Yad Vashem stated tersely that Doctor Wilhelm Gehbert had been tried and sentenced: "For participation in 5,450 murders—four years' imprisonment; and three years' 'loss of honor.'"

Wiesenthal added poignantly that the sentence was served in the early fifties and that distinctively different charges, substantiated by at least two witnesses, desirably those unconnected with the aforementioned murders, would have to be launched if he were to be tried again.

It was disheartening. Elsa fought tears, Freda cursed and Gertrude's bowels erupted in diarrhetic reaction.

Hannah said, "My God, we're worse off than before the inquiry. We still don't know if Grossman is Gehbert but that Gehbert has been tried and is free and very likely never to be tried again."

"What new evidence can we produce?" Gertrude lamented. "I didn't ever actually see him kill."

"Nor I," said Elsa.

"No," said Gertrude, returned from the bathroom.

"Excuse me. Even if we had, who can recall names and even if we did, might they not be one of the five thousand four hundred and fifty murders?"

Elsa shook her head incredulously, "five thousand four hundred and fifty murders... and such a ridiculous sentence. I could vomit."

"Son of a bitch," Freda said, barely audible. "Four years... that's one thousand four hundred and sixty days... one day served for every three murders."

"Not including leap year," Sophie observed irrelevantly, biting deeply into her lower lip.

It was Gertrude's turn to hostess, and her husband walked in late still in work clothes, the coarse material grimed and shiny from the handling of scrap metals. He groused that he was hungry, and Gertrude groused back that he could damn well go into the kitchen and scrounge something out of the refrigerator. He was so startled by this unseemly display of truculence from his usually docile mate that he did precisely that and ravenous as he was, settled for a cheese sandwich and a beer, mumbling under his breath that the lousy Mah-Jong game would one day break up their marriage.

After the interruption, Hannah continued to fret. "Gehbert must have been tried by his mother."

"He had no mother," said Freda. "He was spawned off a urinal."

"Maddening, unfair," said Elsa. "What does 'loss of honor' mean?"

Hannah grimaced. "Does it matter?"

Freda reached for a cheese snack, bit into it but had no taste for it and set it aside. "If it wasn't so fucking bitterly grim I'd bust out laughing. You all know what this means, don't you?"

"Forget it?" Elsa said tremulously and as if being challenged, echoed herself. "Forget it?"

"Goddam shame if we do."

"Who said forget?" said Gertrude feistily.

"Then," said Freda, "it's down to what it was in the very beginning."

"What?" From Hannah.

"For us to handle this in any way we see fit."

They were listening avidly.

"We verify Gehbert beyond a shadow of a doubt. We know that he carries with him the ultimate identification."

The women regarded each other solemnly, knowing exactly what Freda had reference to; the atrocity context it bore for each when forcibly introduced to it many years ago.

After a long moment Hannah said softly, "The dog bite."

"The dog bite," Freda affirmed.

Gehbert, each recalled inwardly had been attacked by a dog and bore a scar, an ugly two inch welt in his left shoulder.

"What do you think?" Gertrude, acridly. "He will take off his shirt? Excuse me Herr Gehbert, we would like to see your scar?"

"No," replied Freda, "I am sure that he will not accommodate."

"If he goes swimming," Hannah offered and let the thought complete itself.

"This is November," Freda answered. "It will not warm until May or June. Does he swim at the beach? Or does he have a pool? Or perhaps he does not swim at all. We would have to keep him under surveillance and get close enough to see the scar."

"That would not be practical," said Hannah.

But there was a way to find out if Papa Grossman bore such a wound and each thought of it and collectively dismissed it as unthinkable. Therefore it was not articulated, and it hung between them and they despaired.

"I have a headache," said Gertrude. Between both ends of her anatomy she was wrenched.

For the first time in twenty years their game broke before eleven o'clock.

Z

Wherever the Jew has wandered, whatever his condition, his identity has persisted. It is not his personal dedication to Judaism but his very existence that instantly recalls his peculiar and particular status in the world.

Jews may protest their Jewry, may reject it, and many in denial have allied with their tormentors to their own destruction. Enemies from Haman to Hitler have tried their most vicious to erase them by physical means that came terrifyingly close. But Jews have outlasted oppressors from antiquity to the present, for their haters do not heed history. It is this virtually institutionalized enmity that unites Jews, for Jews are not even permitted the luxury of melting away. Hitler's proclamation that anyone with a forebear as far back as 1812 to be as fully Jewish as a household of rabbis proved assimilation to be as fragile as a bubble. All are Jews by Persecution.

But it is a truism that victims seek victims and the Jews, despite their historical role as scapegoats, are not an exception. Their bias, however, is bloodless, more comedian than conquistador. Not action, but attitude. They prefer to barb with the word, shrivel with a look and to disdain with a gesture. And who is a favorite target? Their lance is self-abnegating humor and the cutting edge of derision for other Jews. Who else?

The German Jew has always regarded himself to be the most advanced, aristocratic and intellectual, faintly contemptuous of his brethren. He derides the English Jew who derides the Spanish Jew, who derides the French Jew, and through a descending order of the disapprobation, Russian, Roumanian, Hungarian and other assorted Jews reserve for each other, all seem agreed that the Polish Jew is the most woebegone. This lowly Jew may be the precursor of the Polish joke.

Sophie Langbein was a Polish Jew. She had been born Esther Polatsky, but in her nineteenth year she had, in a desperate act of survival, assumed the identity of a dead friend. In a world of large frauds it was a small deception.

Now she stood in her bedroom and examined herself, naked to the waist, gently probing her breasts, pendulous and heavy veined, as disproportionate in configuration as the rest of her body. She was plain faced, with washed-out hazel eyes set wide apart to accommodate a stubby nose with flared nostrils, a mouth with thick lips that revealed disassociated teeth with cleavage, and too-thin hair that resisted management; big boned, thick waisted and wide assed, with splayed feet. It was not a body designed to give or to receive joy but a chitinous shell that absorbed punishment and as such, despite the indigence of childhood and the Holocaust, was a monument to durability. But breast cancer was so prevalent, no longer a closet topic, openly discussed these days, hence the self-examination; she nonetheless felt that if her life continued its pattern, it would betray her into malignancy.

As she probed she ruminated.

It was said that her mother carried Esther to the tenth month, the child reluctant to expel, as if knowing the travails that awaited her. She was finally a breach delivery born on a luckless and star-crossed day, Friday, July thirteenth, on a mat of straw. With Esther's first suck of air, her mother gasped her last and died.

The harrowing birth presaged the harrowing life. Esther's father was a shoemaker; but true to tradition, the shoemaker's children had no shoes. Leather and canvas, expensive and hard to come by, were reserved for those who could afford to pay, mostly the *goyim*, for the twenty or so Jewish families living ghetto-like in the village were impecunious. After a respectful mourning period her father remarried. Thereafter, with annual regularity, there came children until by the time Esther was thirteen, she was surrogate mother to twelve half-brothers and -sisters, five of whom succumbed in infancy.

Brodz was a flyspeck village near the Russian border and had been, even unto the second and third decades of the twentieth century, a *shtetl* hangover not unlike that immortalized in *Fiddler on The Roof.* The streets were unpaved, muddy when it rained, billowing dusty when dry. Esther's family lived behind the shop, kerosene lit, outside privy, and drew water from the community pump serving the Jewish enclave. To the eve of World War II, Esther had never used a telephone, seen a motion picture, knew indoor plumbing or refrigeration or tasted packaged food, nor had she ranged more than twenty-five kilometers from her place of birth. Schooling was hit-and-miss, and she grew up without a childhood of toys and pranks, for it seemed her stepmother was forever bedridden with assorted aches and childbirth. She felt keenly that she alone, among her brothers and sisters, had only the father in common. Her stepmother was not unkind, indeed she was grateful for her stepdaughter who, however ungainly, was resilient as a weed, holding the household together, cooking, cleaning, mending, tending to the young ones. Papa, by this time relentlessly ground down by poverty, his hands blackened and stubbed, his body permanently hunched and shriveled over his last, moved through the wretched hovel called home like a somnambulist. A life of nineteenth-century penury.

The only relief from this stark existence was the holidays. Worship was communal theatre. Somehow, there were new dishes, withdrawn from sagging cupboards, ancestrally handed down, every cracked piece of crockery cherished, goodies pooled and cooked and baked in celebration of—what? Deliverance? But even for Esther these high holiday periods were not festive. It simply meant more work since Mama, as usual, was indisposed or big bellied, and it fell to her to make the family contribution, if not in substance, in service.

But fear was never preempted, for there were pogroms. Bands of Polish youths would swoop in and with mindless ferocity, terrorize them. They would plunder, burn, rape and occasionally kill, but never totally destroy, for to do so would leave little for the next depredation, for their own lives were almost as impoverished as their victims'.

The Jews protected themselves, but not by organized opposition, for whom could they appeal to? The authorities would listen to the Council of Elders, almost comical with their long beards and dangling *payesses* and outlandish long black coats, the prayer shawls worn underneath at all times, shake their heads, commiserate, promise to look into the matter, and look the other way. So they developed a survival sixth sense—as a mariner detects the slightest shift of wind—when another raid was immiment. They would board their shops, hustle the young ones inside and hide the women and await the inevitable—and pray. The locusts descended and the locusts departed, the Jews ventured out, assessed damage and injury, thanked God for minimal infliction and resumed their meager lives—until the next attack.

If the Jews of Brodz believed they knew the depths of despair, they were to know an even greater inhumanity by the German scourge. They swept all in their goosestep path, leveled the hovels that were homes, separated men from the women, the young from the old, the able bodied from the weak, and tore children from their mothers...

Esther survived the trip to Auschwitz-Birkenau, survived the shock of her family rent forever, dispatched elsewhere, never to be seen or heard from again, survived the specific night of debauchery, unlike other nights as bestial but so cumulatively stupefying as to numb recall, when she was ricocheted with two other girls amongst an orgiastic officer cadre.

But that *one* could never be forgotten. He was the

handsomest man she had ever seen, tall and slender, with kindly blue eyes, and she believed that she'd detected a flicker of compassion in them. But there was none. It had been the light in the room, fleetingly coating his eyes in shadow, but with a tilt of his head the softness vanished, the lascivious leer reassertive, for it had never left. He beckoned her to his crotch and pushed her face down to the swollen member. Terrified, repulsed, daring to guess what was expected of her, she recoiled and threw herself to the floor, retched, and coiled into a tight ball and cried out to a dead mother. Sinewy fingers pulled at her, beat at her, and he thrust himself into her and when sated, threw her like a bone to the others. Of those she had no memory, but *that* one, he of the betraying blue eyes, she remembered clearly, the Adonis face forever chiseled with Mount Rushmore clarity deep into her psyche. It had been her introduction to sex.

Wilhelm Gehbert.

She survived all the nights and days of unspeakable horrors, unable to comprehend when liberated, why, out of the thousands who had perished, she was alive at all. She could not recall her rescue, for she lay emaciated and dying in filth. She could be expected to be dead in hours. Yet, through timely intercession and kindly ministration, as much of the spirit as with medication, she miraculously revived and recuperated in the ensuing weeks. But she could not think coherently.

By then, brought back from the brink of death, she sought death. Family dispersed, if not exterminated, friends eradicated, no one she knew from a village that no longer was had survived, without education or recourse, a future that stretched before her as bleak as the past had been, she threw herself before a truck. It was a clumsy fall and the truck barely nudged her. She tried starvation, but when she inopportunely fainted before the quarters of the American Red Cross, was intravenously revived. She slashed her wrists but bled so lethargically she was discovered in time and repaired.

Then a lifeline appeared. She met another very like herself. Sophie Wilewski was a year older. Not uniquely, her life had been similar to that of Esther's, a carbon copy amalgam of paltry village life, large family, hand-to-mouth existence, pogroms and concentration camp. Sophie had also survived Birkenau, subject also to experimentation but had been spared Gehbert's lechery. Possibly on the seventh day he rested. But they did not know of each other until a chance meeting at a refugee relocation center.

Esther and Sophie instantly magnetized to each other, each the mirror image of the other. They clung to each other, bolstered each other, formed a bond as inseparable as Siamese twins, the meanwhile trying to learn of their families and in turn forlornly hoping to be located by survivors. But in the immediate postwar period chaos prevailed. Staffs of the various agencies were eagerly well intentioned but undermanned and overwhelmed, unable initially to cope with and to execute a survivors program, the dimensions of the problems encountered having been seriously underestimated as each passing day revealed, in escalating horror, the calamitious scope of Hitler's bid to annihilate a race. Merely classifying thousands of homeless, bitter, bewildered, hysterical and sickly refugees was a major accomplishment. Disease was rampant, and the prevention of plague was a chief priority. Many who survived the rigors of prison perished in freedom.

Esther and Sophie were each other's family. Sharing the intensity of search, thus renewing life through each other, they pledged their lives, one to the other, vowing never to separate till death do them part. But within weeks of the vow separation came sooner. In two guises: Sophie's health, and a search instituted by a never-seen uncle residing in Detroit, Michigan. Sophie's elation was tempered by dismay. She could not, would not leave her friend for a stranger in a strange land.

Esther, masking her despair at the prospect of losing one so dearly loved, so recently acquired, countered that a relative in the United States was not a stranger and could be no more strange than their own native land had been to them. Sophie could not be persuaded. To leave Esther was unthinkable. To face the future without her was terror as raw as what had transpired in the past.

Esther persisted and urged her to reconsider, bereft at the thought of her own future without Sophie, resolved in her secret heart that after Sophie departed, she would finally find surcease, that her next effort at self-immolation would not fail.

Then Sophie said yes, she would go, but not without Esther. She would contact her uncle, surely he would be generous and not spurn the request to accommodate another. Esther pleaded that Sophie was tempting the Fates, for conceivably the uncle *could* refuse. Worse. Delay might cause him to withdraw his offer to her. Would it not be better for Sophie to go to Detroit, Michigan, and then send for her as soon as feasible? She pleaded and cajoled until finally Sophie relented, fervently promising that she would move heaven and earth and not rest until Esther was sent for, exacting an equally fervent promise from Esther that she would keep in touch with her at her uncle's address in Detroit.

Added to this was Esther's concern for Sophie's health. Sophie did not look or feel well, and of late her condition had worsened. Both did not know that Sophie was unknowingly in the last stages of pneumonia. A racking cough, dizziness and depleted strength were so prevalent among refugees that so long as she remained upright, Sophie did not regard her condition as exceptional. She stubbornly rejected Esther's plea that she seek medical aid. Her fear of hospitals and doctors as an outgrowth of the Birkenau experiments was apoplectic. Not only would a hospital stay postpone departure but she was absolutely convinced that once she entered she would never return.

Sophie's apprehension was misplaced. With a body debilitated by malnutrition and a heart weakened by excruciating crushing pressure, it could not withstand the added dread of departure. In the chill of an early morning, an hour before train boarding, on a wooden bench in a drafty station, pocked with gaping holes caused by Allied bombs, among milling hundreds expressing fears and joys at the trains entering and leaving in recently restored service, Sophie collapsed. She convulsed and died in Esther's arms.

Esther sat benumbed, her own heart close to explosion, and

railed inwardly at the abominating curse that relentlessly stalked her. Doomed were those whose lives she touched. From the first killing moment of her entry into the world, lacerating loss of family and friends, herself a victim of incomprehensible bestiality, now to be so abruptly and cruelly shorn of the one person who was dearer to her life than she held her own to be, a stark lifetime of anguish and desolation, this moment, of all the abyssmal moments encountered, cradling her lifeless friend to her bosom, was Esther's nadir.

She had planned to take her life after Sophie's departure, but Sophie's death in this context fortified and accelerated the desire to do so immediately—she would die, must die, here and now, will it and welcome it, and death would be an inverted triumph and altogether fitting in that the harrowing and torturous sagas of Sophie Wilewski and Esther Polatsky would culminate its release in each other's arms; resistlessly yielded to a dark mantle, engulfing her as blood furiously pulsated in her ears and threatened to fragment her brain—

At the instant of her lids closing, her vision slitted to the skimpy valise still clutched by Sophie . . . at that instant an electric current pierced and evaporated the thickening shroud, a deeply imbedded life-seed rekindled, nurtured and flash-fanned through her. She bolted upright.

No! Sophie Wilewski's death must not waste! Not become yet another hapless, anonymous casualty of a madman's dementia. Serve it must!

Reflexively, she acted with uncharacteristic cunning to take the first major step to irrevocably alter the future course of her life. She pried the valise from tenacious fingers and where Sophie had died on a backless bench, two walls converging in the furthest corner of the station, propped her upright. Then she crossed Sophie's hands in her lap. She appeared to be dozing. Next, Esther confiscated her identification tag and certification-of-travel papers, clutched the valise tightly and shamelessly walked away. She did not look back.

Sophie Wilewski, nee Esther Polasky, was on the train. Not till it grunted out of the station did the tears come.

In Detroit, Esther, henceforth Sophie, was lovingly greeted by Sam and Ruth Wilewski. Sam was a furrier. Their own family was grown, two sons and a daughter, married, and with families of their own. Sophie fit easily into their lives. She knew enough of the other Sophie to fill in or improvise details when inquiries were put to her; otherwise amnesia was implicitly implied due to incarceration too painful for recall. Sam, who had emigrated to the States the year before his brother married and had not seen him since, did not press. It was a *mitzvah* that a remnant of his brother's family had been resurrected from the dead.

Sophie found work as a seamstress. Nights she went to school and displayed an energetic aptitude for the English language. Her pent-up hunger for learning was not only educational but entertainment as well.

After a year, Sam and Ruth felt that the Detroit winters were becoming too severe for their brittling bones and opted for retirement in sunny California. There were sufficient relatives and friends who had preceded them to Los Angeles to make the change an easy transition. Sophie went with them and continued with seamstress work and night school.

Here she met Max Langbein. He was a salesman for inexpensive lines of ladies ready-to-wear dresses. Max was unprepossessing in appearance; short, stocky and prematurely balding. He lived with an aged mother, long widowed, her main support, supplementing a meager monthly social security payment, a sore point with him since he had two married sisters who did not contribute. He was hedonistic, wore flashy clothes and had an inexhaustible store of off-color jokes. Women found him obvious, unattractive and often obnoxious with his unsubtle ardor. It was a major frustration, for he had the drive of a stud and fancied himself to be a swinger. Since there were few takers, he had to pay for his pleasures, a major drain on his limited salary.

His eyes fastened on that big one, newly hired, in the plant, Sophie Wilewski. She met two requirements. She was Jewish and she was docile. She kept to herself and hardly spoke to anyone unless directly addressed. Marriage would liberate him from his mother's constant carping. If he joined the family state, his sisters would be forced to share in her care and disposition to an old age home. Sexually, she was unappealing, but what the hell, that could be taken care of on the outside.

For Sophie it was to be a loveless union. She observed and knew him well, and her antenna was up. The girls in the office snickered at this would-be Lothario, but he, too, filled certain requisites for her. She would have her own home and her own family to fill the aching void of her lost one. Also, it became apparent that if she did not strike out on her own, she would, in spinsterhood, be burdened with the Wilewskis who were becoming increasingly cantankerous with age. Their own children, geographically removed, maintained minimum contact with them, assured that cousin Sophie was on the spot and would always remain so.

She had no illusions of romance. Sex was repellent. No man, no matter how handsome or caring, would ever erase the indignities that had been heaped upon her. She would be sufficiently compliant upon demand. So long as Max was discreetly clandestine and remained clean, the relationship would serve.

Home became a succession of apartments and finally the purchase of an ex-GI's crackerbox home in Culver City, so prevalently tract-constructed in the immediate postwar era. A primary factor in its purchase was the retention of the favorable low interest rate insured by the government, since Max qualified under the GI bill, having served briefly in the armed forces, never leaving the States. With the vagaries of the dress manufacturing business, good times and bad, it was the only one they were to have. Two grown children later they were still in it. Despite its hemmed-in walls, inadequate closet space and architectural defects, it pleased her. She was a cleanliness freak and the home sparkled. She was not envious of those who had more. It was more than she ever dreamed of having, a far cry from a dirt floor in Brodz to inside plumbing in Los Angeles.

Her children, boy and girl, were snotnoses. They bickered with each other constantly, but presented a common front against her. Their music, the drug scene, the sexual permissiveness and peer group influence appalled her. She did not understand them, they did not understand her and displayed not the slightest interest in her girlhood travails. The Holocaust was ancient history, religion was bunk and that, along with the severity of something called the Depression, which their father had undergone, was dismissed with the callous disregard of youth as hearts-and-flowers.

Max's idea of family was very direct. He had done his wife a favor by marrying her, she in turn never questioned his road proclivities. She managed uncomplainingly to make do with whatever monies he saw fit to bring home, managing somehow to put aside a sum for emergencies. When he returned from frequent out-of-town trips, usually sexually sated, he insisted upon peace and quiet. As for the children, only one way to deal with them. When his son displeased him, he thrashed him, and when his daughter annoyed him, he bullied her. When he was home for any length of time and his sexual appetite overcame him, his wife would unexcitedly provide relief. Sophie never spurned him, possibly because for months at a time he made no demand. They seldom discussed the past.

In truth, Max was just a little in awe of the cloddy woman he had married. She consistently went to night school, partaking of adult extension courses, and devoured subjects of the widest range that had, as far as he could see, absolutely no relevance to their daily lives: Aristotelian Philosophy, Theatre Arts Appreciation, Comparative Religions, Eastern World Cultures, Psychology and Reality, English for the Foreign Born, Intermediate English, Advanced English, English this, English that, Great Literature, The Influence of Pulp Magazine Fiction, History, Astronomy, and at least a dozen more he could not recall. Woman's place is in the kitchen and in bed. Too bad there aren't courses in Giving Head or Fornication. He'd sure like to teach *that* class. He would occasionally chide her but not oppose. As for her nuttiness on Mah-Jong, well, he understood. Everybody's turned on by something. He was ape for big tits. If she was content, so was he. She had her nights, he had his, and it would be foolish to upset the status quo.

The fact that Max could not bring himself to acknowledge was that his wife was better educated and more knowledgeable and spoke better English than he or the children, native born. It was this reserve of glacial sovereignty within her that he could not penetrate, that possibly kept the household from becoming unglued. Even the children sensed this and would push their mother only so far and no further.

The touchstone of Sophie's life was the Wednesday night game. It was Family Night. She truly loved Elsa, Freda, Gertrude and Hannah as she did not her own. As deeply over the years as, for a few bittersweet months long ago, she had loved the original Sophie. Among them, Elsa was probably the most affluent, to judge by her big house in Toluca Lake, Freda the most attractive and assured, and she surmised that Gertrude's and Hannah's lives were in order, as reasonably complacent as one might expect, all things, past and present, considered. But not to anyone, not to her husband or children, nor even to the players, did she ever disclose the incident in the train station where she had shed her original identity and assumed another.

So: Fat Sophie—modest, nonacquisitive, lover of learning and Mah-Jong, adversity's child from the moment of her birth, absorbent as a sponge, a born survivor.

Her fingers probed and pressed and then she sighed fatalistically. They found lumps, the size and consistency of uncooked peas, one on each breast.

On Monday following the Wednesday, Freda went again to Papa Grossman's.

It was a visit calculated to take advantage of its least busy night in order to increase her visibility. Due to the Monday night paucity of patrons, she was able to situate at the same table that she and Vicki had occupied on the previous visit. That would serve to enhance remembrance. The decision to embark upon this unsavory but necessary mission did not evolve easily.

Earlier, her body damp and cool and tinged to a glowing pink by a needlepoint shower, she had surveyed herself nakedly in the mirror. She was not displeased by what was reflected. Considering the abuse to which her younger body had been subjected—the receptacle for countless jackhammer ejaculations of faceless assailants, probed, poked and permeated by instruments, blunt and pointed, her now-body, despite assault and age, displayed remarkable resiliency and was relatively scar free.

Her breasts were full with large aureoles and the curve of her thigh, she knew, could still entice, augmented by long slender legs with almost too thin ankles and buttocks unpocked by cellulite. Still, the clock ticked its inexorable tock, and undeniably, there was concession to time, if not abuse; the barely perceptible overlay of belly fat, the lacy network of filigreed veins under translucent skin, the crinkled skin at the elbows and the slight droop of an ample bosom. But strategically corseted, men, all ages, still reacted. Their heads swiveled when she entered a room. She was aware that she could pass in the dark.

Which is precisely what she would do if unavoidably pressed to it. To personally verify the dog bite to absolutely authenticate the despised man. Of the five women, she was certain that only she was capable of the ultimate sacrifice to cause. She was unwed, with no real responsibilities to anyone but herself.

She knew too, without conceit, that despite being the eldest, she was the most attractive. Only Elsa, the youngest, could possibly qualify, but Elsa had neither the temperament nor the unattached state to undertake the loathesome venture. Lana Turner was fifty-four, Olivia de Havilland close to that, Ava Gardner, others still provocative, Bergman at sixty and the perennial love-goddess, Dietrich, into the seventies.

At first, she thought to hire a prostitute. But there was the off-chance that Grossman/Gehbert would react with distaste to a professional and reject her. Very likely that would not be the case, but however remote, there was that risk. Or if accept her, she might mistake a birthmark or abrasion for the scar, or if he was unmarked, fabricate, thinking to tell her what she wanted to hear.

Also, he was older now, the weatherings of time could make him reluctant host to a languorous libido. She mused that with the innumerable women he'd impaled, it was surprising that his overworked cock by now was not eroded. Whatever, she was possessed and determined to confirm his true identity, however contaminated she already felt by even the thought of contact with him. Still, if the tiles fell right, perhaps she could get him to reveal his chest without sacrificing herself.

Perish the thought, Freda Friedkin. A stiff prick knows neither pride nor conscience. You wants to know, you pays the price. She ruled out recognition. He couldn't possibly, over the gap of time and women, recall their first brutal encounter with any specificity.

She was fortified by this: 5,450 murders.

Four years' imprisonment—three years' "loss of honor." One day served for each three murders.

If it was to be done—and it had to be done—she was the one to do it.

Bizarre.

She would, after thirty-two years, attempt to seduce her seducer.

She'd called the restaurant and asked would Papa Grossman be there tonight? Assured that he would as usual, she'd hung up without identifying herself.

The minutes dragged. She was nursing a second glass of May wine and looking to the entrance with subdued and seemingly worried pretense, as if expecting someone to come through, glancing again and repeatedly at her watch. She'd arrived at a quarter past seven, it was now quarter to eight, and she had not as yet ordered dinner. When the waitress approached again, she apologized. She was still waiting.

Waiting, yes... but it's not the outside doors, it's the kitchen batwings. When will the bastard come out? Horrendous thought: suppose he does not for the rest of the evening. She was fearful that she would not be able to work herself up again to do a reprise. Worse than contact was not contact.

In the midst of contemplating alternative action, he came out of the kitchen, sauntered among the patrons, then came over to her and nodded.

"Good evening," he said pleasantly. "You are back."

He had, as she had hoped, recalled her, but she feigned surprise and rewarded him with a smile.

"I enjoyed my last visit."

"Are you expecting the young lady?" She arched her eyebrows in puzzlement, and he added, "She was young."

"Ah yes. That was my granddaughter. My goodness, that was weeks ago."

"Surely, not your granddaughter." His surprise was genuine. "I would have thought your daughter."

"Thank you."

"You are waiting for her?"

"No."

"I see." There was a slight beat. "If I am not impertinent—"
and hesitated.

"Yes?"

"But you are waiting for someone?"

"Is it obvious?"

"Madame keeps looking to the door."

"Well, yes. Late, I'm afraid."

"Unforgiveable."

"Perhaps my directions were not explicit."

"It can be difficult for a woman to drive the canyon."

"I am not waiting for a woman," she replied, assuming just
the slightest coyness.

"Then even more so. If I were delayed, I would phone." She
did not reply and he studied the gold band on the fourth finger of
her left hand. "Your husband?"

"I am a widow."

"I see." And as she reached for another sip of wine, he said,
"I hope that you will not give up."

"Give up?"

"Waiting."

"Well, it is embarrassing. I do not like to eat alone."

He gestured to a chair opposite her. "May I?"

She tilted her head noncomittally. He sat.

"Perhaps more wine until he arrives. You must try a fine
Pouilly-Fuisse."

"Oh no," she said, cupping a well-manicured hand over the
glass. "I am not a drinker. I have already had two glasses, and I'm
afraid I'm feeling a bit tipsy."

"It does not show, believe me."

"Another sip and it will."

"Then I urge it," he smiled and said gallantly, "It will be
most becoming."

Followed by an impasse, and she was fearful that he would
be impelled to leave if the void could not be filled, and she groped
for what to say to hold him, but he did not allow the moment to
become weighty. Apparently, he too was reluctant to relinquish
conversation.

"I am trying to place the accent."

"Oh—Berlin," she said, making it sound offhand. "I was quite young when my family left."

"Ah, quite so. It is barely noticeable. Myself, I am from Alsace." She nodded and thought: up an aardvark's ass you are, butcher.

"Do you know it?"

"No," she said and took another sip. "I do not think back to those times. I have little remembrance or interest in them." And hoped that would forestall further discussion along those shoals.

"Good," he agreed. "I believe that too. There is only today."

"I agree." She placed fingertips to her forehead, shut her eyes briefly, opened them again, and he was staring disconcertingly. There was a deceptively deep penetration in the pale blue of his washed-out eyes.

"You must not do that," she chided.

"What?"

"Staring at me like that."

"Was I?"

"Yes." And looked unflinchingly at him.

He emitted a throaty chortle and said, mockly abject, "I am sorry. Forgive me." She looked again to the entrance and he continued, "Madame is not thinking of leaving?"

"I am thinking I am not feeling well."

"Then you should order something."

"I am not hungry."

"I understand."

"Perhaps I bore you."

"I cannot believe that could ever be," he responded, and again his eyes burrowed.

"Perhaps I'll feel better when I return." She rose and he got to his feet. "Excuse me."

She threaded through the tables and once inside the ladies room, she inhaled and expelled deeply. The son of a bitch was baited. She felt no elation. If he was still there when she returned, she felt that the rest should go as well. For no reason that she could think of, she washed her hands, then dried them with paper napkins from a stack on a wall shelf, and poising herself to return, looked once more into the mirror.

The young face looked back at her, soulful and sadly reproachful...

Incisive stings of pained recall... the roundup... one of a thousand frightened wretches sardine-packed into ten sealed freight cars... seventy-two hours of a dark, sweltering, claustrophobic lurching through an unseen countryside... no food, no water... fear engulfs like pus bursting a massive boil... bladder and bowls erupt... the vomitous stench... those already dead imprisoned upright within the prison, unable to fall... doors finally slide open to disgorge its stinking, dehydrated cargo... watchful machine gunners under the camp gateway sign: *Arbeit Mach Frie*—"Work Creates Freedom"... the dead carted away, the dying and debilitated to be disposed of... this younger one in the crusted dress still maintains a sensual residue of womanhood... led away for "special treatment"... stripped, hosed, dried and covered with coarse cloth to be presented to Dr. Wilhelm Gehbert... tall, handsome, cold blue eyes in a sculptured face... no sooner presented, the door closed, without amenity the fly unbuttons, the bulging obscenity uncoils like a liberated spring...

"Suck!"

Stupified...

"Suck, Jew-cunt!"

Legs paralyze to the floor... she is outside her body... he slaps her... she topples... pain spears from jaw to temple... the sack she wears folds back to reveal a spread of milk white legs. In split second lucidity, she knows that to survive is not to resist. Twenty-two and she had never known a man... and he is now thrusting between her legs... she is flaccid... passivity feeds passion... up, down, up, down, his body heavy upon her with spasmed panting... a curtain of fire... an eternity... and finally, the slamming of essence against vaginal walls—

There was a sound, jolting her back to the present reality, realizing that she was again wringing her hands under the tap.

"Out, damned spot, out—" MacBeth? "All the perfumes of Arabia will not sweeten—" She quickly dried her hands, matted the napkins tightly, almost savagely, into a tight ball and flung it into a container, composed herself, and without a sideward glance to the arrival, went out.

5,450 murders.

Four years' imprisonment—three years' "loss of honor." One day served for each three murders.

If he was still waiting.

He was waiting.

He was sipping the highly touted Pouilly-Fuisse. He rose and lifted the glass and said, "I took the liberty to officially join you," adding, "Feel better?"

She sidled into her chair, nodding, and looked pointedly to the entrance. "There was no call for me?"

"I'm sorry. None."

"Then," she sighed, "he may not come."

"I cannot believe that."

"I am ashamed to say. One half hour late."

"Please," he remonstrated gently, "do not be ashamed."

"I think perhaps...I am stood up."

"He may yet come," and then said without conviction, "Perhaps he encountered trouble. A flat tire or out of gas."

"I think not," she said flatly and with a studied grace, caressed her forehead. "I am afraid I have had too much to drink. I think I should go." But she made no move to implement.

"Perhaps some fresh air."

"Yes," she said, leaning back in the chair, knowing that the next vital and key move would be his. The room was beginning to close in on her. "I am afraid my evening is wasted."

"It need not be," he ventured, searching her face for encouragement, and thinking he'd detected it. "It is a slow night. I am not needed here. If Madame does not think me bold—"

"Oh no. You are most considerate." She turned the corners

of her mouth upward and favored him with the barest hint of an invitational smile.

"Then I suggest a drive. It is most agreeable outside."

"That is very thoughtful." And just the right note of coyness. "Are you sure that you want to do this?"

"It would be ungallant of me to do otherwise."

"You are very gracious."

"My car is parked behind the kitchen. A BMW—blue."

She thought: A BMW. Made in Germany. A small consistency. She favored him with a wider acquiescent smile, and he rose again and helped her to her feet with courtly grace, one hand gently placed under her wrist, the other supporting her elbow. The second time in thirty-two years he'd made her skin crawl.

"Are you all right?"

"Oh!"

She realized that she'd almost given the game away. By what she was setting into motion she would have to, before this Stygian night was over, more carefully discipline her reactions.

"I'll find it."

"In a few minutes then."

His head bowed and she half-expected that he'd click his heels and *"Sieg Heil."* She brought up her purse and unclasped it in a movement to pay for her wine.

"Please." He gestured that payment was unthinkable.

"Thank you," she said demurely, and quaking inside, she turned abruptly lest he perceive it and moved, not too quickly, for the doors. The back of her neck told her that he was watching her egress, anticipatorily savoring the promise of the night.

Outside, she opened her purse, assuring herself of the comforting presence of the .22-calibre pistol within and moved it to just below the clasp for handier access, and went around to the kitchen side. There were several cars parked within the Reserved for Employees area, saw the BMW, opened the door of the front passenger side and slid inside.

He came out in moments. Minus the chef's cap and shapeless cook's jacket, he appeared shorter. He still bore a respectable head of hair, only mildly recessive, still dark and possibly dyed, save for the sideburns. If so, it was an artistic job. He had changed into a shirt, and impeccably added a tie and wore a camel-colored cashmere jacket. He got into the car, was pleased to note her presence, acknowledged it with a smile, started the car and wordlessly drove off.

It was dark now, the road sparse of vehicles, serene and clear, with lights from the hillside homes owlishly blinking in the night. She sat deep in the orthopedic comfort of the seat to brace her spine. They drove in silence as her mind raced ahead to forecast the result of what she had fatefully embarked upon. She was mindful of jeopardy, but the immediate obsessive goal outweighed peril. He had been either bitten by a dog or not bitten, and that was either the beginning or the end of it. She hugged her purse close and yielded to the slap-slap rhythm of the tires on the tarmac.

He drove leisurely, familiarly, and at length spoke. "It is a very nice night."

She "Mmmm-ed" to the banality.

"I think even there are stars. One does not often see them any longer in the city."

Starlight, shmarlight, she mused. He was no more interested in a night with or without stars than she was.

The road ribboned through a verdured isolation uncommon in a megalopolis. Whatever its detractors may say, Los Angeles is a rare city and is, despite its architectural abominations and the rapacious bite of the bulldozer, colorfully crisscrossed by myriad hills and canyons interrupting its parking lots where coyotes and fox and sundry wildlife roam freely above the din of traffic, just a short distance from freeways.

He said, "I do not know your name."

"Anna," she replied easily.

"Anna," he repeated softly. "Anna—?"

"Just—Anna." Her tone was slightly peremptory, conveying the hint that a more personal identification would be forthcoming if the evening fulfilled its implication. Then she reversed the query. "Why are you called Papa Grossman?"

He chortled. "I am not a papa. I have no family. I have never married."

"I did not mean that——"

"For the restaurant it is comfortable. A personal identification but no more meaningful than Jack-in-the-Box," referring to a nationally franchised hamburger chain. "An image. Home. Family."

"Warmth," she said dryly.

"Exactly. For people to come back." And pointedly, "You came back."

"Yes. Perhaps"—her voice husky—"it was meant to be."

"Thank you," he nodded. "I am Walter."

Walter, Wilhelm—Grossman, Gehbert.

It was common enough, the retention of the initials. Those hiding often feel an umbilical compulsion, despite elaborate severance, to cling to some remnant of a disavowed past. The "Papa" cognomen usually called to mind someone like the late character actor, chubby and jello jowled, S. Z. Sakall, who vulnerably regarded the world with Kewpie doll wonderment. But this man beside her, Grossman/Gehbert, was as far removed from that image as fire from water. Too, "papa" was an endearing universal term. Consciously or otherwise, it would be another consistency for Gehbert. Still another rape.

Soon they were twisting up a narrow gravel road, passing a few houses set well back from the road and presently halted before what appeared to be a smaller modified version of the restaurant, built, she surmised, about the same time.

Through this, through eyes half-slitted, she'd tried to note landmarks; a cluster of staked mailboxes, a huge overhung tree set apart from others, the stone fence at a sharp curve—just in case.

"We're here," he said, the engine shuddering to a halt, and got out, went around the front of the car and helped her out.

"Uhm," she said headily of the heavily scented air. "Jasmine."

"Yes. Much grows wild here. It must be seen in the daytime to be appreciated."

She did not feel it incumbent to respond. Guiding her by the elbow, he escorted her up a wide step rise composed of four railroad ties onto a protuberant stoop.

No dog barked. She did not expect him to own one.

He took out keys, inserted one, opened the door and allowed her to enter first, directly into a large beamed room glowing softly by a single lamp light.

"Be comfortable," he said, "I'll make a fire."

There was no chill in the room but he went to the large fireplace, molded of various size natural stone, turned on the gas feed, and in moments the eucalyptus logs were crackling. She noted the room; neat, various periods of furniture mismatched in exquisite antique taste from the sturdy Louis XV sofa to curiously, a collection of vari-hued miniature Venus statues punctuating the room on tables and shelves and housed in curio cabinets, ranging in size from a few inches to a little over a foot high.

She thought wryly, 5,450 murders and not a tear shed, break one of these and it would undoubtedly crush him.

Music lilted into the room from somewhere out of shadowed corners, and presently he was before her with two snifters of brandy.

"Tchaikovsky," he said, proferring one, and as she accepted she replied, "Yes. I recognize it." She wondered that before this night was over, would she detest "Waltz of the Flowers" as Sophie did "The Blue Danube"?

He gently jostled the brandy to raise its bouquet and raised the snifter to her in toast fashion, and she accommodated by repeating the action.

"Dreams," he said.

"Dreams." She tilted the snifter, barely wet her lips and awaited his ploy.

"You are admiring my Venuses," he said, pleased.

"They are lovely."

"Thorwaldsen—Gibson—Covano. Most are reproductions.

I cannot afford originals." He shrugged apologetically and appeared quite disarming for the confession.

She thought: and probably a collection of pornography as well, and necrophiliac at that. She said, "I have no hobbies. And I do not collect."

He stared at her and said, "You said a wasted evening. I hope not so far."

She returned his gaze unflinchingly. "No. I am enjoying." And expected that she would not have long to wait for his move.

All of two seconds.

He took her snifter and set both aside, then removed his jacket and draped it on a chair and loosened his tie, then crossed back to her. She wore a three piece ensemble, fingertip length jacket, blouse and skirt of fine giana material. Without a word he peeled the jacket from her. Resistlessly, she squared her shoulders to allow it to slip easily, an action calculated to jut her buxom charms, her breasts rounding and straining tautly against the clingy jersey fabric of the buttoned blouse. She shook her head, and her hair cascaded wantonly, shoulder length, and turned invitingly, facing him directly, tantalizingly haloed in the soft glow of firelight, anticipatorily poised like a grillwork Venus perched atop the hood of a motor car.

She half expected assault, but his kiss was undemanding, feathered.

Jeanette MacDonald and Nelson Eddy... Where are you? "I am calling you-oo-oo-ooo..."

He pulled her close and his passion escalated. He kissed her eyes, nose, back to mouth, as she suppressed her gorge. She ran her hands along his chest, disengaging three buttons of his shirt, to dip her hands inside, caressing the soft wool of his chest, to finger her way to the left shoulder to ascertain a telltale welt, but the goddam fucking tie kept getting in the way, and by the time she could ease a hand past the matted chest, he'd pulled back.

He yanked at his tie and flung it away. Fire glints danced in his eyes, lascivious. He quickly pulled off trousers but no longer meticulous, kicked them into a heap. His shorts followed, then shoes and socks—but the shirt stayed, the top three buttons unfettered, the bottom three still secure.

As she once more stretched her hand to his chest he parried it, pulling her in close once again and pivoted her so that her back was to him. She could feel his hardness pressing through her skirt. Muttering inaudible endearments in their native tongue, he felt with one hand for the button of her skirt and with the other, cupped a cushiony breast. With one-handed expertise, the button easily yielded, the skirt was proficiently unzipped, and it fell to the floor in an accordion heap. She wore nothing underneath.

She shifted to step out of the orbit of the skirt and to face back into him, but now she was anchored by fondling hands on both breasts. The constricted attempt to turn served to inflame him as he flicked his tongue along the nape of her neck, face buried in hair, seeking an erogenous ear lobe.

As he snorted into her ear, his huffing assumed the decibel count of a runaway engine, she ceased movement and quite rationally unbuttoned her blouse rather than risk its being shredded. It would be expensive to replace. But there was a more important reason to keep it intact. Its full sleeves covered the Birkenau tattoo. She bent away from him and his hands withdrew and slithered along her hips. Reaching back under the loosened blouse, she unhooked the barely supportive strapless brassiere, and as her breasts blossomed in release, it fluttered wispily to the floor.

She had intended to make him shed his shirt before it might be necessary to remove the blouse. He first, and she would go no further if the scar was revealed. She would act then, do what had to be done. If, however, the shoulder was unblemished—the wrong man—well then, bloused or unbloused, the poor man need never know how precipitously he had come to pay for lust, and that he might justly deserve the reward of release, however unfeeling on her part, for unwarranted suspicion.

She had strategically rested her purse, unclasped, to one side of the sofa at its base, with the resolution ensconced within. Either flopped back or preferably on her feet, it was within two steps reach. Vertically, she could swoop down to it, or if less desirably positioned, ferret out the weapon, brandish it, shock him into immobility and shoot him, appropriately and symbolically, in the groin.

But he was agile as a cat, and as she was fleetingly reviewing procedure, he nimbly maneuvered her with carnal finesse, pivoting her deftly into him and capitalized on her momentum to bend her back, down and onto the billowy eiderdown cushion of the Louis XV sofa. She realized in quick appraisal, en route and off balance, that her head would come to rest on the opposite side to where the purse reposed.

She agitated under him attempting to reverse herself, but her thrashings only served to further stoke him, a misconstrued paean to macho prowess that he could bring her to such early arousal. It was futile and she quickly reconnoitered.

"Darling," she cooed with silky loathing, trying to coax him off by pulling on his hair as he dipped his head between her thighs, "Take off your shirt."

He was unhearing, impervious to pain, orally immersed. She felt wet and maggotty.

So much for Plan A. Improvise Plan B. Knee him in the gonads. But here too, she was thwarted for execution was not possible. He was positioned heavily over her, his bulk cleaving her legs as she frustratingly flailed them in inefffectual arcs.

She shifted mental gears. Plan C. Simulate passion—grunt and groan—sneak a cramped hand to the elusive shoulder—verify—ultimately he'll subside for oxygen—causing a switch in position—whereupon leap up—dive for the purse—reinstitute Plan A.

"Oh love! Love!" (DIE DIE!) Joylessly undulating, "More, more!" (If there is a God in Heaven, Nate's God, anybody's, forgive my apostasy and strike this cancered cuntlapper from the face of the earth—a heart attack—massive—settle for small—a stroke—!' But the God she felt had abandoned her thirty-two years ago was also not in this room. The unvoiced plea went unheeded. Grossman's/Gehbert's hands and tongue continued in multiple. The only stroke was his.

He did indeed shift position; with surprising alacrity, magnetically guided, he abruptly inserted.

So shocked was she by the alien object thrust into her that she emitted the first unguarded sound genuinely uttered by her all night, a barely audible gasp—"Mama..."

He tremored inadvertently upon entrance, and she felt his body abate and sag forward, momentarily spent by effort and ecstacy. Just then the bottom buttons of his shirt ripped their moorings. It was the specific moment to roll out from under, but his sudden insertion had impaled her figuratively as well, and she was sloth. Before she could recover from surprise and engineer the rollout, he recouped and was pumping with renewed vigor.

Maddened, inwardly berating herself for lost opportunity, she arched her back in instinctive protest and cried, "Son of a bitch!" grasped at his open collar with both hands, clutching firmly the right extremity with her left hand and with her right, yanked at the left. The shirt ripped laterally, neck to armpit. The endeavor cost; she collapsed and closed her eyes as if to blot out the ugly man-machine exerting in her. Oblivious to the tear, he reacted to the arching by placing both hands firmly under her buttocks and pincered them to enable a deeper press. She was supine now, torpid, yielding to his pulsations. Her eyes fluttered open, and his left shoulder was exposed to her at eye level mere inches away.

If she'd had any notion that he would be chronologically decrepit, his performance belied it. The quiver in his loins would do a young satyr proud...firelight danced...the Venuses glinted...Tchaikovsky played on...

Academy Award nomination for the Best Actress of Any Year for her valiant and death-defying performance in a once-in-a-lifetime role—that of the Sacrificial Angel to Avenge Inhumanity—the one and only:

FREDA FRIEDKIN
In
GOOD TRIUMPHS OVER EVIL

The envelope please. But she had seen too many movies. Or the wrong ones. A farcical fantasy bordered in black.

So intense was her scrutiny, eyes riveted to the heaving shoulder, that she had become detached from and outside her own body, which at that precise moment was undergoing the most profound and intimate collaboration.

The revealed shoulder proclaimed the irrefutable fact.

Walter "Papa" Grossman *was* Dr. Wilhelm Gehbert.

10

When Freda left Gehbert after her abortive attempt to kill him, she was in an absolute daze.

Her first orgasm in over thirty years was so totally unexpected, so consummately overwhelming, that she was swept with vertigo. From the first early weeks in Birkenau when she had been passed from Gehbert to the officer cadre, she had become so resistant in mind that when compelled to yield, she would constrict to forestall the paroxysm. They could vent themselves upon her, but she would derive no pleasure from their vileness. Later, with Nate, she had sincerely tried to induce climax but was unsuccessful. He had gone unsuspecting to his grave.

She had dug her nails deep into Gehbert's flesh and drew blood. Without conscious will, she continued to upthrust her body as he lay, panting, atop her. She was bereft of all sense, the here and now of it, unwilling to relinquish as she continued to propel, piston-like, under him.

Finally, spent, she subsided, breasts heaving, eyes shut, purring rapturously. He slid from her, drenched. Of all the women, beyond remembrance, he had not encountered anyone like her. A wildcat, with a sexuality that belied age. Then he smiled wryly at the myth and puffed with pride. His own was not to be belied.

He left her to shower, dressed, and then returned to her. She was supine on the couch. Only now her eyes were open, wide with wonder. He reached over and gently brought her to a sitting position. She pulled him down beside her and clung to him and caressed his face, her own suffused in radiance. The fire dimmed, Tchaikovsky played out, and no words passed between them.

Then she rose on quaking limbs, gathered her garments, and silently padded to the bathroom. She revived under the shower, dressed and returned to two refilled brandy snifters.

Gehbert spoke the first words since Ecstacy.

"You enjoyed?"

"Mmm," Freda murmured.

He came to her and held her close and kissed her lightly. She nestled in his embrace and could not believe what had happened, knowing only that for so long denied, there had to be, was certain to be, more. She pulled slightly away and studied him with luminous eyes. His face was soft and as full of yearning as her own.

"Did I hurt you?" she asked.

My God, did she just say that?

This is Freda Friedkin?

B 366753!

That is Wilhelm Gehbert!

Did she *hurt* him?

The Butcher of Birkenau!

He smiled and shook his head. And she thought, I can't believe it could be like this. I'd heard but I could not know. It's come late in my life, but it's here, and now and I must not let go.

"We will meet again?" he asked with an unlikely qualm, that hers was a one night stand, a summit reached not to be scaled again. Realizing, that out of all he'd experienced, he had not, until this woman, whoever she is, thought of any woman beyond his own need.

She thought: He's not what he was. I am not what I was. Things change. People change. Change is the essence of life. Was it only moments ago—an hour, two—that her resolve to kill was as firm as Gibraltar, swept away, unthinkable now?

He brought her out of her reverie, repeating, "Will we meet again?"

"Yes," she said without hesitation and was not appalled.

Not until later when he drove her back to the restaurant and she sped away did the full impact of what had transpired hit her. She stopped roadside and got out of the car. There, in the cool night air, with the dew heavy on the ground and dripping from the trees, Freda vomited.

11

On her wedding night Hannah Epstein had, passionately immersed, moaned without awareness, "Paul...Paul..." The bridegroom's name was Leon.

He was puzzled and hurt but never mentioned it. Through a twenty-six-year union which bore three children and four grandchildren, and alone now for the first time since their first year of marriage, their ardor had not lessened. But of late, Hannah detected a decided coolness and Leon's reluctance to bed. She wondered if he was seeing another woman.

Hannah Prinz was an only child, reared in a comfortable house in a pleasant neighborhood in Wurzburg, a gay city in baroque and rococo, located on the right bank of the Main River southwest of Frankfurt. Pleasant, that is, until her sixteenth year when she had two awakenings. The boy next door and the Nazis.

Paul was eighteen, and until she was fifteen he was brother and protector and teased her furiously. But when she budded there was a change. She teased. Both families were friendly, and though they thought the children too young to consider marriage, looked favorably to it in the future.

Within the year Paul was dead, and Mama and Papa. She had escaped the same fate, for at the time she was visiting an aunt in Bamberg. Six months later she was dispatched to Birkenau.

In the bleak week of the triple deaths, she went to sudden womanhood, discovering also that she was pregnant. Only then did she learn that her father, who seemed a vague, loving man, whose world seemed circumscribed by his jewelry shop six blocks away and the large house, a pipe incessantly clenched between his teeth, had been a member of a clandestine organization gathering information on the welling atrocities of the Nazis against the Jews, not yet fully proclaimed to the world. Gentle Mama had been auxiliary. Paul had been a messenger, running with gleaned bits of information to secret printers and archivists. So covert were their activities she did not even remotely suspect this other part of their lives. Nor did Paul's parents know.

Paul, it was reported, did not die easily. Chased by the SS, he had led one to a dead end and strangled him before he was clubbed down. To the end, a week later, he steadfastly refused to cooperate and in an excess of zeal, was beaten to death, for which the local gauleiter was upbraided by his superiors. Dead men tell no tales, and he was demoted for exceeding the refinements of torture to extract information.

Papa had received visitors the week she was away, and she would never know whether it was fortuitous or by design that she had been sent to Bamberg as a favorite niece to an ailing aunt. The visitors were polite but insistent. Names please. Papa dissembled. What names? They would return tomorrow. They returned, more insistent. Papa knew no names. They smashed furniture. Tomorrow they would not be so polite. Meantime, he was not to go to the jewelry shop. That night they learned of Paul's death from his grief-stricken parents, who berated the Prinzes for leading their only child to an untimely demise.

They were Jews who abjured Jewishness, seeing not, hearing not, German nationals first and foremost, the pox would go away, if only all Jews would understand that these bully aberrations come and go. It was beyond their ken that their son, flesh of their flesh, by rite of circumcision, found his own individual way to join with the Zionist youth movement, and the Communists and with those of no political or religious persuasion, Jew and non-Jew, who could not let basic decency go by default. They were a woeful couple who would die hating their kinsmen more than their oppressors.

That same night Prinz, while his wife was heavily sedated, put a bullet into her brain and then turned the pistol on himself. Miles away, the aunt, apprised, tried to console Hannah, who tried to gas herself. Hannah failed because the kitchen had too many openings. Three months pregnant, she aborted, and that was the first anyone knew of it.

From then on she channelled herself to a more direct purpose. She would die, she knew, but not uselessly. She became an active underground worker. Her motives were simple. For Paul and the baby, and after them, her parents. They should be avenged, no matter by what means, no matter what the cost to herself or to anyone else. But despite her zeal, the underground, regrouped and tattered, was wary and careful in their use of her, for she was the marked daughter of marked parents. She ran errands, carried messages, occasionally a slab of plastic explosive taped inside her thighs.

She was captured by a fluke, in a roundup, a random scooping up of people from the streets. On a non-errand day she was netted in a sudden sweep in a marketplace with scores of others, men, women and children. It was not known that she was an activist, but she was Jewish; so a woman, she was herded to Birkenau; being young, funneled to Gehbert.

Hannah was deliberately passive, and other than venting himself, he found her less than satisfactory, and as with all the others, promptly forgot her. But she did not forget him. He was the second man to possess her. The contrast between Paul, idyllic, and Gehbert, venal, was stark. Night after night under the most deplorable conditions, including medical experimentation, which fortunately were not so extensive as to permanently impair her, she fantasized how to kill Gehbert. But, of course, there was no chance of this. She seldom saw him—only when he'd strut the grounds on inspection, always accompanied by a dog.

Auschwitz-Birkenau was more than a concentration camp; it was a liquidation center, the dominant slaughterhouse of the German Third Reich to make it Judenrein (Jew-free). Every day 8000 prisoners were killed, replenished around the clock by daily freightloads of packed arrivals to maintain a roughly constant inmate population of 250,000. Hannah marvelled that she survived. The ferocious hatred of all Gehbert represented and the bittersweet remembrance of Paul sustained her. And luck.

Liberation.

More than one-third of the Jewish population of the world had been annihilated. Two-thirds of the Ashkenazi Jews (German Jews, as distinguished from the Sephardim, the Jews of Spain and Portugal) had perished. Those remaining alive were no longer being converted into fertilizer and soap. The Americans, British and Russians gave them food, clothing and medical care, but beyond immediate relief measures, no unified plan existed for their future. When the magnitude of the German solution was finally revealed, the world was horror-struck, fumbled in ineptitude, for the Jew was still a problem, an irritant and embarrassment. So they were gathered from the death and slave-labor camps, from the forests where they hid and from the rubble of ghettos, and herded into new camps to face an uncertain destiny. Death did not await them but rot did. Many committed suicide, unable to cope with a despair that stretched as bleak into the future as the remembered past.

For two thousand years Jews had shunted from nation to nation, no matter the form of government or religious ethic, tolerated to a more or less degree but always a thing apart, subject to political vagaries, unable to join into the mainstream. Where was acceptance now? Among the ruins of the Third Reich, Germans were still killing Jews. Poland was vile toward the Jews; much of the population had collaborated with the Germans even as they themselves were being degraded. The Soviet Union embraced a manifesto promulgated by a Jew, but czar or commissar, hostility was pervasive. France was still Dreyfus country. Only the Scandinavian countries, Holland and Switzerland were hospitable, but their resources were limited. The United States was a disappointment. It had welcomed countless of the oppressed, the homeless and the wretched of the world and had virtually depleted middle and Eastern Europe of Jews during the latter part of the nineteenth century and into the twentieth, an exodus unmatched in the annals of migration. But now it foundered on its own generosity behind the imposition of a quota system. The British were aberrant. They accepted Jewish troops from Palestine to fight in the British army through the campaigns of Italy and France and Africa, but beseiged as they were, still found arms and shipments to keep Jews out of Palestine.

The blunt truth is that the Allied forces did not fight to save the Jews, or the Gypsies, who had the dubious distinction of being the only other race to officially share genocide, or any of the political and religious categories deemed inimical to the Third Reich, but to prevent a foreign paranoia from invading and infecting their own native lands.

The United Nations Special Committee on Palestine stated for the survivors to the General Assembly:

> We know of no country to which the great majority can go
> in the immediate future other than Palestine. Furthermore,
> that is where all of them want to go.

Palestine! The messianic dream of a homeland. It was a land as scruffy as it was fiercely contested. Surrounded by Arabs and closed out by the British, resistance groups tore at British garrisons and ran their blockades in leaking tubs. The Jews, tenacious as weeds, kept coming, an endless stream of men, women and children. The British could no more stem the human flow than King Canute could reverse the ocean tide.

Hannah joined the Haganah, the underground Jewish Defense Organization, which worked within the camps to mobilize the refugees. She assisted those willing to risk the secret steps to embark upon the harrowing journey, planning at a later date to join the hegira.

Harvey Prinz altered her direction from east to west. He was an official of ORT, Organization for Relief and Rehabilitation Through Training, the officially designated body of UNRRA to service the Displaced Persons Camps. Although Prinzes were not uncommon, Harvey Prinz felt possibly there was a blood tie to Hannah Prinz, vaguely recalling from his childhood adult conversation of a possible connection to a family branch in Frankfort. Hannah was uncertain, she had never heard discussion of relatives in the States. With the pride of a Columbus, he embraced her as long lost even before the fact was established and wrote to his family in Miami.

Prinzes there were uncertain but the query was forwarded to the eldest living Prinz, an ailing octogenarian, residing in a convalescent home in Los Angeles. He thought Hannah to be the daughter of a son whose father had been a cousin and, unsolicited, sent fare for her passage. Hannah was touched but reluctant to go. An ancient relative, however generous, in a strange land, held little charm. The local Haganah leader persuaded her. English had been her second language, she could be of greater service to the homeland by working with trusted citizens, Jewish businessmen and the like, in the procurement of funds for illicit arms being secretly shipped to Palestine.

Harvey, sympathetic to the cause, facilitated arrangements. Before leaving for America, Hannah was impelled to revisit Wurzburg, where Charlemagne had held court in 788 and Frederick Barbarossa had married Beatrice of Burgundy within its walls in 1156, and the Allies on a March night in 1945 had destroyed 85 percent of the city. Devastation everywhere. Her father's jewelry shop was rubble as was the residential section housing that had been her home and Paul's next door.

She poked in the ruins of both houses. What could she hope to find? An intact ashtray? One of papa's innumerable pipes? A crystal bead from a chandelier that once regally illuminated? A skillet handle protruded from a mound of debris. She nudged it with her toe. It fell away to reveal a torn—what? She bent to the object, upon touching it, gasped, knew it even before wholly seeing it. Coated with a fine film of plaster, a remarkably undebilitated photograph of Paul, preserved and unfaded, revealing sparkling dark eyes under an unruly mop of thick black hair that defied a comb, the finely chiseled nose upended, the head tilted back in a wide smile showing even white teeth.

Giddiness washed over her as she unbelievably devoured it, hearing again the deeply resonant laugh mustily echoing in the tunnels of her ears, swayed slightly and as quickly evaporated, turned it over. On the back, equally unravaged, was boldly scrawled "To my Beloved H."

God, she remembered now. She had taken the picture some weeks before the fateful one that had demolished two families. Now she held in her quivering hands a renewed piece of life, a tangible momento outside memory that long ago she had tingled to a boy-man who lived, loved and had given her life. Very carefully, she wrapped it in a handkerchief, tucked it into her purse, and not looking back, walked quickly back to the station as if fearful an unseen hand would snatch it from her.

She arrived in Los Angeles two days after the funeral of the beneficent relative, a victim at eighty-six of a hit-and-run driver. He left no estate, having virtually depleted his life savings to send for her and had been charitably buried by his synagogue. It was a shocking introduction to the new country. Alone and friendless, feeling an inestimable loss for one unknown, who gave so fully and was now beyond her repayment. Unless, it was to be fervently believed, he went to a higher reward for his loving act.

She registered with the '38 Club who alleviated her immediate distress, found her a place to live, a small furnished apartment on Normandie near Melrose Avenue and placed her as part-time saleswoman with the then newly constructed May Company store on Wilshire Boulevard, one of the largest department chains west of the Mississippi, which then, as now, catered to the large Jewish sector in the Fairfax area. Importantly, she established contact with a lower-echelon banker at the Bank of America, a memorized name, Herman Balin, and the code phrase *Dahm Y' Israel Nokeam* ("the Blood of Israel will take vengeance").

Herman Balin had been alerted to expect her. He was the Los Angeles coordinator for converting donated dollars into arms that were channeled to Palestine from secret port facilities and airfields in the States, Mexico and Canada. Paper work was kept to an absolute minimum, and phones were not trusted. Hannah became a vital link in the procurement network, a courier, back to running, carrying large amounts of clandestine cash in a knitting bag culled from moneyed Jews and sympathetic gentiles, the pious and the atheist, in polished offices, restaurants, posh apartments and run-down flats, and in that most serviceable of trysting places, the automobile.

But even in fabled America she looked over her shoulder. For America the Beautiful played the international game, principally to appease its main ally, Britain, officially frowning upon illegal shipments, although minor officials of various government agencies, where they could, looked the other way. Her part-time job at the May Company served as cover, and she was paid by Balin in cash, for services rendered, nominal amounts augmenting her limited weekly income, enabling her to live frugally well.

It was over for her on November 29, 1947, when the United Nations formally recognized Israel and the United States took over the shipping of munitions, thereby improving its balance of payments. Prior to this she met Bo Epstein, a former American pilot who regularly flew cargo. At a mobile assignation, to give him certain forged papers, he'd brought his younger brother. Because Bo's hand was recently broken and he could not drive, Leon, completely trustworthy, was his driver.

Leon Epstein was short and ebullient and smitten with Hannah at first sight. He felt an unreasoning guilt for his lack of involvement in America's greatest war, the armed services regretfully rejecting him because of a punctured eardrum. He had worked on the assembly line at the large Lockheed plant in Burbank all during the war. When it was over, laid off, enriched by inflated wages, he was able to send himself through pharmacy school with ease, which had not been the case when his studies had been interrupted in his first year by the hostilities. He loved his adventuresome big brother and assisted Bo in minor, but important, ways with the use of his car and by sharing his apartment whenever Bo came into town.

Innately shy, Leon wore ardor on his sleeve but could not articulate. Hannah respected his sincerity, was drawn to him, and ventured an initial advance, inviting him to her apartment for a home-cooked meal. It went well, he was encouraged and they began dating. Paul was a forever candle in her heart but it would be a disservice to shackle herself to memory. She was a resilient, aggressive woman with a normal social and sexual appetite, Wilhelm Gehbert notwithstanding; she would not allow that searing trauma and the mindless medical atrocities he symbolized to hobble her future.

If Leon was physically unprepossessing, she, more than most, could appreciate the manly grace of his sensitivity and gentleness. She did not reveal the past to him, but he was aware of what she had undergone because of her runner activity and tie to the '38 Club.

They were married in 1949 in a Reform service and went to Las Vegas, burgeoning in a postwar boom, for their honeymoon.

Her unaware utterances of "Paul, Paul!" on their wedding night baffled and wounded him. She was writhing in someone else's arms. In the ensuing weeks she repeated this several times and then subsided. Because he did not know how to handle it, he said nothing, for she did not lack fervor.

He discovered Paul many years later. Lubricating a resistant drawer in Hannah's bureau. It had been necessary to empty it prior to turning it over in order to sandpaper it. Underneath silky things was the original picture and a larger restored one. He panged at the bold inscription: "Zu meine Geliebte H." His smattering of German was sufficient to translate "To my Beloved H.," jealous for the lingering hold a slender and handsome youth had upon his wife; restored the drawer to its niche, and said nothing to her, but from that day his lovemaking became more insistent, which did not displease her.

However, she noticed a change in him, an uncharacteristic jealousy if she seemed to spend unaccounted time or enjoyed the company of other men. She was mildly disturbed but basically had no complaints—his devotion was touching and the envy of other women whose husbands were less courtly.

Now that the kids were gone, adjustment was the key, a normally trying period in a marriage of duration such as theirs. Suddenly two strangers confront each other in a household as silent now as it was formerly boisterous. Statistically, more divorces occur then than in the first year of marriage. But they bridged this period without difficulty. For all the familiarity between them, the years notwithstanding, they could still find stimulation in conversation and titillate each other under the sheets.

Leon pursued her with undiminished ardor, urging her into bed at all hours of the day. Since he worked a split shift she knew to expect an attack, front and rear, at any time, particularly if she was temptingly bent over a dustpan. Only themselves in an apartment, their love was no longer circumscribed. She had not the maintained physical beauty of Freda nor the enduring cuteness of Elsa, but she did keep herself well groomed, and felt attractive with no more than the usual aches and pains customarily associated with women her age. There was a joke between them; she would not forgive him if he ceased to regard her as a sex object, women's liberation notwithstanding. At her age it was a compliment to be relentlessly stalked by one's husband.

But not lately.

Leon seemed preoccupied. He panted less and sulked more. Occasionally his lack of inhibition had irked her and she'd rebuffed him, but gently lest she ruffle his manly pride, for she basked in his affection and shared his appetite. Was the Gehbert matter, kept secret from him, more telling upon her than she was aware? Ever since it had arisen she had been somewhat tense, but that certainly did not, she self-appraised candidly, affect her performance. She was puzzled. Leon was no great shakes as a looker, but as a lover he made points. Short, almost bald and paunching, he had little vanity, disdaining a hairpiece and binding underwear. Her antenna was up. What was it? Another woman? It's possible, she supposed. Nature is capricious. At a time when a woman undergoes menopause and dimunition of desire, a man's libido flares as a herald of withering gonads. Was he taking his male fire elsewhere, conserving himself for a younger woman? That could not be dismissed; obvious to think that, but her self-esteem would not allow her to dwell upon the possibility. It had to be something else.

She was close to the truth but not close enough. Ever since Gehbert had reentered into her life, Hannah had returned, after a quarter century dormancy, inadvertently and unknowing, to lamenting in Leon's arms..."Paul...Paul..."

Two days later, Gertrude hostessing.

The women were astounded by Freda's flat, fervent and all-out declaration that beyond any scintilla of doubt—"Papa" Grossman was none other than the infamous Butcher of Birkenau—Dr. Wilhelm Gehbert.

Her manner of conveying this without delineating the specifics told them more. How she had obtained incontrovertible proof. None asked, but each felt sullied for the sacrifice one among them had made to verify it. Discount morality, but the exposure to peril, foolish or not, had to have been enormous. And the unilateral action made each feel just a bit guilty for it.

Silence... Then Hannah said solemnly, "The ball is in our court."

"Yes," said Elsa softly. "Now we know."

Then Sophie spoke. "Let us consider very carefully from this point on what we are to do."

"Well... what?" Gertrude was uncertain.

"Look," said Freda with some asperity, "We've thought about it and talked about it, but we've never actually said it."

"Said what?" Hannah probed.

"He dies."

The women sucked breath, and Sophie bit into her lower lip.

"Dies?" Elsa echoed dumbly.

"D-I-E-S! Dies!"

They studied her, studied each other.

95

"If you believe it, say it. Each one says it. No euphemisms, no beating around the bush. Say it. He dies."

Elsa was the first to corraborate, barely audible. "Yes."

"Say it!"

"He dies," Elsa said staunchly.

"He dies," Gertrude said.

"Dies," Hannah followed.

"Dies," repeated Sophie.

"Louder. Together." Freda was relentlessly solemn. "Mean it."

The women were grouped around the bridge table on which the tiles were fanned, and Freda pounded it. A low collective rumbling, gut-emanated and worked through five throats, mushroomed and exploded. "Dies! Dies!" Whipped to pitch, they stamped their feet, pounded clenched knuckle-white fists on the table, its spindly legs threatening to collapse, the tiles leaping and clacking under the assault like burning crickets.

"Does he die?" Freda exhorted with cheerleader fervor, "Yes! Yes! Yes!"

And the chorus responded, "Yes! Yes! Yes!"

"Who dies?" she croaked. "Gehbert dies!"

Mesmerized, the chorus echoed in deep-throated unison, "Gehbert dies!"

"Again. Bounce it off the walls!"

"Gehbert dies!"

Harry, Gertrude's husband, came running out of the kitchen, to be simultaneously joined by Jeffrey, their son, erupting from the bathroom, a textbook in his hand.

"What the hell's going on with you dames?" Harry demanded.

"Chee-rist!" said Jeff. "Even in the can it sounded like a sonic boom."

They had been so intent and emotion-laden they had completely forgotten there were others in the house. Abashed, they looked sheepishly at each other and then to Freda for retrieval.

"Well, what the hell is it?" Harry persisted.

Freda feigned a cherubic innocence. "You hear anything, girls?"

"I'd dropped a tile," Hannah said sweetly.

"Nothing, Harry," Gertrude said. "Nothing."

"Nothing? You got to be kidding. I'm not deaf."

"Me too," Jeff chimed.

"Nothing," Gertrude repeated. "Nothing, I said."

"How can a guy study?" Jeff groused but made no move to leave.

"Be a good kid, Harry," Freda said and proposed, "Go for a walk. Take Jeff. It's time you two had a heart-to-heart."

"Huh? I don't want to go for a walk. What's this heart-to-heart?"

"I gotta study," Jeff said in shared perplexity.

"Then go to a massage parlor."

Harry clucked dryly, "I'd go but Gertie won't let me."

"You say that in front of Jeffrey," Gertrude said, "Shame."

"C'mon, ma, I'm no kid."

"Both of you go. Then report back to me."

"Freda!" Gertrude admonished.

"Sh! I'm working for the CIA. The massage parlors are a front for Billy Graham, right?"

"Right. Would you believe that he reports to a godfather who modestly fronts as a dentist in Culver City?"

"Huh?" said Jeff, suddenly losing interest, shaking his head, and returning to the bathroom. Harry continued in the spirit, reluctant to return to the solitary confine of the kitchen to which he had been relegated due to the cancellation of his weekly bowling game.

"Freda Friedkin, you are a true patriot."

"Fucking right."

"You are also foul mouthed."

"I was raised in a convent."

"Well, you just blew your cover. Those tiles—the dragons, winds and bams—they're really code, right?" He was enjoying the turn hugely.

"Sweet sucking Jehosophat!" Freda threw up her hands in mock dismay. "The firing squad for me."

"Don't worry about it. I know Irving Kushner."

"Who's he?" Elsa interposed.

"You don't know Irving Kushner?" he said aghast, then added airily, "Code name for John Wayne. Your secret is safe with me."

"Thank you, Harry Simon, thank you."

Gertrude wearied of the badinage. "Will you two shut up? Let's get on with the game. Harry, go for a walk or fix the faucet. It's been dripping for weeks."

Harry chose to go out. Whether for a walk or to a massage parlor did not become a matter of record, and in any case, he did not report back to secret agent Freda Friedkin. The room sobered and Hannah said, "We've got to be careful."

"The next important step," Freda said, "How does Gehbert die?"

"How?" Elsa repeated, "I think——" and when eight eyes focused to her, trailed off with a hapless shrug.

"Shoot him, knife him, poison him," Gertrude shrugged. "Point a gun, bang, bang. Like on TV."

"I do not think it is that easy," Freda observed. "We are five women, four married, with families and responsibilities. For as much murder that we have seen or been exposed to, we do not know, I think, how to kill."

"So many people do it, it can't be difficult," Hannah said. There was no humor in the statement.

"I mean," said Freda, "We are a group. It is not a secret if five do it, and five to do it would be awkward."

"One?" Elsa ventured.

"One, I think is best."

"Which one? You?"

"Yes."

The room was very quiet again.

Elsa resumed. "No, Freda. You have done enough."

"We are talking of killing," Freda quietly replied.

"No. I am against one taking action. Either we all commit or none commit."

"The floor is open."

"I—I don't know," Sophie floundered. "Max hates guns. We don't have anything like that." Then perked brightly. "Sears Roebuck has a sporting goods department. I suppose it would be easy to buy one."

"Or Big 5," was Freda's dry rejoinder. "And maybe they give green stamps too."

Sophie frowned. "I'm trying to be helpful."

"Sorry."

"I think Freda is right," Elsa said. "None of us has killed. But I would certainly try in this case—regardless of consequence."

"Consequence!" Sophie aspirated. The word and its implications geysered between them.

"I think," Hannah spoke, "If we commit—then to hell with consequences. I do not overlook it, but the percentage of unsolved murders is on our side. I am not brave and I do not want to be foolish, but it is something to be done or not done."

"Brave!" Gertrude said, "We must be clever. On Starsky and Hutch the other night I saw——"

"Forget Starsky and Hutch," Sophie interrupted. "It's a lousy program."

"You say."

"Ladies, ladies," Freda rapped the table. "Agreed, Gehbert dies. Agreed we will do it. The one who is chosen decides how to do it."

Elsa shook her head. "Not you."

"Me." Freda was direct. "For several reasons. I am a widow, alone, no family to speak of, basically responsible only for and to myself. I am the eldest and have fewer years to look forward to if I am caught. I care very much to live out the years that are left to me, but I am not overly concerned. I would be fulfilled by that bastard's death by my hand."

For a brief moment nothing was said. Then Hannah shook

her head. "I think not. Equal risk, equal blame."

"Then you force me to reveal the most compelling reason. I have terminal cancer. I do not expect to live the year."

There was an audible gasp in the room. Elsa was the first to shed the shock. "I do not believe you. Not until I see a doctor's report."

Her perception transmitted, and Hannah said with relief, "Shame on you, Freda." She grinned. "Good try. But even if that was the case it would not matter on principle."

Freda returned the grin. "Would you believe my ass itches?"

"Mine too," from Gertrude. "Stick to the point. I agree with Hannah. Five executioners—" she lingered over the word culled from endless hours of viewing television cookie-cutter melo-dramas. "Five would be too many."

"Freda said it," Hannah corrected. "But I'm sure we all agree."

Elsa eyed Freda perceptively. "Tell me, Freda. You went to Gehbert. If you want to be the one to do it now, why didn't you do it then?"

Freda was unequivocal. "I failed."

"Then nothing has changed. You have the same chance, one-fifth, as the rest of us."

"Wait, wait!" Gertrude suddenly said. "A thought. Suppose we hired someone to do it for us?"

Sophie pursed her lips and tugged at an earlobe.

"That would be expensive, wouldn't it? Assuming that we could find such a person."

"Hang the expense. We have our Mah-Jong fund, and if we needed more we could all chip in."

"I don't know," Sophie was doubtful. "Max is tight with money. He does all the banking. I only have what I can skim from kitchen money." She looked cow-eyed for having revealed this innermost privacy. "I mean it couldn't be more than a few dollars at a time on installments."

"There's something more important," from Hannah. "If he were caught, he could implicate us."

"Or blackmail us," Gertrude added, "And there goes *all* our kitchen money."

"There is only one way," Freda said. "I'd leave the method to the one who is chosen."

"Are we going to talk all night, or do we choose?" Gertrude said nervously. "Harry may be back soon, and Jeff may come out of his room. Can't we get to it and get it over?"

"What do you suggest?" Freda asked.

"Lots," Hannah offered. "A secret lot. So that any four of us will not know who the fifth is."

"Sophie pursed her lips in thought. "What do you think, Freda?"

"You know what I think," Freda replied. "What if the one chosen is least qualified to do it."

"I don't think that is a matter for discussion. If one is chosen, one does it however it is done," said Hannah.

"Then," Freda conceded with an elaborate sigh. "We should have some rules."

From Elsa, "What kind of rules?"

"Perhaps it is not necessary to state, but we must be extremely quiet about this. Tell nobody. Not our husbands. Not our families. And if anything goes wrong, we all hold ourselves responsible to protect that one."

It was agreed.

"Also, a time element. Say, a week for each one of us. A deadline five weeks from tonight to kill."

Hannah was dubious. "Why limit ourselves? It may be done in a week, two or three, or even the sixth."

"It has to have some form," Freda insisted. "Suppose this: whoever is chosen finds herself unable to do it or has a change of heart. What then?"

They agreed that it would be desirable not to prolong suspense and that the mission should be accomplished within the five-week period. Hannah, fully aggressive, summed up. "If the person chosen cannot do it, for whatever reason, then it is over, finished, kaput. There is to be no guilt, no stigma, and that person is never to reveal who she is."

They nodded in silent assent, but Freda made a final effort to dissuade them. "Please reconsider. Excuse me, but I still think I am the best qualified."

Hannah refuted her. "It is said that anyone given circumstance and emotion is capable of murder."

To which Elsa dryly amended, "We have circumstance and emotion."

"Right, right. Let's draw," Gertrude said anxiously. All rapped knuckes on the table in loose parliamentarian sanction save Freda, shaking her head, stubbornly refusing to yield, which annoyed Gertrude. "Goddam it, Freda. You are only one vote."

Elsa interceded and implored Freda to make it unanimous, whereupon Freda merely shrugged half-heartedly and went to the telephone in the hallway entry, tore five small sheets from a four-by-four six-inch notepad, scrawled a small swastika in the center of one and held it up for their scrutiny. The other pieces remained blank. Then she creased each piece, compressing them to equal-sized wads.

Just then the telephone rang, the shrill sound startling them. Gertrude took it up. "Hello . . . Yes, he's here." She cupped her hand over the mouthpiece and shouted, "Jeff—rey! For you-oo!", listened to the earpiece, waited for her son to pick up the extension in the inner hallway, then hung up. She went to a side table and took up a candy bowl, dumped its paper wrapped miniature chocolate bars and extended it to Freda. Freda dropped the wads into it. Then she took the bowl from Gertrude and moved to the center of the room, and held the bowl aloft above eye level.

"Alphabetically?" she queried, and Hannah Epstein endorsed the procedure by being the first to step forward and wordlessly reached up to withdraw a wad. She stepped back but did not unfold it. Then Freda one-handed hers, fisted it, and the others followed in order: Sophie Langbein, Gertrude Simon, and lastly, Elsa Spahn. Freda returned the empty bowl to its original position on the side table.

Each woman in silent withdrawn isolation gravely unfolded her wad, stared fixedly at it, and digested the enormity of what separately and together, they had initiated and embarked upon; and the heavy responsibility to the one now specifically committed to fulfill the sacred and secret deed of belatedly ridding the world of a diabolical sadist.

There was no sound in the room. Hushed, the drip-drip of a distant faucet magnified and permeated. Each rewadded her individual lot and secreted it on her person or placed it into a handbag. Gertrude replenished the bowl. Elsa turned on the radio from which a coincidentally apt muted rendition of Cole Porter's "Anything Goes" emanated. Elsa studied her fingernails with fierce concentration. Hannah tugged at her girdle, and tugged again. Sophie giggled, and trying to supress, could not restrain, and her lumpish body convulsed, the rolls of fat, belly to bust, jellied as if she were belted to a massage machine. At length, she abated, teary eyed, and blew her nose to signal her return to control.

It remained for Freda to break the tension by bellowing, "What the fuck are we standing around like dummies for?"

Whereupon they sat down, gathered the tiles, and played one of their best games in the twenty-year span.

13

Gertrude beat fiercely on the man's face with savage exultation until it was mashed to a bloody unrecognizable pulp. Then it was suddenly replaced by Gehbert's face, clean shaven and mocking, unmarked despite the relentless rain of blows. Until her hands swelled to boxing glove size and covered with bright red slime, fell upon him weak and spent, and he thrust into her with the ease of a rabbit in heat. She clawed at him, but her body betrayed her will and she flailed ineffectually as a baby, herky-jerky, as if manipulated by an unseen puppeteer. She cried out, but no sound was forthcoming, his penis swelling obscenely within her until it threatened to rip her apart.

She awoke abruptly when pulled upright, even then continuing to struggle and pummel.

"Gertie, baby, hey! Easy, easy."

She realized she was in her own bed and in the comfort of her husband's arms.

"Again?" Harry said. "Christ!"

Gertrude shivered, orienting.

"I thought you were choking to death," he said.

"I'm all right now," she said.

"You scare the shit out of me when you have a nightmare. What the hell you dreaming about?"

"I—I don't remember."

But she did, retained with ice-cold clarity, the gurgling plea of the doctor whose face she pulped with orgiastic delight, only to be supplanted by the granite of Gehbert's face and his heinous thrustings.

"Is it the same one?" he asked, not knowing what it was, for when they had happened before, she had not confided.

"Please, Harry."

"Okay. But you ought to talk it out, or see a doctor. I'll call Fleischman in the morning."

"They'll go away." To divert him. "Get my robe. I don't feel sleepy now. What time is it?"

"Almost three o'clock."

"I'll make coffee."

She would drink and read to stay awake, postpone sleep until drugged by exhaustion. What could she tell him? Harry could be a bull with his temper but quickly endearing if he felt she was troubled, would subside if he noticed his rage cowed her, become contrite, more often than not unable to recall minutes later what had set him off in the first place.

He did not know about Gehbert, or the plot to murder, or fully about Birkenau, of her gnawing fear of insanity, that she had been a prostitute, a betrayer of Jews and had killed with relish. He did know of Ben Frankel. If not for Ben, they would not have met. It was so long ago that Ben had been part of another Gertrude that she had ceased thinking of him.

Gertrude Now was not Gertrude Then. The body, she recalled reading, replenishes itself totally, seven times in the space of a lifetime. Didn't Shakespeare say something like that in one of his plays? The seven ages of man. Wise man, William Shakespeare. Older Gertrude, the Now Gertrude, and the younger ones, each different, representing varied phases of her life. There was the Child Gertrude, innocent and unknowing, emotional eons ago, the young girl ravaged and become bestial at Birkenau; the fierce skeletal survivor prowling the war-torn countries of Europe with Ben and the others in Manson-like fury with gun and grenade. (Talk about your hippies and communes, this was 1945!) Then with Ben in Toronto, an eyelash wink in remembered time; then Los Angeles and Harry, the wife-mother-grandmother years, the longest span. That was six.

The seventh was Now. Gehbert resurrected and the recurring horror of the nightmare, and the dormant fear of insanity reawakened. Was it worth his killing at this stage and time of life if there was never to be peace? Can the Gehberts of the world be destroyed? Chop one down and hydra-headed they respring and multiply. How do you kill memory? And wondered if the others, Freda, Elsa, Hannah and Sophie underwent similar torment.

Over coffee, sending Harry back to bed with her assurance that she was fine now, he had to be up early, and she'd like to be alone, she sat brooding and sipping in the kitchen darkness. And wondered if by some miracle that if Gertrude Now (Seven) could meet and talk with Gertrude One through Six, would she recognize them or even want to acknowledge that there had been certain other Gertrudes, and inventoried back to

GERTRUDE ONE:

Mother, a Jew; father, Aryan; avid Jehovah's Witnesses. Twin older brothers, Rudy and Hans. Life in the small town of Limburg, near Bonn, pleasant but uneventful. In light of subsequent events, idyllic. Apart from skinned knees and childhood ailments, only a single mild disturbance.

Until ten she'd never seen Mama's mother although there were occasional vague references to her "condition," and because of it, she was in a special place. "Crazy," her brothers said, not unkindly, for they too had never seen her. On a summer Sunday they visited her in a large imposing building perched, she recalled, in a park-like setting two hours drive away. The resemblance of this withered white-haired woman to her mother was striking. The old woman did not recognize her daughter or son-in-law, was in fact oblivious to them, mostly humming to herself and licking ice cream cones, for which she seemed to have an insatiable appetite. It was an uncomfortable half-hour of vacant staring and monosyllabic responses. During the drive back her parents were unusually quiet, and the twins, older by two years, subdued. She felt nothing but withheld her chatter, respecting the unusual moodiness of a usually boisterous family.

GERTRUDE TWO:

Members of Jehovah's Witnesses refuse to join political parties, salute the flag or say oaths of allegiance, and refuse to fight when attacked, citing the words of Jesus to Pontius Pilate (John 18:36):

> My kingdom is no part of this world.
> If my kingdom were part of this world,
> My attendants would have fought.

For misplaced loyalty, the Third Reich decreed catastrophe. At sixteen, with the sudden fury of a flash flood, the entire family was carted away on a cold November midnight for the "good of the state." Birkenau for mother and daughter, destination unknown for father and brothers...

A Gehbert selection and discard after a one-time use...

Mama went into a malaise. Assigned to sewing shirts for the army, she became listless and uncoordinated. Life was not only uncertain day by day but moment to moment, depending wholly upon the whim of oppressors as to whether one lived or died. Her utility impaired, she was a certain candidate for the oven. Gertrude Two became fiercely protective, the child becoming the mother to her mother.

Prostitution brought surcease—temporarily.

It was the one aspect of Birkenau that was not coercive. Professional prostitutes were disqualified, a provision difficult to understand, since a professional would have given more pleasure than tender-aged girls. Also disqualified were women showing signs of aging, usually those over thirty. Recruiters spoke glowingly of life in the brothel; enough food, good housing, sainted supermen to sleep with. Gertrude Two was wary. She knew that respite from the rigors of Birkenau was often brief. She also knew that if a disease were contracted, it was back to the barrack without medical treatment, to the hell of starvation and the added dread of a sick and dying body. She knew all this but opted for the expediency that would prolong her mother's life. With a supple body, she was in a marginal position to negotiate improved treatment.

Meeting one problem created others, however. Within the barrack a tattered standard of dignity prevailed among the inmates. Unable to vent themselves against those responsible for their hapless condition, she was scorned and pilloried, reviled, cursed, spat upon and beaten. She retaliated savagely with fists and reported miscreants who hoarded food and scavenged clothing and cigarettes. There was also an additional torment. Coarsened female guards, many with minor criminal records, demanded their pound of flesh. Brutalized and isolated, she was forced to submit to them to insure her mother's care.

In the end the inevitable was merely postponed. Mama retreated deep within herself, not even recognizing the child turned bestial to protect her, and finally was forwarded to the medical section for a freezing experiment, an ideal subject for she had not will to protest. She died after hot-cold water immersions to determine what extremes of temperature the human body could endure.

Gertrude Two went into shock and self-loathing. Revulsion rendered her sexually flaccid. With a constant supply of fresh young girls, she was discarded and sent to the medical section. She escaped mutilation and death when the program was temporarily discontinued due to a rumor that the Russians were about to close in. This proved false and the program was resumed, but by then there was a large backlog of new arrivals to process, and through a bureaucratic oversight, she was sent back to the barrack, still able enough to work in a quarry. Reprieved, she resiliently survived for three years, seven months and three days.

GERTRUDE THREE:

With the collapse of the one-thousand-year Reich perhaps a million Jews were left. Europe, no longer home, but a graveyard.

She existed but in Limbo. No family, no friends, no comfort in Judaism or Christianity, half-Jewish but not Jewish, brought up to revere Christ, but Christians killed Jews and other Christians; floundered, and magnetized back to Limburg in search of sanity. If her father and brothers survived, they were sure to seek her there. But they did not show, and there was no information on them, and it became too painful to wait in familiar surroundings for ghosts to materialize.

She recalled the one and only visit to her grandmother, went there, a place to go. It was untouched by the war, anachronistic in a sylvan setting, most of its inmates blissfully unaware of the devastation lived through. Grandmother was no longer there, but she was shocked to find Rudy, one of the twins. It would have been better not to have found him at all. He was barely recognizable, skin and bones, the once alert face and teasing eyes and athletic body totally slack. She might as well have dropped from Mars, for he did not know her. Nor was he aware of self, curled into a persistent fetal position, forcibly unfurled by attendants who daily walked him and tended to his amenities, for he was totally incapable of fending for himself. Like his grandmother, as their mother, he was insane.

She drifted ... haphazardly falling in with a group of Jews who were driving on to Palestine. Their goal was meaningless to her, but they offered the umbrella comfort of numbers, the herd instinct ... living day by day, hand to mouth, off the land, stealing what they could, terrorizing small villages and farmers, for there was no money for purchases, but taking what they felt was owed to them ... to join with other clusters, accreting into a quasi-military group under Haganah leadership, staying to side roads and forests, moving at night, in small detachments by different paths, a rendezvous point set every three to five days ahead, snaked out over vast distances, on foot, in stolen vehicles, gathering guns and grenades, swelling by the hundreds, until they were thousands. From Hungary they came, and Rumania, and Poland and Germany, a lemmings-like tide, infiltrating the barred border of Czechoslovakia ... managing, this inexorable and shadowy mass, to avoid Allied patrols, the Russians, the underground Poles who still enjoyed an occasional pogrom, and above all, the Germans. For German defeat did not abate German hatred. In the chaotic aftermath of capitulation, remnants of the once mighty Werhmacht sought to surrender intact to the Allies (but *not* to the Russians) and were still formidable. These ragtag but renascent Jews evaded encounter, not because they lacked an avenging spirit but confrontation consumed time and removed the precious cloak of their shadowy migration; also no amount of dead Germans could compensate for yet another dead Jew...

A major event of this period turned out to be Ben Frankel...

One day, as so many did, he simply materialized. Tall, almost cadaverous, unsmiling and lithe, a coiled spring of a man, he conveyed by presence and personality an innate authority welcomed by the leaders of the hegira. It was gleaned that he had been a Canadian pilot, downed in an early raid and imprisoned for the duration. He spoke little, but was in constant movement, very good with the children. He thought no more of her than he did of the other women, but looked after all with a sexless passion. Nor was she drawn to him. He was too remote, as if harboring some private knowledge that could not be imparted.

And Auberfeld...

A picturesque village nestling near the Czechoslovakian border. Apart from farming, its chief industry was a factory in which Jewish slave-labor had been used to turn out shoes and boots for the Werhmacht. Inevitably, the prosperous war years ended and "their" Jews disappeared. The villagers did not anticipate their return and certainly not an advance unit of seven men in a battered truck who asked for and expected to obtain food and water, call it a form of reparations. Ben led them, and they were met by the obermeister heading a phalanx of fifteen solid citizens, including five former SS men who had proudly donned their black uniforms to remind these upstart Jews, wars won or lost, their proper place. Three of the seven were killed before the others managed to scurry back to camp.

By noon, thirty armed Jews returned to Auberfeld, Gertrude

among them. The obermeister had convened a large representative group to a meeting in the town hall to decide whether the Jews should charitably be allowed to slink away or whether more should first be slaughtered as a warning to other Jew vermin what to expect in the way of Auberfeld hospitality. The building was ringed, and Ben and two others entered the council room and raked the room with gunfire and killed all twenty-six occupants. The Jews then swarmed into the village like an invading army and for the next two days helped themselves to food, fuel and water from the docile villagers.

Here at Auberfeld, Gertrude Three killed a man with her bare hands.

It was a chance meeting on the street, two people bracing to avoid a collision, momentarily suspended movement, and looked fully at each other. There was instant recognition between them. He had doctored at Birkenau. His project had been the fertilization of the human female with the sperm of animals. The female inmates were artificially inseminated with the sperm of dogs, cats, horses, pigs and apes. The only results of this insane quackery were infections and death. Gertrude had been twice inseminated and would undoubtedly have continued as a subject until contamination set in but for the reprieve gained by the false rumor that the Allied forces were almost at the gates.

They froze to the spot, she in shock, he in terror. Then he recoiled, barely perceptible, but the movement doomed him. Uncertainty evaporated and with a wounded cry she leapt for his throat. He was larger and stronger but the surprise meeting and the sudden fury of her attack overwhelmed him, he could not pry her fingers loose, as if magnetically clamped around his throat, gurgled and clawed back ineffectually, and forced to his knees, she beat at his face with an insensate rage until it was no longer recognizable. He died at her feet.

There were others in the street, Jews and non-Jews, but none went to his aid. Her mind reeled in letiferous glee, she *exalted* in the kill, continuing to hammer at him as he lay supine. She was finally pulled from the corpse by Ben and two others, who needed all their strength to accomplish the feat.

Through Austria into Italy, following the Adriatic, to the final debarkation point for the survivors, the port of Pescara. A leaky tub awaited them in the harbor, squatting bug-like on the placid water and looking no more seaworthy to run past the British blockade to the promised land than a soup kettle.

Gertrude Three was depressed. She had no interest in continuing on to Palestine with the virtual certainty that it would be an interrupted journey and incarceration in Cyprus. Palestine was a game preserve for an endangered species. Nor did she believe in its four-thousand-year-old mystique. She felt no more Jewish now than she had at the outset of imprisonment or the shared travail of other Displaced Persons. She was neither more Jewish for it or less Jewish for being half-Jewish on the maternal side. She felt now that with the excitement, the intensity, the drive through Middle Europe abated and the goal reached, completely lost.

Propitiously, Ben sought her out. She admired him but despite what they had been through together, did not feel close to him. They had not spoken since Auberfeld on any level other than what duty and exigency dictated, and was totally unprepared for what he offered.

"Would you like to go to Canada?" he asked.

She was not certain that he was even addressing her, for he had come silently upon her as she looked alone and brooding to the sea.

"Toronto is my home," he continued. "I'd like to return. If you care to, come with me."

"Why me?" she puzzled.

"Why not?" he shrugged. "We'll get married. That'll get you across, beat the quota."

The voice was passionless, a favor conferred without patronization. He'd perceived her turmoil and allowed her the dignity of refusal. No declaration of love passed between them for they felt none, they discussed the matter with the romantic fervor of inquiring the time of day. She accepted without hesitation.

GERTRUDE FOUR:

They left the group at Pescara, many tearfully sentimental at their leave-taking, a few appalled by the heresy of their not continuing on to Palestine, and made their way to Rome where Ben presented himself to the authorities. His identity and service was confirmed (missing in action for over four years) and they were married by a Jewish chaplain, Ben's wish. Within six weeks they were in Toronto, where Ben's large family welcomed him back from the dead and joyously embraced his bride. Frankels, Canadians and a contingent from the States, partook in a week-long celebration.

Ben went to work for an uncle in the burgeoning postwar field of plastics. His reserve increased, becoming even more withdrawn, it was impossible to think this quiet man had ruthlessly mowed down twenty-six defenseless Germans without a twinge. Husband and wife did not stir each other, sex was occasional, more ritual than fulfilling, but their basic relationship was respectful, he provided and she cooked the meals and kept the house. Neither dwelled on the past and the future was rudderless.

Eighteen months later Ben Frankel was dead.

Then she finally understood him, revealed when he wasted away in the last weeks of his life. The black spot on a lung, incurred during his prisoner-of-war years, had virulently spread to finally consume him. He'd known then that he was marked for an early death, knew this when he'd joined the refugee trek, knew that he would not go to Palestine because he could not bring life and vigor to its birthing; had sensed her despair and offered a haven, a free choice on her part, for he did not want to burden her with a knowledge that would bring pity to him and guilt to her.

She sincerely wept for a good man, so young, who said little but did much. His wartime insurance helped to cushion her sorrow plus a substantial amount he had set aside for her in the custody of his uncle, who was the only other person outside the medical profession to know his secret.

She was not at loose ends. One of Ben's three sisters, the

eldest, Idelle, whom she had met at Ben's homecoming and liked immediately, invited her to come to Los Angeles for a visit, stay as long as you like.

GERTRUDE FIVE:

Los Angeles. Before the war, Idelle's husband had dealt in junk, during the war the plebian word was elevated to much-needed scrap metal, after the war, graduated to metals salvage. His assistant was earnest, muscled, hard-working Harry Simon who was immediately attracted to her and directly proclaimed that after she observed a respectful mourning period he would marry her. She was amused by his panache, as extrovert as Ben had been introvert, and did not encourage him, which lack of forthright rejection he construed to be nondeterrent.

In the ensuing year she was surprised to find herself increasingly drawn to him but was fearful of remarriage. With Ben there had not been a strong man-woman tie, the relationship had not been loving, merely serviceable. Harry would expect and demand more. She wondered how much to tell him and pondered his reaction. The mind's-eye scene was beyond soap opera:

GERTRUDE: Harry. I must tell you about my past—
HARRY: (grandly) Now is all that counts, baby.
GERTRUDE: I was raped.
HARRY: (sadly) Poor kid. Terrible.
GERTRUDE: I was a prostitute.
HARRY: (understandingly) It was rough, huh?
GERTRUDE: Also lesbianism.
HARRY: (unrepelled) AC, DC, eh? Are you squared away?
GERTRUDE: It was ugly. All ugly.
HARRY: (nobly) All is forgiven.
GERTRUDE: I was injected with animal semen.
HARRY: (shocked) The bastards!
GERTRUDE: I killed a man with my bare hands and enjoyed doing it.
HARRY: (heartily) He deserved it.

GERTRUDE: I may not be able to give you children.
HARRY: (pragmatic) Then we'll adopt.
GERTRUDE: My grandmother, mother and brother went insane. It runs in my family. It could happen to me.
HARRY: (grandly) Forget it.

Forget it? Not likely. If her measure of the man was correct, he would not turn away. But was it fair to burden Harry, or any man for that matter, with the grotesqueries of her past? It would be difficult to comprehend her own life's script had she not lived it. In the end she decided too much candor would be unsettling. She wanted an absolutely clean slate for a reborn life, it was owed to her, not realizing until Gertrude Seven that life unexpectedly fertilizes events into monstrous weeds unless the seed is thoroughly uprooted.

GERTRUDE SIX:
Wife, mother and grandmother. Early, she became pregnant but aborted spontaneously in the third month. She became pregnant again and it happened again. She was pleased that vital parts were in working order, secretly relieved that she was unable to carry to term for fear of transmitting misbegotten genes. But Harry yearned for children, and with the advent of the third month of another pregnancy, she apprehensively took to bed to hold the fetus and barely stirred the entire thirty days. A daughter, Janet, was born, perfectly formed and healthy.

She hoped that a single child would satisfy Harry, if he wanted more they would adopt. But careful as she tried to be, there was another unwanted pregnancy. This time she did not take to bed in the third month but increased her activities in strenuous attempts to induce a spontaneous dislodge, aiding and abetting by drinking gallons of an old wives tale brew, a vile concoction of yeast and cheap wine, guaranteed to scourge the insides. It merely caused cramps, the fetus adhered. Pathologically unable to consider abortion due to the remembered horrors of

Birkenau's medicos, she resigned herself to carry the full term. Jeffrey was born, a healthy specimen.

She did not conceive again and devoted herself as a wife and mother, with the usual viccissitudes in both departments, ever wary for signs of aberration in the children (and herself), but there were only the generational differences. Janet was now married and in the past year had presented a grandchild. Jeffrey attended junior college with less brilliance than tenacity. The '38 Club brought her into contact with Freda, Elsa, Hannah and Sophie and their deeply abiding friendship. The Holocaust years were long gone, seldom thought about now, Harry never pursued the subject and Janet and Jeffrey, as with many of their contemporaries, had found it difficult to believe, despite the evidence, including their mother's tattoo, that such barbarism had actually transpired in the twentieth century.

Indeed, considering the relatively even keel of the life later led, it was difficult to relate back to Gertrude Two, Three and Four... Until Gehbert resurfaced... and the nightmares... into:

GERTRUDE SEVEN:

Sipping coffee in the early morning of a shadowed kitchen, ruminating on reawakened horrors, knowing that if Gehbert did not die she would perish. For so long as he lived, so would the Damocles sword fear of insanity gnaw at her innards. Irrational perhaps. Her grandmother had gone insane before the Nazi bacillus, but then Mama and Rudy might not have, despite predilection, if not for it. So far as could be self-determined, she was not displaying symptoms, could detect none in the children, but now the added dread of transmittal to a beautiful grandchild. Perhaps the evil strain had bypassed her, but would she ever be sure? If Gehbert died she could be, the bad seed interred with him, and she would live in peace the rest of her days.

It had been weeks and weeks of a persistent headache and the recurring nightmare and running to the bathroom, ever since Elsa had declared Gehbert's presence, five weeks since the lot had been drawn to eradicate it. Whoever had been designated had thus far not fulfilled, although five weeks had been allotted for the deed. Then riding collective emotion, five weeks seemed ample time to pull it off. Actually two days remained to the last week, but if the past four weeks portended those next two days, then it would not be done.

Chilling thought: Suppose the one selected was unable to kill and was waiting out the two days. If his demise was not accomplished by then, it had been agreed that would be the end of it. The thought of Gehbert continuing to exist without awareness that he'd even been *threatened* was intolerable.

Who had drawn?

On a capability scale of one-to-ten, let's see: Freda? Cosmetic, sharp, outgoing, talked a good game, but does a barking dog bite? Seven.

Elsa? Attractive, subdued but certain, if committed she would have the tenacity of a terrier. Eight.

Hannah? Up, down, alternately sharp and bland, an emotional plunger, if she was the chosen one, it would have been done at the outset, but since to date it had not been performed...Five.

Sophie? Really an unknown quantity. One really never knew what she was thinking, how could she put up with that slob of a husband? She'd have the stomach for it, the quiet ones get things done. Up there with Freda and Elsa.

Herself? Right this minute, the sum total of all the Gertrudes, an immodest ten. She could not guess how the others would guage her on *their* scales, but then they did not know Gertrudes Two and Three. In truth, even she'd forgotten, well, not quite, pushed back behind a deliberately blocked memories curtain, but now, front and center. To the others she knew that Gertrude Six, which was the only Gertrude they knew, appeared clownish, ate too much, broke wind constantly, wondered if all that early fucking created loose kidneys? Was it an occupational hazard for prostitutes, catching up in later life? What did loose kidneys have to do with farting or fornication? Silly.

Where was she? Oh yes, the scale. Other than the Birkenau denominator what really, down deep, did they know of each other? Put another way, how could one know, however intimate and given dire circumstance, what another was capable of doing? Could they, or anyone, believe that she had beaten the life out of a man and three men had to forcibly remove her from the corpse? She could not believe the others to be capable of such ferocity. Or to have become prostitutes—both ways. That too was beyond belief. Still, she could only conjecture how the others had managed to escape the ovens. High stress resistance? Bought themselves off as she had done? Blind luck? The guilt secretly felt because each had survived where others had not. During the years of intense Mah-Jong play, they had been wise not to dwell upon the monstrous years.

Until Gehbert.

She knew they were as churned up as she by the lack of result to date, the difference being that she was activist. Freda had made the ultimate verification, had volunteered to be the chosen one, one couldn't expect more of her, especially if she had not drawn the lot, and even if she had, was as likely to get cold feet as the others when it came to pulling the trigger. Fatalistically they would all accept the imposed five-week parameter.

Four weeks and five days now and it would go to the full five, and the son of a bitch would live forever, outlive them all. That absolutely must not happen. Having killed, she could again, no psychological or emotional hangups to overcome. Harry had a Colt .38 at the junkyard that she could easily obtain. At Auberfeld, that day she had ridden in with Ben and the others, her weapon had been a stolen Thompson submachine gun with its cartridge clip of .45s that kicked straight up with a full burst of its fifteen rounds. She'd learned to fire it laterally in controlled spurts of threes—brrp!—allowing it to rake across her body on a level line. Compared to it, the .38 was a toy.

So fuck the rules. Auschwitz-Birkenau hadn't been governed by the Marquis of Queensbury. Therefore: Be it resolved that Gertrude the Seventh would assure the demise of one Walter "Papa" Grossman, alias Wilhelm Gehbert, the Butcher of Birkenau.

Not exactly keeping the faith, but the others would never know, including the lot holder who was committed to silence. It would take careful planning. Today she would go to the restaurant, observe the area and Gehbert's movements, take it from there.

There was enormous, almost giddy relief in the decision, contemplating the how of it, savoring the finality, a goose-pimply elation not felt since Auberfeld; she knew, as the kitchen lightened with the fingering rays of early morning sun, that when it was done there would no longer be fear.

The five weeks were murder.

Nothing happened.

Wednesdays came and Wednesdays went. Papa Grossman's restaurant continued to flourish, and his Monday nights picked up. The Wednesday nights were downers.

Freda, Hannah, Sophie, Gertrude and Elsa continued to hostess the weekly Mah-Jong game on the rotating basis. At each weekly session, each woman would upon entrance pay two dollars into a fund set aside and apart from the money played in the game. The fund over a period of time would accrete to hundreds of dollars to some vague goal, such as a group vacation to include husbands.

There had been only one such vacation, and it was a disaster.

They went en masse to Palm Springs for a three-day weekend. The Weather was expected to be seasonally warm. It was perversely cool. The sun barely peek-a-booed. Swimming or lounging around the pool was an invitation to pneumonia. Proximity did not make for endearment. Basically, the husbands did not take to each other. Or like each spouse's playing partners. Harry Simon thought Max Langbein was a glob. Max had gotten falling-down drunk at the wedding of their daughter and thrown up into the punch bowl. Gil Spahn, the youngest, a mere stripling then in his early forties, thought the husbands were dullsville and characterized Freda as a crude and overcosmeticized broad. The image he saw in the mirror was athletically trim, fashionable and agressively virile.

But these broad-spectrum dislikes did not exacerbate, for it was not that important to each man since the wives enjoyed each other. That was the common denominator. Each respected his wife's night out with no questions asked, either because it was felt that this weekly liberation made for tractability in the kitchen for the balance of the week or allowed them, in turn, an unchallenged night out on the town.

Still, they made the best of the bad weather and vibrations. Harry Simon and Gil Spahn were golf nuts and for the three days were virtually incommunicado on the greens. Nate Friedkin, then alive, unfettered by business concerns, read and slept luxuriously. Max Langbein and Leon Epstein tried to stoke up a poker game but were unsuccessful; even their wives were disinterested, so they retreated to television sets. The women found that if they did not play Mah-Jong—which they had resolved to forebear, for after all, this was to be a vacation—and did not talk about their children, and since the common bond of early travail under Naziism was implicitly understood never to be discussed, as well here as in the city, the days and nights were a prolonged bore.

A change of scenery did lend itself to renewed conjugal bliss between husbands and wives, but this too palled after a morning or two. They were not of a generation to even remotely consider an orgy. The use of liquor was moderate, drugs nonexistent and wife switching unthinkable. So the first group excursion was the last, without ill effect for it.

The fund evolved into informal insurance and was used as such when the need arose. Freda kept a record of each individual's contribution and banked the money into a savings account. At one time, Sophie, hard pressed, withdrew her share to pay for glasses for her youngest child and to partially defray the expense of an orthodontist. As did the others similarly avail themselves. No questions asked. The user would then start over by paying the two dollars.

Wednesday night had been as fixed as the sun. Each woman

looked eagerly forward to the one night in seven that allowed her to cope with the remaining six. Famine, flood and family exigencies were tolerated Thursday through Tuesday, but never on Wednesday. Vacations, holidays, religious and secular, illnesses and emergencies were manipulated to be seldom in conflict, and save for an occasional hostess-switching to accommodate an unforeseen intrusion or inconvenience, there was a remarkable consistency of attendance. The game was tranquilizer, psychiatric couch and lover. The 136 tiles blotted out the world.

But not these past five weeks and into the sixth, Elsa the hostess. Nothing more was said about Gehbert in all that time. Four did not know the designated fifth. It was as if the matter of Gehbert had never come up and did not exist. But each avidly scanned the newspapers and listened to the radio and viewed television news programs for some word of his demise; be it bullet, knife, mace or mallet, strangulation, suffocation, arson, poison, car accident, a fall or push off a cliff, bow and arrow or snake bite.

Freda told off-color jokes but only rote laughter was induced. Sophie worked her lower lip furiously. Hannah's arthritis flared, elbows to hips. Elsa complained of headaches and her husband, unaware of cause, but feeling its effect, took more cold showers. Gertrude noticed that she was going to the bathroom with greater frequency.

They played as intensely but not as well. For the first time since the inception of the group, their play was sullen and without zest. They snapped at each other. The offender would become contrite; the others would overlook it, being susceptible themselves to irascibility, understanding the underlying cause for it during this trying period, but the pattern persisted.

Mah-Jong has a long and puzzling history, largely obscured by uneducated guesses as to its origin, and clouded by legends. It has for centuries been the favorite game of the Chinese, and tradition has it that its name is apropos of the sound made by the tiles clicking together during the game. *Mah* means flax or hemp

124

plant, and is said to refer to the sound of the plant's leaves clicking in the wind. *Jong* means sparrow, and supposedly recalls the chattering of the bird.

The hostess for the evening furnished the Mah-Jong set. Twenty-five to thirty games were played in the four-hour period from 7:30 to 11:30. Each player's investment for the evening was three dollars, total fifteen dollars. Prices ranged from twenty-five to thirty-five cents for each hand. Each player had her own card on which were inscribed the rules issued by the Mah-Jongg League and revised yearly. The goal was to duplicate a hand as designated on the card. Not all games produced a winner, but by evening's end one could lose the three dollars or pie for the total amount of fifteen dollars. However they were so evenly matched that this was a rare occurence. By the end of the year the wins and losses usually leveled out to the original amount each player started with. But their enjoyment for the year was incalculable.

Was.

Freda knew just where the blame lay. On Freda Friedkin.

She could not sleep, was not eating, losing weight, her eyes shadowed and her skin was drawn; guilt-ridden and filled with self-loathing. Ever since she had palmed the swastika-marked lot and deceptively assumed the task of killing Wilhelm Gehbert and failed miserably the past five weeks to carry it out.

15

The situation was untenable. Freda harbored dark thoughts of suicide.

She meant to kill Wilhelm Gehbert if the dog bite confirmed him. But in so doing she submitted to him—and experienced her first orgasm in thirty years—by the very same man who first violated her and was responsible for the block.

That was on a Monday night. By Wednesday, humiliated by the experience, she knew that she had to try again and not fail. On that Wednesday when the lots were drawn, she had substituted a blank piece of paper for the marked one. The deception was simple. She had torn an extra sheet of the notepad just as the telephone rang for Gertrude's son. It was sufficiently distracting to instinctively swivel all eyes from her as she was composing the lots to enable her to make the switch with ease. When the lots were drawn, there were five blanks. The marked lot was in her sleeve.

She had gone back to Gehbert fiercely determined to kill. Instead, reawakened as a woman, she submitted one more time—and another time—and again and again—and as the weeks slipped by she wavered. Belated passion flash-flooded and each time washed away resolve. She'd succumbed to raw pent-up lust with nymphomaniacal fervor, undergoing the torments of an abysmal hell; betraying herself, the Mah-Jong group, the memory of her beloved ill-fated family and the horrendous medical

125

experiments that Wilhelm Gehbert had vilely instituted at Birkenau, of which she had been a subject.

The past could never be far from her, but it had not been allowed, thanks largely to her husband, to intrude upon her subsequent life. It was past, not to be forgotten, but relegated to perspective. The world had gone on and so had she. Only now the world stopped and marched back in time as night after night she consciously recalled the nightmare, to whip herself, to dismally fail, to reconjure a firm resolve only to fail again....

1943. Auchwitz-Birkenau.

Three main camps spread over twenty square miles... completely surrounded by an electrified barbed-wire fence twelve feet high... a floodlight every one hundred yards, a machine gun every four hundred... outside the fence a quarter mile of no-escape, bleak, bulldozed and blasted flatland... 6,900 guards under the SS, including 850 Polish and Ukranian fascists, 500 German professional criminals, murderers and perverts, 250 dogs and, shamefully, hundreds of Jew-betrayers of Jews to suppress a quarter of a million prisoners... peaking to 8,000 killed every day... the day-and-night freight cars belching their hapless cargoes so that the executioners were hard put to reduce the inmate population... malaria... the festering body sores .... the spine-breaking work gangs... the starvation diet, fetid water... scorched flesh and smell of urine, stinking indescribably... stomach and bowel ailments rampant... to relieve oneself was life and death at the inadequate concrete troughs, the floors ankle deep in mud, a slippery mixture of feces, urine and blood, sliding, and falling to frantically gain a place, the weaker ones trampled into the muck, losing clogs and soiling the prisoner clothing for which there was never wash water, herded by the numbers by the day, the troughs closed at night....

She winced and involuntarily shuddered at the searing recall of that night... weak, debilitated, her kidneys exploding... squatting, supporting her back against the barracks wall... discovered by a hefty trustee, a German prostitute, responsible for the fiction of sanitation and subject to reprisal if it is not upheld... screaming vile epithets, pulling at her, beating her... but she withstood and completed... pulled to her feet, the bony hands at her throat... somehow, the spark of life-force rekindles, fever flares in outrage, she claws back... so surprised is the trustee she goes flaccid... moments later lies dead face down in the muck... staggering back to the barracks... to await the worst the morning will bring... it does not come... the trustee is one more death overlooked by the sheer weight of numbers and bureaucracy oversight... and another takes her place...

She had killed.

Within Auchwitz, Birkenau was the female complex, a portion set aside for medical experimentation. The one who made it a landmark in the misuse of medical science was Dr. Wilhelm Gehbert. He'd convinced higher authorities of his ideas of the usefulness of prisoners in experimentation on behalf of the Master Race, in line with that of Dr. Josef Mengele, who was to become the chief docotor at Auschwitz and specialized in what he called "the science of twins" and who tried to artificially create Aryan children with Aryan features and blue eyes. Gehbert was given a free hand over a wide range of insanities, which were applied elsewhere as well. The classifications of skeletons, men and women, of various nationalities and races; heads severed and stored, sterilizations, how long people can live only on salt water, hot and cold immersions, freezing, innumerable tests to see how people could die of a variety of causes, injected with poison or subjected to deadly diseases, complex and impossible forms of bone and skin grafts, demented attempts to redesign the genetic system and to reshape the human anatomy; without benefit of pain killers or sanitary safeguards, a lunatic lampoon of the entire concept of healing and medicine by psuedosurgeons. It is catalogued. German efficiency was equal to German madness. The records are fastidious.

Gehbert's specialization was experiments on the female system. The women were subjected to all sorts of operations, particularly on the female organs. The ovaries and uteri would be removed, or their external organs, such as the clitoris, amputated. Some would be inseminated artificially with a variety of semen and as pregnancy progressed, cut open for examination or to see how and when an abortion could be performed, these abortions executed throughout the nine-month cycle, the rate of success nearly zero, the women dying like flies, in terrible pain from the butchery.

Freda wrung her hands in an agonized dry-wash, regarded herself in the mirror. The younger Freda assailed her in bitter self-colloquy:

—Shame, Freda, shame!

—I know, I know——

—Do, do!

—I try! I try!

—Not enough!

—How long does hate endure? Must the victim become as base as the oppressor?

—Rhetoric! Masochistic bitch! Gehbert does to you now what his bestiality could not do then, and you love him for it—

—Denied for so long——

—By *him!* Like a bitch slavering in heat—crawl, crawl to beg for more—fill your depraved cunt with *his* sperm. How much semen can gush to wash away Mama—Papa—Ernst?

—Beg of you——

—You've killed!

—Not again. I cannot——

—Cannot or will not? Look at me! Remember the "rabbit girl!"

—No, no, no!

—The experiments... to see if the human female could be fertilized from another animal... with dogs, cats, horses, pigs, sheep and apes! Ei! Ei! Pregnant! The idiot joy of insane doctors—ecstatic—they're going to see... the birth of a subhuman Jewess and an animal... Only the X rays reveal... the fetus to be a disappointingly normal human... raped by an intern...

She heard a piteous scream and beat at the mirror until her fists pulped, but the mirror image would not go away, for she too was lost, and with a last tattered shred of dignity said:

—Say it! Admit it! The bitter loathsome truth. The despised man—beast—is my lover.

—No...!

—Say it! Wilhelm Gehbert—is—my—lover!

—Wilhelm Gehbert—is—my—lover!

Young Freda's face segued into an ineffable sadness, a deep visceral cry gut-ripping from her, old, oh so old, parodied into a witch's brew and the one sagged against the other and yearned yet one more time for the final release.

The gun was still in her purse, still loaded; she reached for it, when the phone rang, its harshness so startling her heart stopped. An alien hand reached for it and an alien voice responded to:

"Grandma? Grandma, you there?"

"Yes..."

"Vicki...Grandma?"

"Here."

"You okay, Grandma?"

"What?"

"You sound so strange. You sure you're okay?"

She oriented, adjusted. "Overslept." Her voice coming back. "What is it, darling?"

"Granny. I met the nicest guy——"

"What?"

"I mean, ci-yute! He's in my psych class——"

"Oh?"

"I'd love you to meet him. His name is Graham Block. That's a nice name, isn't it?"

"Yes."

"You okay, Granny?"

"Graham——"

"Graham Block. I told him about you, and he'd love to meet you."

"If you want——"

"Sure. Why I called."

"Well, of course. But not today. I'm sort of—well, under the weather——"

"When? Tomorrow? Wednesday?"

"Wednesday. Is tomorrow Wednesday?"

"All day...Grannny...Granny?" Her voice evinced great concern. "Is something—?"

"I'm fine, Vicki. Please don't worry."

"Okay."

"Darling...I'm glad you called."

"I am too. Graham is, wow, outa sight."

"I mean that. I really mean that. I love you very very much."

"I love you too. Will you?"

"Will I what?"

"Meet Graham. Can you meet him tomorrow?"

"Tomorrow is——?"

"Wednesday. Will you be free? Granny—?"

"Yes, darling. Wednesday I will be free."

16

Grossman hadn't been feeling well all day. Nothing much, a cold, more annoying than sickly. He did not go to the restaurant; it operated smoothly enough without him. Other than an occasional supervisory chore, his appearance was largely ceremonial. The white coat and chef's cap had become a logo, touching base at each table. The customers seemed to enjoy the personal touch as did he. It gave status to old ones, and new ones, lamenting the general lack of service in most restaurants, the quality and high prices, were flattered. His appearance accompanying each serving seemed to assure that the food was good.

Anna had called. She was most solicitous, poor man, he shouldn't be alone in his condition, she'll be over within an hour.

He puffed with pride. Sixty-three and he could still do it. How many over the years? It was impossible to estimate. Bodies and faces blurred, especially those of the old days. He did not often think back. No point to it. He was vastly different now. Perhaps it comes with age. A hobby, cooking, had made possible a new life in another country. Of course, ODESSA had set him up; he was broke after the war. He'd served with maniacal zeal, and idealist that he was, he had neglected to line his pockets as Bormann, Megele, Stangl and the others had done. There was a condition. He had to always, and at a moment's notice, to be on tap for the Resurgence. Euphemism, that. He no longer cared, the fealty that was exacted for a cause he did not believe would surface again in his lifetime was a small price to pay. Half of postwar Germany had not been born then. The younger German was a good deal more discerning. In any case there was no choice, he had to go along. His yearly tithe, laundered through that Texas millionaire to Switzerland and ultimately to the border town in Chile, was his only link to the past. He had no reason to be in touch. ODESSA knew where he was. Just as well. The hard core, older and thinning, were still mad, replaying an old theme like a rehash of an old movie. Had he ever been? Yes. Oh, the basics were still there, just mellowed around the edges, he'd been caught up in a national paranoia, the like of which was not again foreseeably predictable in what remained of his lifetime. But all men created equal? Rubbish. There were still superior minds, superior bodies, the haves and have-nots, the quick and the dead. Survival was the key. He'd served his sentence, was absolved, and since settling fifteen years ago in Los Angeles, he'd been exemplary. Fear of reprisal from some demented creature out of the past had been a real one after his release, but he'd walked so many streets over half the world, and there hadn't been the slightest incident. Muggers and thieves were a greater menace. He was secure, with a reborn identity, good health, a successful business and a mistress.

Anna. Anna Spanger, she'd said. Spanger, Spanger, didn't ring a bell.

Probably not her real name. An enigmatic. She had to be fifty, perhaps more, but that was merely chronological. She was sensual, satisfying, dropped into his lap. As good a reason as any for circulating in the restaurant. Amazing the number of widows and married looking for something on the side. He still cut an enticing figure, he knew, but the coat and cap help, the uniform syndrome.

That first night had been a humdinger. When she finally aroused she was a tigress. The scar did not repel her. It may be enhancing, she keeps coming back for more. He was pleased that she did not probe him on it, but that may be because she draws the line by not revealing more of herself.

He specualted: She said widow, well, maybe. If not, still married with a husband and children, one of the bam-bam thank you ma'am guys—when he got around to it. Like the night she was waiting for her lover to show up and he hadn't and he'd taken advantage of her obvious loneliness. Or the time before when she'd come with her daughter—no, granddaughter she'd said. That's some subterfuge to use as a cover for a rendezvous. Well, he hadn't shown, it was his good luck, now Mr. No-Show is out of the picture and he's in.

But, if they were going to continue, he would have to know more about her. He liked her, even more than that, wouldn't it be strange if after all these years he was actually falling in love. Perhaps even marriage. He didn't have anyone and there were fewer years ahead than what he'd already been through. In that case he'd have to tell her something, but just enough to serve the purpose. Meantime he'd respect the tacit commitment between them and not push for her identity, he could dig into that easily enough. Her driver's registration or vehicle license would serve. He'd see how it would go tonight and start uncovering Anna Spanger tomorrow.

He chuckled inwardly, thinking of another reason why Anna Spanger would choose to remain anonymous. Apart from the titillation mystery holds, if she's really a grandmother, how would it look to her family—sexy granny in the sack? Scandalous!

He heard a sound, and his reveries was interrupted when outside her car pulled up, the headlights beaming into the room heralding her approach. The lights bit off, a car door slammed, and she was at the door. Before she could knock, he swung it open and admitted her. She was carrying a bottle of something in a sack. They embraced.

"I'll give you my cold." He was considerate and nasal.

"Poor man. They're so damned annoying."

"Keeps hanging on."

"I brought a bottle of homemade remedy." She removed a thermos bottle from its cover. "It's a strong herbal tea. It's orange flavored, and I've added a touch of bourbon." She moved familiarly and got a cup, poured into it and extended it to him. "Drink it all down."

As he sipped he said, "I think, Anna, we should talk."

"Not now, you poor dear. Who is there to take care of you?"

"That's what I want to talk about. We know each other yet we do not."

"Hush." She put an admonishing forefinger to his lips, and he playfully nipped at it. "You drink and you must rest."

The hot tea was soothing, and she refilled the cup and then went to the fireplace, probing the logs, sending up a shower of sparks. He like the way she moved. A fine-looking woman, although she looked peaked of late. Probably it took some doing on her part, the strain of family, to run out nights to come here. He felt very close to her.

"Anna. You must take care of yourself."

She looked at him in surprise. "That's a nice thing to say, Walter. Now drink up."

"I mean it. I look forward to seeing you."

"And I you."

"I don't think I can be much good to you tonight. I'm not feeling well."

"I'm glad I came anyway. There's more to life than that."

"Yes. More. We must talk."

"Don't tax yourself, Walter. Rest."

The room was quite warm now and had begun to haze, and he sat on the couch. She bent down and untied his shoes and swung his stockinged feet onto the couch, causing him to lie back.

"I'll just bet you didn't eat a thing all day."

"Was—wasn't—hungry," he muttered, his voice thickening and squirmed reflexively. She was at his fly and unzipped it and withdrew his member caressing it into rigidity. He yielded completely to the sweet sensation.

"Rest ... rest ..." she murmured, her voice mellifluous as she continued to stroke. "Rest ..."

About to drift off, he was roused by the acrid aftertaste. She was studying him with that peculiar quixotic smile he'd noticed the first time they'd met. Then it had been come-hither, titillating, but now he detected a bitter, mocking quality. He bolted upright, renting the curtain of darkness that had begun to descend and speared her questioningly with his eyes, collecting himself, inwardly noting two things: he'd never seen her in daylight and that, stupidly, he hadn't precautionarily thought to ask her to remove the bracelets that she constantly wore even in their most intimate moments, to look at the underside of her right wrist.

She was jolted by his sudden movement and leapt to her feet as if scorched. Trying to further rise, he felt disembodied, uncoordinated, instead, rolling off the sofa to his hands and knees. Flailed at her, glowering with suddenly acquired knowledge, pawing the air ineffectually as if treading water. She had stanced herself out of range, slowly, deliberately, removing the bracelets from her wrist and dropping them one by one, four in all, into her purse, open on the floor at her feet. Bare, she jutted it out, close enough for him to view but beyond the reach of his inept swipes. He could not discern the numbers, but their impact was clear enough, shaking his head to both clear it and to deny their existence.

"Doctor Wilhelm Gehbert!" she spat.

A single lunge and he could grasp her ankle, but though he was thinking clearly enough now, his body was unresponsive and he seemed helplessly rooted to the spot.

"Come to me, lover," she taunted, and measured each word in cadence. "B-three-six-six-seven-five-three."

Goaded to a massive effort, he pulled himself up along the arm of the sofa and managed to get to his feet, swaying, feet wide apart and glared accusingly, less at her duplicity than at his own self-betrayal. She repeated her number in a singsong litany, but he'd noticed that she had taken an inadvertent step backward with his rise. She was frightened, and now that he was on his feet she was no longer fully in control. By God, he wasn't that easy to kill—if he could just keep his lids from closing—maybe he could outlast the dosage—perhaps she'd miscalculated its effectiveness——

"Die, bastard Butcher of Birkenau! If only you could die for one hundred years!" She spit in his face.

He edged forward, first one shuffling, tentative step, then the other, arms outstretched, like Frankenstein's creature, feeling himself getting stronger, each step surer and firmer, eyes riveted to eyes in a relentless exchange of mutual hatred, detecting her fright as he closed the gap, smelling the fear in her. She stepped back colliding with a floor lamp and instinctively but foolishly turned to right it. In the instant of altered direction he lunged. Falling, he grasped her right ankle and his fingers clamped like a vise.

She strangled a cry—what will kill this monstrously evil thing?—there had to be enough in the tea to drop a bull—strained to pull free, but her foot was anchored as if encased in cement—stretched to reach the curio cabinet housing the miniature Venuses, clawed at its puny filigreed handle, managed to unlatch it, springing it open, and pulled. The cabinet toppled against her, breaking its crash to the floor. She recoiled with its contact, and Grossman pulled, and she tumbled back toward him. Still clenching her ankle, he snaked his free arm upward with surprising speed and grabbed her right wrist. She writhed and beat at him with her left fist, but he was impervious to the rain of blows.

She fought panic, the fear knotting in her stomach; somehow, reflexively, disengaged her left shoe, its heel, wide at the base narrowed to an inch and a half, leaned into him, causing him to slacken both arms, and swung desperately down to catch him behind an ear. His grip on her wrist loosened as he fell back. But he still clutched her foot. He was staring fiercely at her, eyes blazing coals of hatred, his chest heaving, working his mouth soundlessly. Quickly, she bent over and with all the strength she could muster, one by one, unclenched his fingers until her ankle was freed. Then she sprang upward, poising the shoe, ready to meet the renewed assault. Instead, he rolled to his side, hunched again to hands and knees, heaved himself heavily to the sofa and dropped leadenly onto it, rolling face upward. She grabbed a pillow, placed one knee on his chest and pressed.

Now he'll die and oh, there was relish to this moment—this shameless, triumphal savoring of the kill—the sheer sweet savagery of execution—and the heady exaltation of success! She pressed hard, her entire body weighted on two rigid arms for what seemed to be an interminable period. Then suddenly, he thrashed, arching his body in a death throe's protest, and for a brief vomitous moment she feared she would not match his last gasp of dying strength. For that moment, as she clumsily continued to knee him down and press at the same time, his body suspended, his arms flapped like broken chicken wings, and then he collapsed.

When she withdrew her arms they ached, and she was perspiring and breathing heavily. She became frightened by a sudden drumming sound until she realized that it was the throb of her heart. He did not stir, those mild blue eyes were forever cocooned, and he seemed totally relaxed, as if in repose. She put her ear to his chest and heard nothing. She searched for his pulse and detected nothing.

Satisfied, gleeful, she rose, inserted the thermos bottle she'd brought and the cup he'd used into her purse. Then she righted the curio cabinet. Amazingly, the glass had not broken and the frail shelves were intact and in place. She wiped it cleanly with a handkerchief, then retrieved the spilled Venuses, wiped each piece and replaced them on the shelves in the approximate arrangement she recalled them to have been in. Unable to repress her agitation, she tried not to hurry as she inspected all the rooms for any signs, any objects or jottings, wiping clean any of those she might have touched, that would indicate that she had now, or ever, been on the premises. Save for the prostrate form on the couch, there seemed to be no evidence that Anna Spanger existed.

Her voice was a deep-throated melancholy croak. "For you, Mama... Papa... Ernst... and forgive me, Nate." She started for the door just as her eye caught an object almost buried in the deep pile of the rug. She bent to it and picked up a three-inch Venus. Almost without thinking, rather than go back to the cabinet, reopen and reinsert the wayward miniature and rewipe again, dropped it into her purse and quickly went out, careful to wipe the door hardware, inside and out.

Her heart beat fiercely in cadence with each measured step to her car, glancing neither to the left or right, not allowing herself a last look back to the hated aerie of the despised man. Irrationally fearful that any out of the ordinary movement from the house to the car would be a giveaway to invisible eyes in the night that could discern her in the darkness and perceive what she had done.

Only when swallowed by the freeway traffic back to the city did the finality of the deed register and the immensity of relief overtake her.

Halfway home she suddenly remembered that Gehbert's fly was open.

12

For the first time in weeks Freda slept, a deep sleep that thoroughly refreshed her.

She showered leisurely, dressed comfortably in slacks, looking in the mirror, liked what she saw, went out to pick up one of the morning papers flipped onto the driveway for two of the four tenants in the building, the first floor Reitzes, 1A, being the other, she was Japanese and he was Dutch and they had two well-behaved children.

She turned on the radio, made breakfast, famished, ate heartily, went through the paper twice. There was no word on Grossman. Nor was anything said on the radio. It was early, a scant twelve hours since she'd left him, and that probably accounted for it; the body hadn't been discovered yet.

It was amazing the change that had come over her. Was it only yesterday—eons ago—that she had been on the verge of—? Then Vicki's blessed lifesaving call that had jolted her back to reality with her exuberant prattle of her newfound boyfriend. It would have been the height of irony, she saw now, the triumph of the darkness that such as the Gehberts of the world represented, if he'd succeeded after all these years in having her do to herself what he could not do to her before. It had been a long, hard, off-balance road and a very narrow escape to her own "final solution."

She went to the food market to buy a few things in

anticipation of Vicki's visit and to fill in for the game she would hostess that night. Returned to the apartment and began to set up. It was fitting this milestone day that she should hostess. She could hardly wait to see their faces when they heard the news.

Vicki, all bounce and verve, came promptly at twelve to show off Graham Block to her grandmother, and her grandmother to Graham Block. He thought she was super, she thought he was very nice, if bland, obviously wanting to make a good impression, a pleasant animated hour with Vicki doing most of the talking, and after a light lunch, Vicki, delighted with her grandmother's approval of her first real boyfriend, they left. Freda felt her old ebullient self.

One o'clock and still no news. Two o'clock, three o'clock, no word. Four o'clock and still no news. She went out for the afternoon paper. Nothing in it. She was tempted to call him, to reassure herself that he would not answer, but she thought better of it. Right now the police could be swarming. Still, it was early in terms of his routine. He usually didn't get to the restaurant until midafternoon to prepare for the evening trade. If he'd complained of a cold, it was possible that he was not expected to be in today at all. It could be days before he'd be discovered. Still one or more of the personnel could be expected to call to inquire to his health.

Five o'clock and the catastrophes did not include him, and she was becoming increasingly nervous. What if something had gone wrong? What if—? Sooner or later the body would be found. Had she left anything telltale behind? Not from last night, but from previous visits? She thought not, she'd gone through the rooms carefully afterwards. Still . . . a hair, a comb or brush or—? No, that's television and the movies where it all wraps neatly at the end. She was very careful to bring her own toilet articles and leave nothing after each visit. Was there someone in the restaurant to link her to him? No. From that first time she went with him from the restaurant, she was careful not to return or to be seen publicly with him, and her visits were always at night.

Neighbors?

His house was set well back. The closest was at least one hundred and fifty feet distant and obscured by foliage. Bless Topanga Canyon, one of the last enclaves, ablaze with larkspur, poppies, toyon and purple lupine.

Six o'clock. It was full news time, radio and television, and both were on, flipping each to catch local segments. Nothing. She prepared something to eat and wasn't hungry. Christ, *was* the son of a bitch dead? Had she really done it? Let's hear it from ABC, CBS and NBC that Wilhelm Gehbert is dead! dead! dead! The history of the world since the first recorded word has been the Wilhelm Gehberts. Correction. It is possible, going back ten thousand years, that the first scrapings on cave walls may have been "lousy Jew."

THOU SHALL NOT KILL.

That one at Birkenau...Had she really? The trustee, a victim like herself, only a bit healthier for her exalted position as keeper of the latrine...strangling her...countering demoniacally...pushed? slipped? face down into the muck, spent, to suffocate in three inches of shit.

THOU SHALL NOT KILL.

They say it comes back. A deep-seated crisis and you've never left. God watches, God knows, dear God...6:30 now and it tore at her. To calculatingly kill...She'd read somewhere, miss three meals a man lies, miss six he steals, and nine he kills. The world's food supply rests on three inches of topsoil. Armageddon is only seventy-two hours away. We all live three inches from topsoil...Could there have been another way? What way? Someone else? Who? Four years puny sentence and "loss of honor" for 5,450 murders! Square that, God! If you command THOU SHALL NOT KILL you should have added another: WILHELM GEHBERT SHALT NOT HAVE BEEN BORN. At the very outset, when the original couple proved defective, you should have broken the mold and recast a new product. Any good manufacturer knows that.

THOU SHALL NOT KILL, FREDA FRIEDKIN!

A neck nerve throbbed, her armpits were wet, and she feared

142

she would hyperventilate but it passed. The minutes snailed. Earlier, she had eagerly looked forward to the arrival of the women, to see their faces when they'd burst in on her to exchange the joyful news, but now it was dreaded. They did not know, and no longer believed that it would happen, and she must contain and hold herself as solemnly. To face them, knowing that what was so fervently desired was now the irretrievable fact, they were all deep into it now.

Hold it! Don't lay it off on the others. You did it! By your hand and only by your hand, Freda Friedkin!

How would she make it through this night—or tomorrow—or the next day if they don't find him soon? Or have they already and are deliberately keeping it quiet because *they know*—they're biding their time—they'll be coming for you, Freda Friedkin, in their own good time!

There was time to call, postpone the game, not feeling well, anything—what time is it? My God, 7:30! They'll be here any minute. Hurry, you miserable creeps, hurry—

Elsa was the first to arrive, and within ten minutes all were there. Their mood-of-the-week carried over, making brave small talk to veneer the strain. Curiously, Freda felt relieved almost at once with their arrival. Her mood altered abruptly, the comfort of the herd, palliated by the presence of bodies and voices. The die was cast. There was nothing to be done but wait. What the hell is this self-colloquy business? The monster is stone cold dead. That's fact, and if you want to retain your goddamned sanity, cut the inner dialogue. She turned the radio up, ostensibly to better hear the music but to make certain that every word on the periodic news-spots would be clearly heard above the sounds of play.

The games were evenly played. Intense, chatterless and poorly. Freda was bursting, anticipatorily awaiting each news announcement; deflating when the half hours passed without disclosure; restraining from proclaiming the accomplished deed that had to, just had to become public before they broke for the night or truly she would go out of her mind.

When Sophie uncharacteristically let a flower that could have meant Mah-Jong, and the game slip by, not hearing or noticing a vital tile being discarded, she threw up her hands and shouted "Goddam it! That's it! I can't concentrate. Call it quits! Either we officially declare—"

"Shut up!" Interrupted by Hannah.

Sophie was astounded. "What—?"

"Listen!" Hannah hissed. "The radio!"

Immediately quiet, the words in a tailed-off announcement of a newscast filled the room. "—the proprietor of Papa Grossman's restaurant in Topanga Canyon was found dead in his home. Cause of death has not been established." The dulcet voice went on to capsulize other local and national mischiefs, and then the music resumed.

They were stunned . . . it had happened . . . the incontrovertible fact proclaimed to the world . . . Walter "Papa" Grossman, nee Wilhelm Gehbert, was dead, dead, dead!

Gertrude was the first to unfreeze, rising abruptly and knocking over her chair to announce, "I have to pee," and ran off. Elsa grabbed a handful of unsalted peanuts and fired them singly into her mouth, and Sophie actually drew blood from her lower lip. The invisible heretofore oppressive weight lifted from them and evaporated the tension. Freda just sat, mummified, grinning beatifically.

Gertrude returned and they exchanged covert glances. Who among them had done this dastardly lovely thing? One out of five had achieved dimension and distinction, a silent Joan of Arc immortality that must not go unhallowed this night of nights. Freda unkinked, rose, and went to the refrigerator, withdrew a bottle of champagne, popped it expertly and filled five goblets.

Hannah beat on her knees, accompanying to a litany. "I'm going to scream, I'm going to scream, I'm going to scream. I just know it, I'm going to scream."

"Hold it! All of us." From Gertrude, orchestrating. "One—two—three!" They all screamed. "Again!" They screamed a second time, louder and longer. Followed almost immediately by a metallic banging emanating from the elongated wall heater and a muffled voice from below welling up through the air shaft. "What the hell's going on up there?"

Elsa cupped her hands and directed to the floor, "Screw you!"

"Hey!" said Freda. "Alienate your neighbors. Not mine." Then turned to the others. "A toast," she proposed with unrestrained glee. "To the late unlamented Butcher of Birkenau. May the mangy prick rot in hell!"

"For a thousand years," Sophie amended with ghoulish delight.

They drank to that.

"To that one among us who so nobly performed this magnificent deed to rid an uncaring world of a vile bastard," Hannah swooped her arm up, slopping herself, drained what was left in the goblet, and refilled it. A nondrinker, she was making an exception to honor the landmark occasion and was already giddy.

They drank to that.

"I honest to God didn't think it could—would be done," Elsa confessed and winked broadly.

Sophie winked back with a Cheshire cat grin of her own. "I didn't think so either."

Gertrude beamed. "I have a dream," drawing the words out in the manner of Martin Luther King. "To pee on his grave."

They drank to that, resumed the game, played a tipsy and zestful mishmash, enjoyed each other hugely, and slept well.

The early morning news was a shocker.

Hannah was frying bacon when she heard it.

Gertrude's son was leaving for school, but she was berating him for leaving his collection of *Playboy* centerfolds in clear view. It offended her to see them each time she came into his room to make the bed. She offered a deal, take it or leave it, he could make his own bed and keep the room clean and she would not trespass. Jeffrey figured it was less hassle to put them away. She caught it on the transistor radio he carried as he went out the door.

Sophie was vacuuming, by the time she'd shut it off, the announcement was over and she wasn't at all sure of what she did catch.

Elsa was driving to work and heard it on the car radio.

Freda was still sleeping and did not hear it.

The phone awakened her. It was Hannah, excited and garbled, but settling down, clear enough. Freda could not believe what was conveyed. Within five minutes the others also called. It was agreed to meet at her place at two o'clock to consider the emergency!

It would be the first time ever that they would all get together in the afternoon. It presented no problem beyond a rescheduling of minor appointments, dental for Hannah and hairdresser for Gertrude. Sophie prepared dinner and left a note to her family that she would try to be back by then. Elsa left the boutique to Valerie, her sole employee.

Freda had been roused out of a deep dreamless sleep. But the reality of what had been told to her did not permeate until she padded into the kitchen, turned on the radio, lit a cigarette, sat in the beakfast alcove, and between sips and inhalations, heard it:

"...Police reveal that sixty-three-year-old Walter Grossman, found dead in his home last night, has been the victim of foul play and have in their custody a suspect who was apprehended at the scene. He is forty-two-year-old Martin Renner..."

When they convened, the room looked hung over. Freda had not put away the bridge table or the tiles or discarded the empty champagne bottle that was the fount of so much merriment only last night but now was perched mockingly on a counter top. They were still in shock, a stricken tableau. Elsa said in dismay, "It's a mistake. It just has to be."

"No," said Freda with undemonstrative agitation, "no mistake. Gehbert will rot in hell, but so might poor Mr. Renner. Have you read the papers? He was found a few hundred yards from Gehbert's place in a ditch in a turned-over car, with three broken ribs, unable to account for what happened."

"Unbelievable!" Hannah snorted. "We *know* who did it. *We* did it!"

"One of us," Sophie corrected and insisted, "One of us."

"The same thing." Hannah chided and shook her head in bewilderment. "How can they arrest an innocent man when we know the truth? He didn't do it."

Gertrude stared at the empty champagne bottle and said opaquely, "I think I'm going to throw up."

Cotton-thick gloom blanketed them as thoughts and words welled collectively in five throats but died inchoate. Elsa rose and in the silence, mechanically emptied three or four ashtrays into a single one, then turned to the others in anguish. "We can't let an innocent man go to prison."

"No," Hannah shook her head and swept the room with her eyes. Then put the question to them knowing that they could not answer.

"*Who* is Martin Renner?"

BOOK TWO

MAHJ!

19

"You are Martin Renner?"

The man addressed gazed steadfast at the two detectives through his one good eye, the other discolored, swollen and half-shut. It pained and the heavy tape that bound his rib cage throbbed and made breathing difficult; also it forced him to sit unnaturally stiff-backed as if a ramrod had been run through his spine.

He was of average height with no distinguishing features, slender, with even white teeth, light brown eyes, and a full head of wavy dark brown hair only mildly stranded with gray. His hands were large and the fingers manicured. He was, according to his out-of-state drivers license, Martin Renner, age forty-two, born in Cleveland, Ohio, residing at the time of issuance in Chicago, Illinois.

"You are Martin Renner?" the larger of the two, Milliken, repeated.

"If that is what you say," Renner replied, his voice low and well modulated with a richness and culture-sound that surmounted its midwestern origin.

"That's what it says on your driver's license."

"I suppose."

"You suppose? Don't you know your own name?"

"I don't remember."

"Don't want to—or can't?"

149

"I can only recall since I revived."

"Nothing before the accident?" Milliken asked evenly with concealed disbelief. "Not your name? Why you were in the Canyon? Or the accident itself?"

Renner shut the other eye, probing, attempting to pierce the dark curtain that had descended so abruptly but a few hours prior. When he opened it again, the men had not moved, and his look was beseeching.

"I wish I could. No."

Milliken pulled at his bulbous nose. He was just under six feet, well over two hundred pounds and looked bigger. His clothes were ill-fitting and his beer-fat belly protruded over trousers that rolled at the top to show the lining. He looked as if he slept in them. His paunch was an enemy, and he'd long ago given up evasive action to reduce it. He appeared formidable and looked unmistakably detective. His voice was a surprise, high pitched and deceptively mild.

"Are you in pain, Mr. Renner?"

"My eye——"

"Yeah, nasty. You busted three ribs."

Milliken glanced at his partner. Chevares had piercing eyes under bushy brows that could drill through granite, fixed in a perpetual scowl, and was three inches shorter than Milliken, trim and sinewy. In the department they were called Mutt and Jeff, after the venerable cartoon strip, but not to their faces. They were capable and knew it, and the look between them said it: here we go again, the cagey son of a bitch is going to pull the hoary amnesic bit.

Chevares, quiet until now, snapped, "You understand your rights?"

"You explained to me."

"I mean," Chevares grated with feisty emphasis, "do you understand them? You're entitled to a lawyer."

"No lawyer is necessary."

"Your injuries are a direct result of the accident, right?" Renner nodded assent.

"Okay. Let's run through it again. You don't know who you are? Don't know where you live? Don't recall a family or friends or how you support yourself? What you were doing in the Canyon and why? How the accident happened? That's an awful lot for a grown man not to know about himself. Suppose you tell us what you do know."

"Only that I was pulled out of the car by two officers."

"Prelutsky and Jennings. Listening."

"Brought to the emergency hospital, examined and taped, given aspirin, told to rest—" hesitating slightly, "then brought here to the station."

"Dig back before the accident."

"I've tried. I don't remember." Renner looked from one to the other, and clearly they did not believe him. Or at least not want to believe him. "I'm sorry," he shrugged woefully, "I can't." Then, apologetically, "Excuse me, but isn't this line of questioning unusual for an accident?"

"Yeah, we think the situation is very unusual, Renner. We'd like you to share it with us."

"I'm sorry. What did happen?"

"Thought you'd never ask—"

Milliken nudged Chevares's elbow, and the latter yielded with an artistic sneer. "At about nine-thirty this evening you were traveling in a southerly direction on Casitas Road in a rented car," Milliken said, and interrupted himself. "Jump in any time if we haven't got it right." He resumed, "suddenly this dog crossed your lights—we know that part from the Rosses—people who were looking for the bitch. To avoid hitting her you swerved into a ditch, hit your head and passed out. Mrs. Ross stayed with you, and Mr. Ross ran to the nearest phone to call the police. They came and pried you loose. Essentially right so far?"

"I'm hazy on that but I have no reason to doubt it."

"What happened before?" Chevares repeated.

"I seem to have lost my memory."

"Keep nudging it," said Milliken, "it'll come back. Since you obviously needed treatment and were in apparent shock, unable to identify yourself, Officer Prelutsky asked permission to search your person, which you granted."

"I don't recall."

"We have witnesses," Chevares again with asperity. "The Rosses."

Renner nodded, conceding.

"We know who you are from your license. The car you wrecked is a rental. That gives us your temporary address. The Seakist Motel on Ventura Boulevard. You've been there two weeks. Remember that?"

"No sir. I don't remember anything before the hospital."

It became quiet in the Spartan room, containing a long scarred table flecked with cigarette burns and unmatched chairs worn with countless interrogations, and dingy walls, bare save for an austere clock which read 1:30 A.M. and a large unillustrated calendar. The only other adornments were a telephone and a writing pad. Chevares thrust out with:

"Tell us about the initials: W. G."

Renner registered blank. "W. G.? What do they mean?"

"Tell us."

"I don't know."

"When you were pulled out of the car," Milliken said, "a map fell out. An area in Topanga Canyon was circled. The accident took place within it."

"I don't know about a map."

Chevares reached for his back pocket, withdrew and unfolded a large city map dispensed by service stations, indicated the Canyon area and pointed to the circle within it marked with a black felt pen. Slightly above it, clearly discernible, were the initials: W. G.

"Familiar?"

"No sir." Then helpfully, "maybe it was left by the previous rental?"

"Think hard, Renner." And prodded. "W. G."

"Take your time," Milliken added.

The two men withdrew slightly, and Milliken lit a cigarette.

Chevares did not smoke, his eyes not leaving Renner, boring relentlessly. Milliken slid the pack along the table to Renner who picked it up, removed a cigarette and awaited a match.

Chevares pounced. "How do you know you smoke, if you don't know anything else?"

Renner was startled and looked from one to the other; up till now Milliken appeared to be less forbidding than his partner, but now his eyes slitted almost as fiercely.

"I don't know. Maybe it will help me to think. It's frightening...I mean—if I've lost my memory——"

"W. G." Chevares persisted, reached out and unceremoniously whisked the unlit cigarette dangling from between Renner's lips and flicked it across the room repeating with irritation, "Come on. W. G."

"No."

"No what?"

"It doesn't mean anything. Is it important?"

"Yeah," Chevares cracked his knuckles crisply in the manner of a fighter, which he had been prior to joining the force. "They could stand for Walter Grossman. Ring a bell?"

"No sir."

"He owns a restaurant about a mile from where you were found."

Renner awaited elucidation.

"Also a house off Casitas Road where your accident took place and all within the circled area on the map."

Renner tilted his head as if to alter its position could coax remembrance. "W. G....W. G...." he mulled, then shook his head. "It's just not familiar."

"He was found dead within minutes of your accident."

"Oh..." He gestured haplessly, what was he supposed to say? And he was tiring. "I don't know anything."

Milliken took over. "Mrs. Ross stayed with you while her husband went to find a phone. It's still pretty isolated in the Canyon. And it's dark. He had a flashlight and worked himself to the nearest place, Grossman's house, although he was familiar enough with it, since he lives in the area. He banged on the door. There was no answer. He ran his flashlight through the window, and saw Grossman on the couch. He didn't look right, so Ross kept banging away, thought maybe it was a heart attack, but he couldn't be sure. He ran to the next place, the people were home, and he called the police from there. They arrived and he told them about Grossman. You came to, didn't want an ambulance, so they said they'd take you to the emergency hospital. Recall that?"

"Vaguely."

"You were placed in the police car, and they drove to Grossman's place to look in. Remember that?"

"That we stopped? I guess so."

"Prelutsky and Jennings looked through the window, saw Grossman, and he didn't look right to them either, so they busted in. Grossman was dead."

Silence fretted the gloomy room to let the fact sink in, awaiting a telltale reaction from Renner, but there was only an unaccommodating perplexed look and Milliken resumed.

"Something struck Jennings. The initials 'W. G.' on the map—everybody around here knows—knew—Papa Grossman—your accident and the fact that it happened at the same time just a short distance from him, pointed *away* from his house when he kicked off...so...copper's hunch...he looked around and found what could have been forcible entry to the rear of the house." Milliken inhaled deeply, coughed and gurgled up phlegm, which he swallowed back. "Know anything about that?"

Renner shook his head and mumbled incomprehensibly.

"Louder," Chevares barked, "the acoustics in here are lousy."

"No sir. I don't know anything."

"In short, Renner," Milliken tugged at his nose again. "Since it may be more than coincidence that Grossman died at the approximate time of your accident—or the other way around—and you're not telling why you were where you were—and insist you know nothing of your past life before nine-thirty tonight—forty-two years of living goes into the garbage can—you've got a four-hour running jump into a brand new shitty one."

"That's the ball game," Chevares rasped. "Now what've you got to say?"

The man sitting wanted to scream for understanding, compassion, but that had gone begging all evening—his side throbbed, and the eye was rapidly closing, and he longed for sleep—to sleep away this gross charade until the light of the coming day would bring with it reason and would—must—absolutely have to reveal the grotesquerie for what it was—a bad dream. For if the nightmare persisted, he would surely go through his own skull.

Instead, with as much dignity as one with a lavender-hued protrusive eye, forced to sit stiffly upright due to a corset of tape binding three bruised ribs, in a cheerless room, subject to a relentless probe for over two hours, could muster, he was quietly but firmly audible.

"I have nothing to say."

Within two days, Martin Renner was arraigned. The judge asked for his plea. Renner stared blankly. The judge asked did he plead guilty or not guilty. Renner said that he did not know what was happening. The judge repeated the question, Renner repeated the reply. The judge asked if he was represented by counsel, Renner said he was not. The judge said if he could not afford counsel, one would be furnished. Renner thanked him and said there was no need. The judge asked did he mean to act as his own counsel, and Renner said that he did not understand why he was here. The judge pointed out that a complaint has been issued charging him with Murder One and he was entitled to adequate counsel to insure a fair trial as quickly as possible. Renner thanked him again and again stated he did not know why he was here, he simply could not remember events leading to his arrest. The judge studied his nails. Arraignment was automatic in most cases, request made, request granted, a procedure that usually took no more than five minutes. It had already consumed ten. The judge, slightly bored, decided that since Renner was not admitting to guilt, a plea of innocence would be entered, a public defender would be provided and set a date five days hence for the preliminary hearing. No bail was recommended, the judge affirmed, next case.

Among the handful of spectators were Freda, Elsa, Sophie,

157

Hannah and Gertrude. Earlier, Freda had called Vicki for Graham Block's number, and to forestall curiosity, said vaguely that someone she knew might be in difficulty and perhaps some legal advice could be helpful. Vicki was pleased that Grandma was taken by Graham, he was the scrunchiest, and was certain that Graham, although not actually practicing law, would do what he could. Freda called him, and he was delighted to hear from her because Vicki was the scrunchiest and he knew how fond the two women were of each other, it was a beautiful thing to behold, what could he do for her? And was taken aback by her request for information on court procedures for trying a murder case, but rallied nicely.

Arraignment was usually forty-eight hours after issuance of complaint. A preliminary hearing usually followed within two to five days in Municipal Court, its official purpose being to determine probable cause before a judge whether the defendant could be held to answer to the charge. The District Attorney's office would attempt to make its case, and the defense attorney would try to discredit witnesses, if any, and to assess the strength of the prosecution's case. Upon sufficient cause, the case would be placed on the Master Calendar, usually within twenty-four days for the actual trial. The three separate procedures allowed for further investigations and preparations by both sides but most importantly, to allow for plea bargaining. Freda asked how she could find out where and when a person would be arraigned, and he gave her a number to call.

Aware that his curiosity was piqued, she thanked him profusely, ventured no specific information and hung up. Through two phone calls and five routings later, she learned that Martin Renner would appear in Division 80 of the municipal court, located in the Civic Center, tomorrow morning.

Freda relayed the information to the women. After repeated phone calls and cross-conversations with each other, weighing the pros and cons of appearing at the arraignment, only Gertrude held out for complete disassociation. When it was finally decided that an appearance by one or more on an optional basis could not possibly incriminate, Gertrude was thereupon swayed by a curiosity equal to the others'.

Early that morning, Hannah picked up Gertrude, Freda picked up Sophie, and Elsa, the only one to live in the Valley, drove alone to the parking lot of the International House of Pancakes at Third and Occidental. Convened, they then moved the three cars to a nearby side street, comprising vintage residences with no-limit street parking. Freda and Hannah parked their cars and pooled into Elsa's Cadillac and together drove the rest of the way to the downtown courthouse to save the parking fees of two cars.

It was Freda's first appearance in a courtroom. Gertrude and Sophie had made small claims court appearances, Hannah had been a witness to an automobile accident, and Elsa had served on a jury in Superior Court. They arrived promptly at eight, were seated among a handful of spectators at eight-thirty, but it was not until eleven that Renner was presented. Freda did not know what her expectation was, but the leisurely murmurings on the prior cases behind the balustrade in the hushed room seemed to belie the urgency of law and order so unlike the pyrotechnics of courtroom drama as portrayed on television and the motion picture screen.

What she saw and heard, they all later agreed, was of little value. Renner appeared to be a mild man, a *nebbish*, none could recall ever seeing him before. One eye was discolored, and he seemed to list to one side as if favoring an injury. Certainly, he did not *look* like a murderer. Freda, within the comfort of dear friends, realized with a start that neither did she. Renner's disposition was over in minutes, as hangdog, he was led away. Poor man.

They then drove to Little Joe's restarant on North Broadway for a light lunch. The clatter of its lunchtime clientele was backdrop to their intensely hushed discussion of what next to do. Since this was not basically a place to discuss alternatives, it was decided to continue the discussion at Freda's place to consider further what, if anything, there was they could do if indeed they should do anything at all.

Elsa insisted on paying the check but the others overruled her. They split five ways, tipped generously, and she paid by credit card after reimbursement to allow her to use the deduction. They drove back to where Freda and Hannah were parked, resumed their original pairings and drove on to Freda's apartment, which was centrally located.

They reconvened at Freda's and probed all aspects of their involvement including the obvious course of doing nothing and they would be home free, Renner to fend for himself. The hope would be that despite any case the police believed they had, that simple justice must prevail and he would be freed because they *knew* he was innocent.

But to do nothing was unanimously rejected for several reasons. Simple justice was often no justice at all. Miscarriages were legendary. Even if found innocent, it would be unfair to put him through the anguish of awaiting trial and the trial itself. It was indigestible that anyone should be tried for Gehbert's demise. They self-righteously proclaimed that not only should the perpetrator not be tried, but publicly lauded and richly rewarded for an inestimable service to humanity. Also, inherently and by experience, they were not copouts, could not accept the pervasive Kitty Genovese syndrome of noninvolvement, particularly since they were the guilty ones. Their animus for Gehbert had been so fervent it had not occurred to them to even remotely consider the possible apprehension of the true murderer. Had that happened, however, there was no question whatsoever that they would solidly unite in support, one for all, all for one. They could do no less, must do no less for Martin Renner. He was, they realized, the sixth musketeer.

Embarked upon rescue, the next question was formidable.

How?

They engaged in a dour session of wishful thinking. Where are you, Errol Flynn, now that we need you? Or Agent 007? No godfatherly Mafioso to tap, or dollars to bribe, or any member of the Writers Guild to concoct a daringly bizarre plot, a Mission Impossible, to spring the hapless man?

Their giddiness subsided. The fretful fact was that they had only themselves to look to and what were they? Any mirror could tell them. Five aging women, who for all their bravado were frightened, for themselves, for Renner, with extremely limited resources, and would be hard put even to rescue a kitten in a tree.

"The poor shmuck," Freda shook her head in frustration. "What the hell was he doing in the canyon anyway? Makes no sense."

"No sense is the best sense for him." replied Hannah. "That he does or does not remember anything doesn't matter. We know he didn't do it."

"How do we know that?" Elsa countered, assailed with a sudden thought. There was a stunned silnce, and she continued quietly, "Suppose—just suppose for a moment——"

"What—?" sputtered Gertrude, almost gagging on a mouthful of unsalted peanuts.

"One of us was chosen to do it—still supposing—but couldn't and didn't. We waited five weeks and were at a point where it was almost all bets off, remember? Then it happened. But if the Renner thing hadn't come up, we would have no reason to believe it was not done by one of us. However, we'll really never know unless—" trailed off, leaving the pregnant observation to swell among them.

"Unless?" Sophie prodded.

"We honestly question ourselves and openly admit that the one committed to do it, did not."

They spoke at once, the words spilling out, canceling each other, unintelligible, but the tenor was unmistakable. There must never, but absolutely never, be disclosure, even if failed. That would go to their graves.

"All right, all right," she waved them shut, never more proud of her love and friendship for them than at this moment. "Another thought. The police can be wrong, but they are not fools. They may know something about Renner we don't know."

"On TV the other night, there was this poor slob accused of murder," Gertrude started to say, but Hannah threw her a withering look and she aborted, thumbing her nose at Hannah.

"You mean maybe he's queer and was carrying on with Gehbert?" Hannah ventured.

Sophie puckered thoughtfully. "Who knows? Maybe. No normal man could do what Gehbert did. It's possible, I suppose, that he screwed everything that moved."

"Immaterial, immaterial," Freda rasped and turned to Elsa. "Any more bright ideas?"

"The thought occurred," Elsa sighed. "My own feeling is even if I knew Renner did it, I'd want very much to help him."

They were back to reaffirmation.

After much discussion there was, bottom line, an inescapable approach. The truth. It was armor and ammunition. A confession could be anonymously sent to the authorities. They would recognize its authenticity by details not publicly revealed. Renner would be released. Or would he? Upon reflection, there were hazards. The confession could be ignored out of malice, for myriad reasons, and the trial nonetheless undertaken as a possible stratagem to reach the conscience of the anonymous letter writer to draw the murderer out publicly. That would defeat the original purpose of sparing agony to Renner. If one were exposed, all would be tarnished. Still cloaked in righteousness, they could not envisage peril to be as dire for them as that immediately facing Renner.

Suppose they all confess. Five Joan of Arcs. Here we are, Mr. District Attorney, we did it, we did it, and we're glad. They would have to be believed, covering for each other, not giving away the actual culprit. But perhaps they were underestimating the minions of the law who would be wise in the ways of confessors, also overestimating their collective abilities to withstand interrogation, even incarceration, should one break. They were allergic to imprisonment. The shuddery prospect of being placed behind bars, reminiscent of their captivity in Birkenau, was more than each could bear to contemplate. Another consideration. The possible repercussion within their own families and the devastation of lives beyond their own. Did they have the right to involve others to whom opprobrium would surely attach? In the long run four would needlessly suffer for the fifth?

Well, they'd started something, it was out of hand and there was no turning back, that much was agreed.

Finally, a plan was devised.

Only one out of the five in the room knew the precise manner in which Gehbert was dispatched. That one must continue to remain anonymous. She would write out, that is, type out the confession, for her handwriting could be a giveaway, make five copies, including one for herself, destroy the original, and mail a copy to each from a neutral post office. Each, upon receipt, would study the confession and they would meet again to discuss ways and means of presenting it. Today was Friday. They would meet again the coming Wednesday. Out of the discussion lightning might strike whereby no one need be sacrificed. This was perhaps wishful, but until each had precise knowledge of the crime, it was agreed that none but one knew what the hell they were talking about. Also, they resigned themselves to forego Mah-Jong until further notice, somehow a travesty to continue to enjoy themselves while poor Renner languished in jail.

The meeting broke up. Hannah drove Sophie home, stopping en route to Culver City at Fazio's Market on La Cienega Boulevard across from Montgomery Ward's, to purchase specials on jumbo-sized eggs, diet soda and apples which were plentiful this time of the year. Elsa drove Gertrude to the Farmers Market at the corner of Third and Fairfax and continued on to her shop. Despite murder on her mind, Gertrude walked leisurely about, taking in the colorful environs and the press of people, even out of season, still mostly tourists, supressing a twinge of guilt for stealing a rare deviation from household chores. The day was shot anyway, she would pull something out of the freezer to feed her family. What she really wanted, and indulged herself, was delicious homemade cherry pie a la mode at Du Par's restaurant.

When they had all gone, Freda immediately went to work on the confession.

Freda read the confession carefully. Her palms were sweaty, and she flexed her fingers to keep them from trembling although they had not betrayed her once she started typing.

She had spent what remained of yesterday and this entire morning writing several drafts on a yellow legal pad. It had been difficult to render. Venom had spewed onto it, not so much for a life taken, but for the self-revulsion in committing to paper for public revelation, her fornication with the enemy. Also, to be wary of a subjectivity that would inadvertently reveal her to be the perpetrator. At one point she had written: "In 1945 I am liberated. I emigrate to the United States. I marry. I do not have children. This is not by choice. I had been destroyed internally by Gehbert's bestiality. I make a new life with my husband who is most understanding. Birkenau is a thing of the past." Realized that the passage was a giveaway. Hannah, Sophie and Gertrude had given birth. She and Elsa had not. Reduced to two choices, the others could easily believe that between the two, by personality and by her verification of the dog bite, she was the one who had committed the deed. Certainly Elsa knew that she had not. In the end, it was reduced to: "After I am liberated I emigrate to the United States. The past is behind me." Not memoir but a simple recounting of vital detail to effect the release of an innocent man.

When she was finally satisfied that the letter contained the truthful essentials she typed it. The typewriter had been

167

borrowed from Vicki, who knew her grandmother to be an excellent self-taught typist. Finally, after several false starts, a clean copy with few erasures emerged. It came to three pages, double spaced. She would have five copies made, mailed out and destroy the original.

The confession read:

To Whom It May Concern:

My name is _____. I reside at _____. On the evening of January 20 of this year I, and I alone, killed the person known to you as Walter Grossman.

He was Doctor Wilhelm Gehbert, chief medical officer of the SS (Schutz Steffeln) who directed the medical experimentation program carried out on the women of the Birkenau concentration camp. Tried as a Nazi war criminal for participation in 5,450 murders, he served eighteen months and "loss of honor" (I do not know what that means) or one day for each three murders. This is a matter of record.

That is why he died. He served too little for doing untold and irreparable damage to thousands more beyond even the numbers he was charged with. I was among them, one of many thousands of women subjected to rape, torture and medical experimentation.

After I am liberated I emigrate to the United States. The past is behind me. I do not think that I will see Wilhelm Gehbert again. But one day, by chance, I go to Papa Grossman's restaurant in Topanga Canyon and there I am shocked to see the man I know to be Gehbert. It is many years later but I am certain it is he. I take steps to verify his identity, including one irrefutable fact: a scar just below his left shoulder, the result of a dog bite. There is no mistake. Beyond any shadow of doubt, Walter Grossman is Wilhelm Gehbert.

He must die. I have never killed. I have been exposed to much killing and the thought that I will take a life sickens me. But it is heinous that Gehbert has gone unpunished for his crimes and lives a full and successful life and no one knows or cares. I plan carefully. He does not know who I am. He did not then so this part is simple. He knows me only as Anna Spanger and our contact is only when I call him.

On his last night I go to his home at 11501 Casitas Road. He has a cold. I bring him tea in a thermos bottle. He is grateful that I am interested in his welfare. In the tea is a depressant. Chloral hydrate in syrup form. I had called a pharmacy and asked if there is a record of its purchase many years before. I am told that records of prescription drugs are destroyed after three years. So I am safe in using it for I know it cannot be traced. One tablespoon is a half ounce. I learn that two tablespoons can be a lethal dose. I am inexperienced in such a matter and cannot confide in anyone, so I guess three tablespoons will insure the purpose. But there is a problem. Chloral hydrate has an immediate aftertaste. Fortunately it is scented and I tell him to *expect* an orange flavored bitterness. I have also added bourbon to help disguise the taste.

The thermos is one pint or two glasses. He drinks it all. I think that he will go into a coma and then I will suffocate him with a pillow. I prepare for this when he lies down on the sofa and I take off his shoes. This next is not easy for me to say, but I know that it is a vital detail to authenticate this confession. I open his fly and allow him to become exposed in anticipation of a sex act. As expected, it lulled him.

But then it does not go as I expect. He is strong. He rouses himself and suspects what I have done. Finally, he knows, not who I am, but what I am. Still, I have miscalculated, almost grievously. He attacks me and we struggle and I fear for my life until I beat him off. Finally, the poison takes hold. He falls on the sofa. Then I suffocate him with the pillow. He dies.

I wipe clean whatever it was I may have touched, including the curio cabinet containing miniature Venuses. It had fallen during the struggle. Nothing was broken. This is mentioned because my knowledge of the Venuses further indicates my presence with him. I had arrived at 7:15 P.M. and leave at 8:20 P.M.

That is how and why Wilhelm Gehbert died. I admit to the above without coercion and totally of my own free will.

I do not know Martin Renner. I have never met him. I have no knowledge of him whatsoever other than what I have read or heard in connection with Gehbert's death.

Signature

Well, it was done and she felt better. Of course, she would have to again manipulate to be the one to confess but she was certain that she could manage as easily as she had the first time. She addressed five envelopes, then showered, and refreshed, went to the Gardner Street Library above Third Street to run off five copies on a duplicating machine; inserted each into envelopes, sealed them, then drove downtown to the main post office to mail them.

And she thought, well, the tit is in the wringer now.

When Freda deposited the confessions into the mailbox, it was only the first of twenty-two steps to the final one of delivery to the recipients. The Los Angeles Terminal Annex of the United States Postal Service, located on North Alameda Street, spews out over sixty million pieces of mail every week. Processing is a strange amalgam of old and new technologies, a factory with a strange assortment of tools, where the nineteenth century and the Space Age merge; the muscles of mail handlers who heave heavy sacks in and out of trucks in much the same way mail was loaded on stagecoaches over one hundred years ago, conveyor belts that were new when the building opened in 1940, and electronic gadgetry that bears the stamp of the seventies. Delivery is 97 percent effective. The other 3 percent is misdirected, mislaid or lost mail that has given rise to an ineffectual image denounced by Congressmen and coupon clippers. When thousands of pieces of mail on any given day are not delivered on time, its unhappy reputation persists.

When the five women assembled at Elsa's on Wednesday night, four had received copies in ample time for study. Ironically, no copy was received by Freda. With the aplomb of a Bette Davis, she lamented the crappy mail delivery. Time was taken out for her to study one of the four confessions offered.

Elsa was hostess for the evening. Tiles and goodies were

spaced out in the leathered and wood-panelled den, but as previously agreed, they did not expect to play. Elsa thought it prudent to go through the ritual setup rather than risk questions from her husband why they were meeting if they were not going to play.

Through masterful grimacings and lip pursings, Freda ostensibly finished reading, set the confession aside and said matter-of-factly, "So that's how it was done."

Each looked to the other and tried to perceive the secret heart of the one who had executed, but encountered only the blank look and curiosity she herself felt.

"I'd like to say something," Hannah ventured and the floor was open. "What's revealed isn't pleasant. I don't just mean the killing. I mean, well, what it says, you know," and it was not necessary to complete the thought, for it was understood precisely what was meant. "I mean, okay, that's what it took. Nasty. Between us I'm sure we can all live with that. But to stand up to it publicly," gesturing lamely.

"Jewish princesses," Gertrude muttered.

"Including one honorary member," Elsa smiled. "If that part bothers anyone let's talk about it. Until we actually decide what to do, I guess anyone has the right to change her mind about doing anything. This has to be entirely voluntary."

"Let's cut the squeamish shit," Sophie said with startling asperity. "A man's life is at stake."

"Bully for the broad," Freda cheered.

"We're analyzing," Elsa said. "Let it hang out, as they say. Speak your piece."

Freda chortled. "Gee, you talk dirty."

The uncomfortable aspect was not pursued, and Elsa continued. "Let's take this in some order," rapidly assuming leadership. "We've read the confession. So the question is, How do we present it? How much of it will be necessary to reveal? For instance if we go in en masse, we're all in it, that speaks for itself. If only one, well, she recognized Gehbert and killed him. Just the motive and enough of the means to serve the objective need be revealed. The others and the Mah-Jong game don't have to be mentioned."

"Okay, vote," said Gertrude.

"Vote on what?" Sophie asked.

"First to make it official that we save Renner," replied Elsa. "I know we agreed to do that *before* we read the confession but now that we've all had a chance to study it——"

She was interrupted by a chorus of "ayes."

"Next, do we all go in or just one?"

They looked at each other in uncertainty.

"It's messy," Hannah said. "But if we spread it five ways, there's at least comfort in numbers."

"Right," Gertrude agreed, flicking a peanut morsel from the corner of her mouth, rolling it between her thumb and forefinger, and studied it as if it held some mysterious profundity. "We're up to our navels, and we should spread it, divided by five, we fortify each other through whatever crap would be thrown at us."

"I just said that," Hannah said.

"So?" Gertrude shrugged. "I agree with you."

There was no doubt to what Freda thought, but she wanted to gauge the feeling of the others before speaking, certain of the only decision to be made, to lead them to it, for only she could travel the road. But Gertrude suddenly called for a vote for all of them to confess and fearful of its acceptance she spoke up.

"That," she frowned, "would look like what it is to the police. A conspiracy to free Renner. Obstructing justice. And it might not work."

"What do you suggest?" Sophie asked.

"It's foolish for five to admit to murder when one will serve."

"So who would they prosecute?" Gertrude asked. "Four of us didn't do it. They don't know who the fifth is. They have to let us go."

"Don't you believe it," Freda replied testily. "Look at us. What are we? Five menopausal dames trying to get Renner off the hook and save our own skins. You can bet all your unused tampons no matter how just our cause and noble we feel, the police are going to be a helluva lot smarter than we are. They deal with crackpots all the time." She sought to mask her impatience with the fruitless discussion for her game plan was to channel them to the determined end without revelation or alienation.

"All of us charged with murder?" Gertrude asked incredulously.

"Come off it, Gertie. You think tiddlywinks?"

"Don't jump at me," Gertrude returned with a pout. "I'm in this too, you know."

"Why we're here," Hannah interposed calmly. "If we all go in it will certainly change our lives."

"It already has," Sophie said quietly, "and Renner's."

"Ladies, please," Elsa clapped hands smartly. "Does anyone think it would be a good idea to talk to a lawyer?"

"Great idea, sister Elsa," Freda piped, unable to keep the truculence out of her voice. "I suppose that comes under the heading of Clear Thinking."

"Oh shut up, Freda," Hannah snapped, and Freda retreated, angry with herself for venting lest she obstruct the plan. Hannah continued, "We have decisions to make"—turned to the others—"Who could we go to that we could trust?"

"We wouldn't have to tell him everything," Gertrude said, "Just enough."

"Then what would you go to him with?" Sophie asked. "If five of us have to remember lies or what we leave out, we'll sure as hell screw ourselves up. Then why go to him in the first place?"

"Who? To whom? Who?" Gertrude sputtered. "I don't know any lawyer to go to."

"Let your fingers do the walking through the yellow pages," Freda chimed. "Go ahead. We're listening."

Gertrude looked around, uncertain as to the merit of her proposal. "Well, I'll listen, too."

Of course they knew attorneys; their husbands, either personally or in a business way, dealt with them, but none was known to be criminal. Uppermost, the personal touch, the subjectivity, confidence and understanding would be lacking. There was no way they could possibly convey the intensity of a thirty-year trauma as a righteous vendetta to justify murder even if they were lucky to find a sympathetic legal ear. He'd have to think they were five over-the-hill crazy broads unless he was a publicity hound, and that was the last thing they desired.

"Anyone?" Hannah floundered. "It was your idea, Elsa."

Elsa giggled and shook her head. "Amazing. Four Jews and not a single lawyer in their families."

"Stereotype shit," Freda said dourly. "There's a branch of Nate's family that has been on welfare for a generation."

With a proud tilt of her head, Sophie commented sagely, "Jews revere learning. It has given them upward mobility and ulcers. So my kids can spell but can't butter bread."

"Another thing," Hannah chimed. "Anti-Semitism. Boy, would we get nailed."

"A figment of your imagination," Elsa replied airily.

"Yeah. Six million Jews were figmented."

"We digress," Sophie said.

"Also" Freda remembered. "The Mah-Jong fund only carries $93.27. A lawyer wouldn't scratch his ass for that."

To lay the subject to rest, Freda pledged an indeterminate amount if ever, God forbid, the matter came to trial. Elsa said she too would contribute. Hannah, Gertrude and Sophie, less affluent, felt the economic burden would fall embarrassingly unequal. The consensus was to table the procurement of an attorney to the future depending upon unfolding events and only as a last resort.

"We're agreed that a confession is in order," Freda said, making the move. "Is it agreed? One?"

Hannah was unhappy. "Seems unfair that one should bear the brunt."

"Fuck brunt. We didn't quibble to kill."

Sophie quietly intervened, "I think Freda is right. One would spare four."

"But it's selfish," Hannah persisted. "The ripple effect

would be devastating. For her, for her husband, her family, even for us."

"One," Freda was steadfast. "Does that button it?"

"We didn't vote," Gertrude was back to plopping peanuts into her mouth. "God, I can't let these subversive things alone," she added self-consciously, but it did not deter the rapidity with which she consumed them.

"So vote."

They voted, Hannah and Gertrude for all to confess. Elsa and Freda voted one. Sophie demurred.

"Please, Sophie," Freda pleaded. "No abstentions. Or we'll be here all night."

Sophie gestured haplessly and nodded. "One."

Hannah shrugged with grace. "Reminds me of a B'nai B'rith board meeting. One of the members is ill. By a vote of eight to five they wish her a speedy recovery."

No one laughed. "Screw all of you," she said.

Freda rose from her chair and brushed invisible lint from her wool skirt, composed herself and said, "I'd like to be that one."

"Why?" asked Sophie. "Aren't you scared? I admit I am."

"I am not brave, Sophie dear——"

"I mean, look what you've done," and Freda's heart skipped a beat. Did they know? But Sophie's next words allayed her. "You verified what's-his-face's dog bite."

"Oh that," Freda brushed tribute aside, and returned to her request. "I'll confess and after Renner is released——"

Interrupted by Elsa, "If he's released. We hope so."

"Oh, shut up and listen. Where was I? Oh yes. There's bound to be some publicity, whatever. No matter how it goes, I'd have the least to lose."

"You said all that before," Hannah said. "When we originally drew lots."

"Oh, God damn!" Freda jabbed the air with a finger, annoyed. "That was then. This is now. That was secret. This is not. I'm the one."

Elsa placed two fingers to her lips and emittted a shrill whistle. "Will you lousy broads shut up?" The room quieted, and she gazed steadfast at Freda. "We'll choose again, but this time I don't think you should participate."

"What?"

"Because," Elsa continued evenly. "Because of all of us you can be attached to Gehbert. Each of us, Hannah, Sophie, Gertrude, myself saw him but once in a public place. But you—" She hesitated, but her eyes and voice were unwavering, the meaning clear. "You verified the dog bite."

"Oh shit!"

"The real point," Elsa drove relentlessly, "is that maybe someone saw you with him precisely because you were with him. Until now that didn't matter. Now it does. If your picture appears in the paper it might refresh someone's memory, and you'd be placed, and that could be dangerous."

"Well?" Freda faltered. "Well?", the game plan skittering away. Hannah jumped in.

"There's wierdos out there who even if they didn't see you would say they did."

Freda recouped. "That would work fine. Don't you see? It would give credence to the confession."

"Freda, Freda," Elsa singsonged. "The point is, after the confession and Renner is released for it to appear that the confessor *didn't* do it."

There were slack mouths in the room as Elsa, diminutive but expanding to full assertive height, continued. "She'd claim she didn't get her full rights or her constitutional rights were violated and she—oh, what's the word—take it all back."

"Recant," Gertrude said and puffed slightly at her special knowledge, and threw the moment away when she said, "I saw exactly that happen on Starsky and Hutch when——"

"Pee on your Starsky and Hutch," Hannah snorted. "The idea of all of us confessing would be too suspicious, right?"

"It's already decided," Freda snapped.

"You spoke," Hannah retorted. "Let me speak. Okay. So one

does it. Not anything we'd like to do but something we must do. Right?" The others nodded, Freda maintaining a tight-lipped silence. "It could get ugly. Right?" Again heads bobbed. "Okay. But we embarked upon a situation and we could not forsee that this would happen. So! Come what may, two things. Renner must go free, one of us confesses, and Freda is excluded."

"That's three, honey," said Gertrude.

"Screw you, honey," said Hannah.

Freda bridled. "Who decides I am not included?"

Gertrude and Hannah said in unison, "We do," and pleased by their sisterly chorus, shook hands.

Elsa attempted to mollify. "It's democratic, Freda."

"Put it to a vote," Freda said, disheartened, the result foregone.

"We already have," Hannah confirmed. "Me, Gertie, Elsa. What do you think, Soph?"

Sophie glanced at Freda and favored her with a wan smile, "Makes sense, Freda. Now it's one out of four for the rest of us. Don't be annoyed. "We're really going to need each other."

Freda sighed dolefully. "If you're all so frigging sensible, why don't one of you just volunteer? I'm sure the other three would be relieved to get off the hook." She was churlish, she knew, and diminished by her own pique, but the others, wounded for her, refused to be baited.

Elsa said softly, "Shame on you, Freda. To say a thing like that."

"Freda, quite right. We are not brave," Sophie said, not unkindly. "It appears that we do not even know how to kill. It is a very nervous time and does not help that we fight among ourselves. We are very much going to need each other."

Freda shrugged in disdain, the plan shattered. It had been a simple one. It was a virtual certainty, after discussion, that the only feasible course was for one to be selected to confess, and she had resolved to be the people's choice. She would have, as before, channeled the procedure to the drawing of lots and as before palm one to designate herself. Instead, she had been excluded.

Elsa, Hannah, Gertrude and Sophie were more than friends,
more than family, plain, unsophisticated and loving, bonded
together by shared unspeakable trauma. But she knew, of all of
them, by actual deed and temperament and personal circumstance, that she was best able to withstand the forthcoming
travail. Now, carved out by their misguided sense of love and
democracy to protect her, one of the others could be foolishly
crucified. For a fleeting moment she thought to scream out that
she had done it, override their desire, and go to the district
attorney and assume the full burden of the confession. Although
acknowledging the love that would prompt her to that, she knew
they would deem it an unforgivable breach of faith. They could be
counted on to loyally support her until the case was resolved, but
they would be rent apart and then Gehbert, in his grave, would be
residually triumphant to the end, and that too was unthinkable.

"Vote your fucking heads off," she groused.

The others wisely ignored her, and Elsa asked. "Shall we
draw lots again, same as last time?"

Hannah shook her head. "What for? There was a point to it
originally. Secrecy was of the utmost. This is different. The
confession will become a matter of record. We'll just know who
before the police do."

"Mmm," Gertrude cudded a mouthful of the unsalted beasts.
"What?"

Gertrude swallowed and said, "I was agreeing. Makes sense."

Elsa went to the game table in a corner of the room where
the tiles, fanned out, glistened under a low overhanging light and
proceeded to scramble them, blank sides up, held up a tile, one of
four red dragons among the 136 tiles. "First red dragon?"

Sophie nodded. "Sounds sinister," and moved with Hannah
and Gertrude in silent assent to assist Elsa swirl the tiles to insure
a mix. The tiles click-clacked as Freda, off by herself, glowered
and drummed her fingers on the bar.

"Listen." Unable to contain herself, she shed petulance and
blurted. "Before you dames get carried away, there's something
each of you should ask herself." She entered into the orbit of the

overhang. "Gehbert paid little for thousands of crimes. The winner—" she smiled sardonically, "may pay much for one."

"Oh, for Pete's sake," Hannah rasped. "Think we're enjoying this?"

"Look," Freda was undeterred. "You'll have to tell your husbands. Obviously. What would you say and they say?"

Hannah frowned. "I've thought about that. I guess we'd have to confide."

"Think they're all up to it?"

"I hope so," Gertrude shrugged, but uncertain.

"Think about it," Freda persisted. "Because if he isn't solid, it could break up a happy home. I mean, blind faith is asking a helluva lot of any man."

"Well," Sophie said limply. "That's what we have to have. What else is there?"

"Don't strain it. Because he's just got to ask something of you none of us has asked each other."

"What's that?"

Freda drew a deep breath, ladled out the words. *"Did you do it?* How would you answer?"

Silence pulsated, each looked inwardly, assessing connubial strengths and strains, viewed the others, each solitary and joined. Elsa broke the silence.

"I wouldn't. Gil has to abide by the same rules we do."

"La-de-da," was Freda's dry rejoinder. "Suppose he doesn't back you up?"

"Really, Freda," Hannah said, mildly exasperated.

"No, no, a good question," Gertrude said. "If it's me—well, Harry would—I don't know. He might go crazy."

"If you have to you'll deal with it," Elsa insisted.

"Oh sure," Hannah said, not at all sure just how she would.

"Let's not get carried away," Gertrude was uncomfortable, and amended. "My Harry's very jealous. Even after all these years. And look at me. It's flattering but also a pain in the ass."

"Suppose you get the red dragon," Freda challenged. "And Harry asked you. How would you answer?"

"I'd say—I'd say that—" Gertrude wavered. "Well, that it was necessary."

"Necessary?" Freda echoed, and relentlessly. "Suppose he wants to know if before killing him you had or were prepared to give him head or lay him to do it? Even if he doesn't ask you, the police sure as hell will."

"Oh stop it, Freda," Elsa fretted. "Let's not compound the situation.

"That," Freda returned, "would be your situation. Personally, I wouldn't think much of any man who was more concerned about *that* than did I kill for good and sufficient reason."

Then Sophie spoke. "You're not married. Would Nate have understood?"

"No," Freda replied flatly. "I wouldn't expect him to. But he'd back me up. But don't you see, I don't have to contend with that. Won't you reconsider and let me be the one?"

"Let's choose," Elsa said authoritatively, sitting in dismissal, whisking a tile from the fringe. Without further dissent, the others sat and silently pulled tiles, face down, surveyed them and singly turned them over showing a wind, a bam, a flower and a dot.

"Stupid," Freda mumbled, retreating in chagrin.

The tiles were pulled in rounds of four. Thirteen times they went around, fiercely concentrated, thirteen times four, with no sound save their breathing and the scuffling of the tiles, and Gertrude breaking wind during the eighth round.

"I farted," she said irrevelantly, no one caring in the least.

On the fourteenth round a red dragon appeared.

"My lucky day," Elsa said with a forced bouyancy.

Freda bounded to her. "Elsa. Let me take your place."

Hannah jumped up. "For God's sake, Freda!" but before she could say more, Freda lashed. "You just keep quiet, you've had your lousy vote. This is between me and Elsa," turned back to Elsa and beseeched. "This is the short hair, Elsa. Without shame or retreat. Let me. Please let me take your place."

Elsa fingered the red dragon, studied the faces of Hannah,

Gertrude and Sophie, understanding how secretly relieved they were not to have to confront spouses. No onus would attach to her for yielding.

She said stoically, chin jutting. "Gehbert had to die. My husband will understand. Martin Renner must go free."

Freda applauded. "Bravo, bravo. Bullshit!"

"Crazy!"

Gil could not believe what he was told. "That's crazy!" he sputtered, and repeated, "that's crazy!"

It was the evening of the day after the women had met and Elsa had been chosen by lot to admit to murder.

Gil appeared at seven, had his usual gin and tonic, and suggested that they go out to eat, but Elsa said that she wanted to talk and had ordered Chinese food to be delivered. Gil was agreeable. They ate out three or four times a week because his hours were irregular and Elsa was usually too tired from her day at the boutique to prepare dinner, although she enjoyed cooking when she took the time to do so. He was not a fussy eater and was always complimentary when she placed a dish before him. Home cooking or takeout, both relished the quiet hours that ensued, viewing television or playing records, their taste running to the semiclassical or Broadway show scores. After thirty years of marriage they still enjoyed exchanging amenities and small talk on the day that was. It was a tribute to their basic affection that there was never strain even at those times when long silences would sometimes flow between them as well.

The satisfactory meal was finished and they went into the den where Elsa announced with gravity that she had something to discuss and for him to resist interruption and to withhold comment until she was through.

183

Her presentation was straightforward and without embellishment, from her visit to Papa Grossman's restaurant and her disturbed reaction at sighting the host, felt with instinctive certainty that he was the infamous Wilhelm Gehbert, and presenting her suspicion to the Mah-Jong group. Over the years they had not openly discussed their camp experiences; not all the women who passed through Birkenau were subject to rape and experimentation. But with an osmosis borne out of time and camaraderie, each had come to understand that Gehbert had rapaciously encountered the other. They had individually visited Papa Grossman's, observed him and confirmed that indeed genial Papa could be none other than the Butcher of Birkenau. Of contact with the '38 Club and inquiries put to Simon Wiesenthal in Vienna and Yad Vashem in Israel; their despair at discovering that he had been tried for 5,450 murders and had served the ludicrously minimal sentence of four years, and was therefore and had thereafter been free to roam the world. Of their bitter frustration nurturing a growing compulsion to have true justice rendered but since there was no place or no one to turn to, looked to themselves for a resolution culminating in the drawing, by secret lot, for one among them to bring about the desired end. Their uninhibited glee at its execution only to be astoundingly shocked by the arrest of an innocent man for the crime. His trial scheduled, they could not do other than pledge themselves to his release. A confession was written by the anonymous perpetrator, circulated, and she had been chosen by another draw to admit to the murder.

She finished and cupped her hands in her lap, perched at the edge of the easy chair like a little girl awaiting a parental remonstrance. She gazed steadfastly at him throughout the recounting, and his eyes never once left hers, his brow furrowing with increasing disbelief, restraining himself from interrupting at several points, less from Elsa's requested discipline than from the immensity and implication of a situation so bizarre as to render him speechless. She anticipated that he would be initially shocked but was secure in the belief that once he grasped the situation, whether or not he sanctioned what had been done, he would, as surely as the sun dipped in the west, be supportive.

Gil listened, fascinated at its unfolding but repelled by her complicity, silently and continuously shook his head throughout as if palsied. Finally he rose from his chair, lit a cigarette, inhaled deeply, then stubbed it out, and breaking the silence, proclaimed, "I have to give up smoking." But what he had heard from his lovely wife, so frail looking, of a generally placid mien in all things, save for her aberrant birthday behavior, including their early struggle years and prior to that her camp incarceration, rarely mentioned, had not prepared him for what she presented. He felt his stomach knot.

"Crazy," he muttered again. "Craziest thing I ever heard." She smiled wanly, uncupped her hands, gestured waveringly and cupped her hands again on her knees. Then he exploded.

"Of all the goddamned crazy—! What do you mean *you're* going to confess to murder?"

"I am."

"Wait a minute. You drew lots and you were elected?" She nodded solemnly. "Whoa, back up, Ellie. Grossman—that is, Gehbert is killed. You five dames planned it, but only one of you did it?"

"Yes."

"My God, you didn't do it?"

"I can't tell you that."

"Oh hell you can't," but did not pursue the line. "The fact is I don't think that any of you biddies could pluck a chicken let alone kill."

"It's done and I'm committed."

He seemed not to hear, ruminated. "Who? Discounting you there's Gertrude, Hannah, Sophie and Freda. Sophie? Those quiet ones are the worst. Go along and bam! They explode. Still you never know. Poisoned and suffocated him, you say? That meant contact with Gross—Gehbert. I don't see that with her. The kind of man he was, she'd be too fat for him. Gertrude? She has the drive of a tea bag. Hannah? Well, comme ci, comme ça.

186

Freda? Ah! That foulmouth has the brass to try anything and I must say she's still an attractive woman. Freda. She'd be the one."

"If she drew the lot."

"Oh really, Ellie. Am I supposed to say sure go ahead, take the rap and not know anything more about it?"

"You know as much as four out of five of us."

"There had to be giveaways. Some sign or other. Little things out of the ordinary to peg who did the bastard in. Surely, you have an idea."

"It would be conjecture."

"Christ, El, don't get cryptic on me. Do you realize what you're asking?"

"Yes."

He lit another cigarette and paced the room. Outside the chirp of crickets surrounded the mounting gloom. At length he spoke again and said softly, "No." Then he knelt before her and placed a hand over hers. "You can't do this—this wild-assed thing."

She regarded him lovingly, freed one hand and caressed his cheek. "Gil. You must know that it hasn't been easy for me all these weeks, keeping this from you. And the dread I felt to bring myself to tell you, what I feel now, knowing what I'll have to face. More than ever I'm going to need you."

"Christ!" He bounded up. "Have you really thought out the consequences? To us—yourself—me? How the hell could I go to work, face everybody, especially I'm due for comptroller—"

"Gil. That's wonderful!"

"It's out the window, my wife a self-confessed murderess!"

"I'm sorry."

"Sorry, shit!" bristling, "and when the story gets out—did your wife lay the guy to get close to him?—how do I answer that?"

"You don't."

"Don't give me nobility. Even if I don't believe that you didn't do it—"

"You don't know that."

"I know," he fretted adamantly and immediately wavered. "Hell, what you want to do—I don't know! But the fact that you're willing to say you did—Christ!"

"What bothers you more?" she asked uneasily, "Murder or sex? That I could have done one to do the other?"

"Damn right. Not only another man but with that scum." He slapped his brow with the heel of his hand. "Something just occurred to me. You could, theoretically, have drawn two lots—to kill *and* confess?"

"Theoretically."

"Crazy, crazy. I'm sorry, Ellie, we haven't disagreed over the years. I've taken pride in our relationship and our staying power. And I don't think in all our time together that I've ever dictated a single thing to you."

"No, you have not. Nor I."

"But now you're not asking me, not even confiding, but *telling* me."

She mumbled, "I suppose so."

"For what?" He was becoming shrill. "A bum not worth going to prison for?"

"To free an innocent man."

"Don't be too sure of that. Maybe whoever was chosen hired him. Or called in one of the other hens and *they* hired him. Or maybe none of you did it, and the poor slob had his own reason for knocking him off."

"Yes," she said quietly coming under the rise of his voice, "it could go any number of ways. We discussed all that and each of us could have backed off and done nothing, but our consciences would not let us. We just had to commit ourselves."

"Consciences? Commit?" he echoed. "Ellie, Ellie. After all you'd endured, can you still believe in that romantic horseshit?"

She said evenly, "Precisely because I have endured."

He rolled his eyes in dismay. "Five hausfraus, killers!" and snorted, "Is a jury supposed to believe that?"

"If it comes to that, I hope not."

She tensed forward, silently and prayerfully imploring with

her eyes, the thrust of her body, her entire being. His reaction was greater than anticipated, but she had to believe his basic essence of decency and justice would assert, his love for her overcome opposition. But his voice became even more high pitched in anger as it always did when they infrequently quarrelled.

"You're Catholic," he pierced her reverie. "Okay. We don't work at it. But the other broads are Jews—"

"Gertie is a half-Jew."

"Same thing. What lousy odds, four to one, and you could have drawn *two* lots."

Distraught, "Gilly, please—"

"I heard you out, you hear me out. Jews act as if they own persecution. For thirty years they've kept the pot boiling with their six million dead. Well, three million Catholics died. You don't hear about that. And a helluva lot of others perished as well, but all one ever hears are the concentration camps and the damn Jews."

She bolted upright, springing to her feet as if shot by cannon. His remarks were of such an unforeseeable cast and so vehemently uttered that she felt as if he had physically assaulted her. Never in all their years had she heard Gil speak disparagingly of the Jews, or of any ethnic group. But she could not allow the remark to pass or pretend she had not heard, hoping that he would instantly retrieve the bitter words before the ugliness of what they portended would burgeon. But no apology was forthcoming.

"Really, Gilly," she chided, "do you know what you said? If I didn't know you as I do it could be anti-Semitic."

"I know what I said," he snapped without hesitation.

She clutched at him, pressed her face to his chest, breathing deep of his maleness, as if anchoring to him would blot out the vituperation, but he stiffened, his arms fixed to his sides, offering neither retreat nor solace.

"That's a crappy refuge, anti-Semitism," fueling his own anger, "that blanket covers the world. Well, baby, not in this house." She involuntarily tremored in a massive effort to abort tears. "Whether you did nor did not kill, you're involved in a conspiracy. Worse, had you crazy broads pulled it off without a hitch, you would never have told me."

"I know that has to hurt," she said lamely, "but would you have done differently?"

"Damn right. I wouldn't have gotten involved in the first place. God, what a patsy you are."

She peeled away from him and said staunchly, "I can't back down. I've given my word."

"It wasn't yours to give. A thousand years of Mah-Jong is diversionary, but five dames turn it into a lethal affair. Well, I know what we've got to lose if you persist in this insanity, and you damn well better know it too."

"What does that mean?"

"It means that you are not going to jeopardize what's left of our lives by confessing." His tone had returned to its lower register, painfully controlled. "Elsa," the formal address dire in implication, "God Almighty, I've tried to understand what you've been through. I fought my family over you and don't regret it. We didn't have kids, and I feel no guilt about that. You opened up a plant shop so that you could be your own person, fine. I've put up with your freaky annual birthday rite of getting disgracefully, falling-down drunk because you're unable to overcome a childhood trauma. Despite all that we've built a life together, love each other, more importantly, enjoy each other until—this. It could cost a promotion, even my job, yet you ask me to blindly share consequence without confiding in me. On top of which you accuse me of anti-Semitism! And for what? And for whom? For them—*them!* Four nutty broads who've lost their minds. Willing to throw all that into the garbage can out of a misguided notion that you're personally responsible for some poor shit thrown into the can for a crime you didn't commit, over a victim not worth spit.

If you had done this weird thing, had you laid him to get to him, even so, I might, I just might have backed you had you confided in me, and that's a goddamned helluva lot for any man to say! But no! Instead you choose to ignore me and to confront me with an irrevocable decision. Not only that. I've been waiting for you to at least let me read the confession, but so far you haven't seen fit to offer it."

He stopped abruptly, an unexpected olive branch tendered begrudgingly but in ameliorating invitation to narrow the widening cleavage between them. She closed her eyes and winced, opened them, wrung her hands in an agonized dry wash.

"I—I can't."

He bristled. "Your behavior is beyond me." And added sharply, "No!" She did not respond. "I said no. Are you listening?" She nodded miserably. "Then that's it. Forget it. I think I have the right to ask—no, demand—that you do not go to the police."

"Gil dear," she entreated humbly, "I understand what I'm asking of you. I know your torment. You know mine. You give me love. Please, please, give me faith."

His response skewered. "Don't beg."

She reddened, the pall in the room cotton-thick, braced herself with a deep breath and faced him squarely with what tattered dignity she could muster and said evenly, "I lost my mother, father and sister, and a beloved uncle. It damn near killed me. Your family objected to me but damned if that could destroy me. Now my other family—yes, they are my family—I love them—are threatened. Not physically, but we started something we must finish. We could have chosen to do nothing about Martin Renner, and maybe he would pay and maybe not. In either case we would have been home free. Or would we be? I'd never forgive myself—or Sophie or Hannah or Gertrude or Freda—for remaining silent because, damn it! that's what the world did and all those good German burghers who pretended that the Jews and Catholics and Protestants and gypsies and masons and atheists—*people*—were not being killed! I am not brave, I am not noble, I am scared to death. For Renner. For you and me. But I cannot do otherwise."

She subsided, quaking. He stared at her long and hard in the eloquent silence, then finally broke it, unassuaged. "I am your family. I come first. It's them—or me."

They faced each other over the ghosts of burning memories, resurrected and palpable in the room as the stench of putrescent flesh that would never leave her nostrils; two who had overcome ashes and animus to find each other out of pairings numbering countlessly on the face of the earth, he who was sweetheart, lover and husband; a heart probing and capturing her own as no other could; eyes that looked more deeply and lovingly into her own than any other; they had breathed through each other's pores. But the warm brown eyes were now implacable, the skin ashen, bloodless lips a grim slash in a taut jaw—a sudden stranger, lover come back to me. A clock ticked, the crickets chorused, and his last words were:

"I'll be at the club. If it matters."

She could not believe it. Did not believe even as she heard him rummaging for an overnight bag in the hall closet, would not believe as she heard the scrape of dresser drawers, still not believe the angry steps to the door. In the wake of a thundering silence following the finality of its slam, she finally believed.

And wept for ghosts past and present.

Head Deputy District Attorney Dino Ferrara of Van Nuys wondered what was going on downtown.

Ferrara swiveled his chair and looked out the window of his second-floor office in the Van Nuys City Hall, tented his fingers and puckered his lips in thought. Why the interest from above in the homicide of a comparatively obscure person by an obscure alleged perpetrator? Specifically, interest from cool cat Whyte whom he disliked as much as Whyte disliked him.

Not without reason. He, Dino Ferrara, had been head of OCU, an acronym for the Organized Crime Unit of the city of Los Angeles for four years, an umbrella organization combining specialty groups of officials and citizens to study trends and recommend procedures to combat crime. Without enforcement powers, the prestigious group worked quietly to stop the Syndicate from becoming entrenched in a number of areas. In the one instance by discreetly leaking that a certain judge had surreptitiously disclosed search warrants in advance of a search of a warehouse stuffed with illicit drugs. Most of the contraband had been seized, resulting in the largest drug bust in the city's history. The judge had been pressured to resign for reason of personal health.

As a result, prior to the last election the influential *Los Angeles Times*, by its own proclamation, one of the world's greatest newspapers, had approached him to run for the city attorney's office, but he'd declined. Marie was failing rapidly, and even if she had not been terminal, his taste did not go to politics.

Dino Ferrara was in his late fifties, with a fireplug build and seamed ethnic face, topped by a full head of thick black hair, slightly gray at the temples. Heavy-lidded eyes mirrored an innate repose that belied the terrier tenacity with which he followed through on a case. His voice was mild without trace of the Italian peasantry of his immigrant parents, inordinately proud of his heritage. Their love and the support of close-knit brothers and sisters enabled him to bootstrap through law school to the head of his class.

He liked law enforcement, had not become jaded in it, serving it with a passionate neutrality, respected by all, colleagues, malefactors and victims alike. In the best sense, he wanted law to be what it often was not, equal dispensation to all regardless of race, color, creed and the Almighty Buck. On a wall was a framed original by Interlandi, political cartoonist for the *Times*, depicting a large spiderweb in which a $ sign blithely slithered through entangling filaments, with the legend: "Laws are spiderwebs through which the big flies pass and the little ones get caught.—Honoré de Balzac."

Jonas Whyte had run and been elected as city attorney by a squeak majority. With an eye to the future, he was concerned for Ferrara's viability as a candidate in another election coming up at the end of the year. Now that Marie was gone, Ferrara might be susceptible to blandishment. For Jonas, reelection to a second term would anchor politically. It was no secret that Jonas Whyte longed to be Attorney General for the great state of California. And its governor.

Shortly after the election, he had removed Ferrara from OCU and transferred him to Van Nuys as its chief prosecution officer, ostensibly a promotion, in reality a kick upstairs to a political desert where he could not be expected to bloom. Ferrara accepted gracefully. He needed all the time he could spare to be with Marie. She was two years withering; now two years gone. They had been thirty-two years close. Their three children were into families of their own, and however loving they were, it was unfair to impose a continuing grief upon them by his constant presence. The selling of the comfortable house, located in the Silverlake district they'd lived in ever since the eldest was born, had bordered on trauma. It took him months to make the decision. Now he lived alone in a furnished apartment close to his job and dreaded its walled-in emptiness.

Ferrara thought that without a witness and the possible amnesia that Renner, with a thus far uncovered past and no ascertainable police record, was by no means a cinch case for prosecution. The DA had been pretty intense that Ferrara personally bird-dog the case. Whyte was peculiarly interested in this homicide as he had not been in previous ones in the three years and nine months Ferrara had been shunted to Van Nuys. Walter Grossman was known in the San Fernando Valley area as a genial restaurateur but otherwise lacked the celebrity status to warrant the attention Jonas Whyte was bringing to it.

As for Renner, he was a drab little man. A hidden identity offered dramatic possibilities, but short of an improbable Perry Mason courtroom revelation, it wasn't likely he'd turn out to be anything even the tabloids could run with. Particularly since the Federal Bureau of Investigation did not have his fingerprints on file. The case lacked the built-in interest of a silver-spooned Patty Hearst seeming to renounce her moneyed class to join with revolutionaries, or the sex furies of a Manson. Unless Whyte planned to step in and conduct the actual trial to time out with election coverage, to keep his name perking into the voting booth as the Indispensable Protector of the People in what he believed to be a case of assured conviction.

At the preliminary hearing, Renner had maintained a bewildered innocence and persisted in refusing counsel. Stanley Z. Ritchie, of Hammer and Ritchie, had been appointed to represent him. Good man, Ritchie. Renner will have adequate defense. That is all important, and if and until Whyte actually intervenes, he, Dino Ferrara, would discharge his prosecutorial duty consonant with his oath.

It was near the dinner hour and he thought to drop in on one
of the kids, but they always felt guilty when he stopped by
unannounced or with insufficient notice to prepare dinner for
him, as if that mattered, it was company he sought. For a short
period following Marie's death, it was assuaging that Grandpa
would baby-sit round robin, but that had palled. Now and then he
saw a few cronies or ate out occasionally or brought work home,
but mainly the long evenings were a leisurely scrounging for
dinner and ensconsing himself before the television set. One of
the casualties of the contented life he had shared with Marie was
that she so tended him he was now a lousy cook.

So for the legal lion of Van Nuys, it would be another TV
dinner tonight and falling asleep in the chair before the opiate
eye.

Carolyne Whyte was shocked to learn of Papa Grossman's
death on the eleven o'clock news. She and her husband had been
viewing television as was their wont before retiring for the night.
Jonas Whyte had, however, dozed off. She wakened him and
distraughtly relayed the news.

"How terrible. Such a nice man. Who could do such a thing?
You remember, he catered Ruthie's sweet sixteen party."

Jonas Whyte recalled Papa Grossman from their one initial
meeting, at which Grossman had catered their daughter's party
on the vast lawn of their San Marino home. He was impressed
immediately. Grossman was reserved and unobtrusive among the
well-heeled guests, and his arrangements and food were in
excellent taste and moderately priced. Subsequently they had
gone twice to his restaurant and enjoyed the cuisine and extended
the relationship, Grossman maintaining the fine line between
server and patron without ostentation.

"He was all set to cater next week's fund raiser," Carolyne
Whyte said. She was referring to one of her many activities, fund
raising for a children's disability clinic. "I hope that this isn't
going to be another of your unsolved murders."

The remark nettled him. "According to the news an arrest
has been made."

"I mean," she returned coolly, "will there be a conviction?"

"I'll look into it," he murmured.

Reviewing the case, he became immediately more interested. The scene of the crime placed it within the jurisdiction of Van Nuys. That was Dino Ferrara. There was a homicide leap in the Van Nuys area from ten the previous year to twenty-three, an increase of 130 percent. Cumulatively, nine arrests, no convictions. It was part of the dramatic rise in crime in Los Angeles in recent years, not the largest increase, but right up there with the West Los Angeles and Devonshire divisions, both 150 percent. Van Nuys was boondocks with a relatively stable population, but the statistics were alarming. He'd have to patch some statistical fences, get something going to show his office to be on the ball, light a fire under Ferrara.

He was thinking of reelection and beyond. No formidable opposition loomed, but he did not rule out Ferrara in view of his original support by the *Times*. However, Jonas felt that he might capture their endorsement this time around, especially in view of his excellent record. After his first year in office, Los Angeles topped the state with its conviction rate of 93.6. During the three years he headed the DA's office, it had been number one nationally in conviction, Van Nuys notwithstanding. The *Times* liked to play kingmaker. Of late they had become increasingly liberal (by his lights) and with the phasing out of the old guard on its editorial staff, replenished with younger Eastern establishment journalists, few of whom played the cocktail circuit, he wasn't sure how he was regarded.

Too, the party hacks cottoned to Ferrara's rumpled, fatherly and altogether more benign image, conveying a sturdy pliability that masked the steel of the man. Jonas would be thirty-seven next month (priding himself on looking younger), of an old Los Angeles family, the best schools, strictly law and order, worthy credentials, but his youthful austerity antagonized them. He knew his own strengths, formidably at ease before jurors, not playing to them but against them, intimidating without abrasion. Most felt privileged to enter into his orbit.

It would enable him to keep tabs on Ferrara if he stayed close to the case, get a line on his thinking, whether he'd consider running this time, now that he was an unencumbered widower. Let Ferrara sergeant the case, and if the timing was right, step in and conduct. He had yet to lose a jury trial in twelve years of private practice and public service. He had a gut instinct on this one, and he was not instinctual. Despite Renner's feigned amnesia and any amount of psychiatric evaluation (my experts cancel your experts), Renner was playing to a stacked deck. No identity? No fingerprints record? No social security number? No credit rating? A spurious drivers license? With everyone in the country virtually computerized, one would have to work at *not* being tagged in some manner. Sudden thought: Did Martin Renner ever file an income tax? That would take some pulling out of the feds, but it could be done. On second thought, it would be an asset *not* to prove his identity, prosecution was in the present tense. Don't dig on it, probably fugitive in some aspect, and the defense would have neither the means nor the desire to do so. The jury would have the strong feeling that a forty-two-year-old man was running or hiding from *something*.

There was an option. If Ferrara wasn't running and the case unraveled without undue incident, he'd step back. If it got hot, which didn't seem likely, Renner not a resident, a transient, without funds and friends, no constitutional or social issue to which the bleeding hearts groups could obstreperously latch onto, it should go well. Given these conjectures, the case should not be troublesome. He'd have time to assess whether he could actually coax coverage out of it for political mileage prior to the election. In any case, he'd please Carolyne for following through.

Which might have been the case. Until Elsa intervened.

"Is this Mr. Ferrara?"

"Speaking."

"Mr. Ferrara. You *are* in charge of the Grossman murder case?"

"What is it?"

"I've been shunted all morning, but I want only to speak to the person directly in authority."

"Who is this?"

"My name is Elsa Spahn. Mrs. Elsa Spahn. I have information on Walter Grossman's murder."

"What is that information, Mrs. Spahn?"

"I did it."

Well, he sighed, what kept you? Here they come. There was the one-legged Viet veteran who regularly confessed to homicides that coincided with the receipt of each disability check; and whenever a derelict was found in skid row with his throat cut, the little old lady from Santa Monica came forward and insisted that little green men from Mars invaded her body and forced her to do it. And the dwarf newspaper vendor who regularly confessed to rapes, fancied and real. And the weight lifter who—

"Mr. Ferrara—?"

"Yes. Listening."

"Did you understand me, Mr. Ferrara?"

"I did."

"I want to confess. How do I do that? Do I come to your place, or do you send someone for me?"

Ferrara smiled at the unconscious joke, your place or mine. This one was new, naive. He said gently, "I'd have to know a bit more, Mrs. Spahn."

"Oh, I see. I think I understand. You must get a lot of crank confessions with murders."

"It happens."

"Well, Walter Grossman died in his home at one-one-five-o-one Casitas Road in Topanga Canyon at approximately eight-thirty p.m. of an overdose of chloral hydrate. He was poisoned. By me. Are you taking this down, Mr. Ferrara?" She continued without waiting for his response. "Incidentally, but really the crux of it, Walter Grossman was really Wilhelm Gehbert, known as the Butcher of Birkenau. That's Auschwitz-Birkenau, the notorious concentration camp. Birkenau was the female compound. I'm talking of the Nazis, you know. He was in charge, and his specialty was medical experimentation. I was raped by him when quite a young girl, and was a subject for experiment. I had not seen him for over thirty years, but when I recently did I knew he had to die. He was officially charged with five thousand four hundred and fifty murders but served only four years. That's three days for each murder. That was a horrible miscarriage of justice. That's why I killed him...Mr. Ferrara...? Mr. Ferrara, did you hear me?"

Ferrara had heard and Ferrara believed. Kook or not, the caller had disclosed not only hitherto unrevealed details known only to the police but revealed a motive for the killing, knowing instinctively that new and very palpable elements had just been injected to drastically alter the case. He sat upright, kept his voice even.

"I'm listening, Mrs. Spahn."

"Well, don't you think you should come for me. Or I can come to your office if that's more convenient."

"Mrs. Spahn. Have you discussed this with an attorney?"

"No. I have not."

"I think you should. You have certain rights and are entitled—"

"I know about rights. I don't need one."

"Nonetheless, Mrs. Spahn, I urge—"

"Mr. Ferrara. I am not a child. I have called you of my own free will. I know exactly what I'm doing."

"I'm sure. Still—"

"Mr. Ferrara. I know why you insist. You must be a very able public servant."

"Thank you."

"Well? Do you pick me up or do I come in?"

"Well, if you don't mind, Mrs. Spahn."

"No. I don't mind. I'm not far." Then suddenly, "Oh!"

"What is it?"

"I just remembered. My driver's license expired last week, but I've been so busy I'd forgotten to renew it. I don't want to break any laws."

Ferrara smiled at the earnest irony. "Don't worry. I think we can stretch it this once. May I have your name, address and phone number?"

"I won't change my mind."

"For the record, Mrs. Spahn. And I want to clear you to see me."

"Of course. Mrs. Elsa Spahn. You know how to spell that?"

"Like Warren Spahn?" An absent reference to one of baseball's immortals.

"Pardon?"

"Go on."

"Eight-three-two-seven Bobolink Drive, Toluca Lake. That's near the new shopping center. The phone is seven-six-five—four-three-six-one."

"Thank you, Mrs. Spahn. I'll be waiting."

"In a few minutes."

He did not send for her because the arrival of burly detectives (well, not necessarily burly, which is the cliché, but the stereotype is close enough to be unmistakably detective) might produce a jolt of reality to shake her conviction, her company in their intimidating presence from pickup in her home to deposit in his office might give pause for her to deny that she had anything to say or had even called in the first place. But coming in of her own free will carried its own momentum, and undoubtedly she would be even more anxious to talk.

Now she sat before him, elfin, well dressed and reserved, speaking with a barely discernible accent and as is so often the case with foreigners, graced the language with a clarity of enunciation that would shame most native-born. Ferrara listened attentively as she spoke with deep-felt and controlled emotion, her words being tape recorded and written down. When she finished she sat rigidly back in the stiff-backed chair, crossing her legs demurely and nestling her hands in her lap, a cryptic smile on her remarkably youthful face. She could have been sitting in church awaiting benediction.

Before allowing the confession to be duly witnessed, Ferrara asked, "Mrs. Spahn. You say you do not know Martin Renner?"

"No. I have never met him."

"Is there anything you want to add or delete to what you have already said?"

"No."

"The record shows that your rights have been fully explained and that you understand them."

She continued the Mona Lisa smile. "You have been fastidious, Mr. Ferrara. Am I under arrest?"

It was his turn to smile. "No."

She appeared crestfallen. "But I thought—"

"We'll be in touch."

"Please," she urged. "That poor man."

Ferrara phoned Jonas Whyte to relay the development, savoring the reaction it was certain to elicit. The conversation went about as expected:

"I'll be a son of a bitch."

Ferrara did not debate the point.

"You think she's covering for Renner?"

"All things possible in this imperfect world. She's exonerating him and implicating herself."

"Would she be his girl friend?"

"Renner was brought up to date. He actually appeared bewildered and said, quote: 'If that's what happened, that's what happened.' Not very gallant."

"She was home free. Now she saves his ass." Jonas Whyte's voice clearly conveyed skepticism and disdain for the righteous of the world who muddy up clear-cut murder cases.

"She doesn't consider that she has committed a crime. The worse crime is Grossman—or as she claims—Gehbert living or a Renner prosecuted for allegedly killing him."

"Well, it sure as hell bothers me. Renner picked up on the spot, and this day and age, no fingerprints record or a credit rating or social security."

"I would say that takes a certain talent."

"I have a gut rumble says its deliberate."

"Maybe so," Ferrara dry-chuckled. "But there's no charge for defiance and evasion of twentieth-century technology."

"Crap!" returned Joans dryly. "There was a forced entry. That's not the way a woman gets into a man's house."

"That's been ruled out."

"What do you mean? It's in the police report. You checked it out?"

"I did. The bedroom sill was scraped all right but some time in the past. It's been painted over. Actually, there's no way of telling. I've gone back on all the burglary complaints the last year or so. If someone had tried to break in, Grossman didn't report it. Listen, maybe he lost his keys and broke in himself."

"I see," said Jonas Whyte unhappily. "Well, we're damn well going to hold him until he's thoroughly checked out. And that Mrs. Whatever—"

"Spahn. Mrs. Gilbert Spahn."

"Yeah. Check them both six ways from Sunday."

"I'm already on it. The confession is on the way to your office."

There was a pause and then Jonas Whyte said, "What do you think?"

"Of what?"

"That the two of them did it."

"No opinion."

"I mean, it's a ploy. They cooked this up."

"Same answer."

Within the hour Jonas Whyte pored over Elsa's confession and listened to the tape, then looked broodily to the lushly panelled walls of his starkly huge, deeply carpeted office in city hall, noting the swirls and convolutions of its ash grainings, seeming to connote his unease. On the one hand he should have been pleased—a confession down to the last detail—the case laid out—the victim is not who he appears to be, is killed for what he is alleged to have been—very dramatic, but still a simple felony that could garner publicity mileage—yet his sense of order was ruffled. On the other hand he already had a case. Without Elsa Spahn, Martin Renner would have held to his amnesia in a hapless appeal that would be easily perceived as deception by a judge and jury.

That night the usually unflappable Jonas Whyte, upon entering his home and being greeted by his wife, barely brushed her cheek, snarled at the child he adored and kicked out at the cat.

22

It had been a trying week for Sophie. X rays had revealed a possible malignancy in one breast, elusive diagnosis in the other. She had gone to Hannah's doctor, and he urged immediate hospitalization for biopsy. But she was fearful. Since Birkenau she'd studiously shied from the medical profession. The births of her daughter and son had been her only confinements. This would be her first need for surgery, and she quaked at the prospect of the knife.

She might lose one breast, possibly two. The extreme could be that the malignancy was not to be deterred and her days were numbered. For the first time since leaving post-war Poland, she yielded to an uncharacteristic self-pity. She reflected bitterly on her life, inwardly railing at injustices endured. Destruction of her family in the ovens, a loveless marriage, guiltily unaffectionate of her children, a lifetime aversion to the ungainliness toward her body, which no amount of periodic dieting relieved, even her name and identity not her own.

Curiously, her thoughts went to Elsa. However much she loved the others, she would have liked most to be like her. Without envy she thought Elsa, of all of them, had surmounted early travail with least effect. Slender, remarkably youthful and attractive, economically secure and until the recent shock of her separation from Gil, ideally married. It had been inconceivable that she and Gil would part. But they had and she was troubled by that. Obviously, it had to do with Elsa's luckless draw to confess.

It would be a corrupted triumph for a Gehbert roasting in hell to pervasively reach out and destroy any or all of them. Pain inflicted on one was pain inflicted on all. Perhaps she could set that right, remove the source of conflict between them, herself assume the burden and they would reconciliate. It would be a grand gesture and a noble act. She had long ago taken from another to preserve her life; now she would give to insure another.

In this state of mind, maudlin and moribund, she addressed her husband and children, admonishing them not to interrupt until she finished speaking. She informed them of her condition. Then she confessed to murder. The future would be difficult to appraise. They had better adjust to her certain conviction, to the odium that would accrue to them in job and school, of being the husband and children of a confessed murderess. She told them of the plot to kill Gehbert, and why; that *she* had drawn the secret lot to do so, and had; and that Elsa had drawn the second lot to effect Martin Renner's release. Her cancer now changed that, and she no longer felt bound by the rules. She would righteously renege on the pact made between the players in order to free Elsa. She did not mention the breakup of Elsa's marriage, and her decision to confess was to salvage it.

When she finished, they bombarded her with questions, appalled and vicarious. She fended them. They did not need to know more than what she had outlined. Her daughter wept and embraced her with an outpouring of love as she had not in years, and the boy said admiringly, "You're great, Mom. You've got guts. Real guts." Their wholly unexpected endorsement of her resolve without castigation for murder or its possible effect on their young lives moved her to tears, and she unabashedly hugged them both. Perhaps she had underestimated them after all.

Max said very little, dumbfounded. His mind raced. Their relationship was a shell. They had not had sex for over a year. Sophie, an early riser, had after a hard day's chores taken to falling asleep on the living room sofa while watching television.

The arrangement had evolved without stress. The children seemed not to notice. As with many of their contemporaries, they simply thought anyone past forty had banked the fires of passion. Worn out as she was during the week, she was resiliently animated on Mah-Jong night, hostessing or guesting. Bedding alone did not work a hardship on him. Whereas it was inconceivable to him that any man could become interested in her or she in another, he knew she knew, or at least suspected him, of continuing infidelities. He was regularly seeing a secretary twenty years younger, a childless divorcee, working for a competing firm located on the floor above. It was an ego trip and he fantasized that the day was not too far distant when he would shed his cow-wife and openly move in with her. The kids were a restraint, but in a year or two they would be on their own, and then he would be unshackled. In the meantime he was careful not to flaunt, allowing Sophie the dignity of overlooking still one more transgression. It was tacitly acknowledged between them that she was at least partially responsible for his seeking outside the home what he did not obtain within. The arrangement was placid so long as it remained confrontless.

But the bizarre revelation of murder and declaration to confess to it caused him to shift mental gears. He thought, I don't know if I can believe her. How could she have even gotten close to Gehbert to poison him? She'd sketched the whole thing minimally. I don't know if *they'll* believe her. Maybe she's gone bonkers along with all her screwy Mah-Jong friends, none of whom he liked very much, playing with all those inscrutable Chink tiles. Whether or not her condition was dire or whether she faced imprisonment, envisioning the household without her, one-titted or flat, was for the present intolerable. Unlike Gil Spahn, he could not afford to leave his wife. No children were involved. With two, he was still responsible for their upkeep. Nor could he maintain two households and the major expense of a housekeeper. He was on the same economic plateau he'd been on since his marriage, his head barely above inflationary waters. Younger men passed him and that rankled. The firm wore him like old shoes, but he was too old to challenge it. And Christ! he shuddered at the effect her confession would have upon the job already held. Married to a murderess! They'd snicker at him, an object of derision and pity. Too, he should be panged for her condition, but what really troubled him was that Dora, his upstairs love, would learn of his wife's affliction and in the peculiar sisterhood women, even strangers to each other, evinced for one another, would out of sympathy conceivably terminate him. He suspected she was balling others. At his age, despite cosmetic artifices, he wasn't all that certain he could snare another even in today's permissive flesh market.

Suddenly the image of the late comedian Eddie Cantor bobbed into view, rolling his banjo-eyes and wistfully chanting his signature song out of an old Ziegfeld Follies:

> The judge says you'd better keep her
> It's much cheaper
> than making
> Whoopee.

He knew the grit of his wife and the weakness of his position with her to deter her. Nonetheless, he was affronted. She had completely disregarded him in her decision. He felt humiliated, reduced in the eyes of the children, for they sensed what he felt. He had to salvage, assert himself, he was still the man of the house, and damn it, that had to be respected.

He asked to be left alone with her, then faced her squarely and forbade her to go through with such crazy foolishness.

She said, "Max. Go fuck yourself."

Ferrara listened with disbelief as the woman dictated her confession, disclaiming any participation whatsoever by Elsa Spahn in the homicide. Varied in phrasing, the text was remarkably, if not coincidentally, akin to the prior confession.

"How did Mrs. Spahn know about Grossman—or Gehbert—if she had not done it and you did?" he probed.

"Because I told her. I couldn't keep it to myself." Sophie replied simply.

"Then why would she confess for you?"

"Because she's a dear sweet friend. She knows I have cancer of the breast. Frankly, I fear surgery and am avoiding it. I know that's foolish, I will have to face up to it, but Elsa knows how terribly upset I am and just won't allow me to carry the additional burden of Mr. Renner's arrest."

"Would you have confessed had she not come in?"

"Yes, because of Mr. Renner."

"And if Renner had not been charged?"

"I would not have come in."

"I see. Your friend confesses to relieve you because you are suffering from cancer. You confess to relieve her because her husband has left her because she had confessed. Is that right?"

"It really doesn't matter, Mr. Ferrara. I did it."

Over the phone, Jonas Whyte hit the ceiling. "That clever son of a bitch Renner. He got those two women to come up with the same story disclaiming they know each other. The first confession to get him off the hook and the second to cancel the first."

"I can't say," replied Ferrara. "Mrs. Spahn's story checked out. We couldn't hold Renner in light of that."

"By now he's probably out of the country."

"I've got a search out for him," Ferrara said. "To question."

There was a pause, and then Whyte said in a flat voice, "We'll never locate him." Ferrara did not respond, shrugging mentally. Whyte continued irritably, "Damn it. I told you we should have hung onto him."

Ferrara was about to rebut in kind but prudently withheld the indulgence. "What we have against Renner is circumstantial," he said evenly. "A man who would not admit to guilt. Now we have two who readily answer to the charge. That will satisfy the law. That's what you want, isn't it?"

After he hung up, Jonas reflected upon Ferrara's tone of voice and wasn't sure but that Ferrara was enjoying this latest development.

Leon Epstein felt betrayed by the woman he cherished. Hannah had faltered in her esteem of him not to have confided to a past lover. That had been before his time and it certainly would not have mattered had it been divulged. Was this the "Paul" of long ago nuptial disturbance, the face in the lingerie drawer, that still rankled in retrospect? The shock and pain of her recent outcries as painful in recall as it had been at first orgasm. Was he still alive? Had he come back into her life?

Suspicion gnawed at him and eroded his desire for her. He was fearful of his performance because she no longer aroused him to the degree he had always known with her. Recently he could not sustain erection. It frightened him, this ebbing of essence, his once galloping gonads reduced to a castrated trot. He avoided her. The fact was visible. His penis was as limp as liver.

He had to find out if he was past performance and sought a prostitute. She was young and attractive, liked shy men, the studs were a bore, and put him completely at ease. As she velvet-mouthed him, he erected for the first time in weeks. Inserting, he climaxed in six strokes and could have rammed through a knothole. It was quick and unsatisfactory, and he felt unclean and violated; Hannah had driven him to this.

If this was what he had to look forward to, love on the run, purchased haphazardly, what was to become of his marriage? Rationally, he still loved Hannah. Irrationally, she had emasculated him. Their union was teetering, would end abysmally. He was angry, miserable and self-pitying. Finally, he lashed out in confrontation, the more so because she seemed unaware of his state.

Which, as it turned out was not the case. She was keenly aware of the rift but was also floundering. In a choked voice he spoke of her wedding night cry to a bygone lover and the reemergent cry decades later, of the hidden photographs. The years between them had been a lie, love was gone, manhood gone, best acknowledge that they might at least part friendly for the children, the grandchildren, and the remembered joy between them.

Hannah winced. She had been incredibly stupid, pained that she had hurt him and meant to make amends. She went to the drawer and withdrew the long-ago-offending photographs. About to rip them, he asked her not to, that was not the point, it was not the then of it but the now of it. He would not expect her to rip out that portion of her heart that still held her. She wept and spoke deeply of her early traumas, of family and Paul. What was happening between them she now realized was the baleful result of Gehbert revisited, and related the events from his discovery in Topanga Canyon to the double drawing of lots concerning his death; first the killing and then the confession to free Renner by Elsa, and now surprisingly and unplanned, Sophie had also confessed, only hours before, absolving Elsa.

Leon shook his head without castigation. "Why would Sophie break the agreement?"

"She has cancer of the breast. I know because she asked me for a doctor and I recommended Klinger. She's supposed to check into a hospital. Instead she went and confessed, thinking I suppose to help Elsa because Gil had left her."

"I wondered about that."

"I guess he didn't approve of what she did."

"What happens now?"

"I don't know. They won't mention the others. I've talked to Freda and Gertrude, and we're very disturbed by what she's done.

We're meeting tomorrow at Freda's to decide what next to do."

"And what do you think that will be?"

"I can only speak for myself. I don't think I can stand by."

"What does that mean?"

She breathed deeply and expelled softly. "That I confess and absolve Elsa and Sophie," adding quickly, "Obviously I'm concerned how you would react."

"Suppose I say no."

She smiled ruefully. "I would understand."

"It's too much to ask of anyone. Not only of me but of yourself."

"I know." She gazed steadfast at him. "You haven't asked if I did it."

"Did what?"

"Did I kill Gehbert?"

"Did you?"

"You'll never know."

Silence. The moment teetered. Then he shrugged elaborately. "So I wouldn't ask."

A great warmth suffused her, the chasm between them evaporated in the communicating sunlight of her candor, she wanted to rush to him, to embrace him, to kiss his feet, but he had turned from her, went to the phone and dislodged it and turning back, beckoned. "Come here, woman." She complied with alacrity and he pulled her close.

"Bitch," he murmured, a benediction, and a half head shorter, reached to nuzzle her ear. She kicked off her shoes and looped her arms around his neck and pressing tightly against him, gyrated her pelvis. The dam burst and they became awash with a resurgent love that swept away all antagonisms like so many matchsticks and right then and there, tore the clothes off each other and made shameless love on the living room floor, the years shed as if they were adolescents in heat, and this time and for all times hence, it would be "Leon...Lee...Lee..."

The same evening that Hannah confided to Leon, Gertrude's husband demanded to know just what the hell was going on?

There were frantic calls from Freda and Hannah in the wake of Sophie's violative action, confessing on her own. Initially Grossman's murder had scant reportage, relegated to a back page mention in the papers. Elsa's confession alleging to the victim's true identity moved it to the third page of both dailies as a feature story. The double identity exposé is classical journalism. The Man of the Year heaped with civic honors by chambers of commerce turns out to be an underworld kingpin; the saintly philanthropist is really a child molester and the genial restauranteur who cooked people is a periodic staple with reader deliciousness. Sophie's confession moved the story front and center.

Harry was certain Gertrude knew all the facts; all the women being that close, how the hell could she *not* know? Her nervousness of late and nightmares attested to that. It wasn't by accident, he recalled, that they had that one time gone out of their way to eat at Grossman's restaurant. If she was in trouble, and Freda's call and then Hannah's seemed to underscore all their involvement, then he damn well wanted to know about it.

The floodgates erupted and weeping, she told him of all her Gertrudes, trying dispassionately to speak of passionately horrendous events, not sparing herself, the words spewing out in catharsis. Of Birkenau and volunteer prostitution and lesbianism

215

under duress; an informer; the group killing at Auberfeld and her murder of the doctor; Ben Frankel's pivotal role at this crucial time in her life; above all, the haunting fear of insanity, particularly the transmittal of misbegotten genes to children and grandchildren; outlined the plot to kill Gehbert with religious adherence to not revealing whether or not she had drawn the original murder assignment or to guess who had, and the subsequent ploy of Elsa chosen to free an unjustly accused man. It had worked. Martin Renner was released. Elsa was held but was prepared to ride out the charge—until Sophie's misguided and unsanctioned act. Both now faced an uncertain future.

Harry listened, slack-mouthed, stunned, trying to jigsaw the bizarre revelations into the familiar portrait of the one person in the world he thought he knew as well as himself; devoted wife, loving mother to his children, a grandmother now, who shopped twice weekly at Ralph's and Von's and Mayfair and constantly complained of high prices and ferreted out coupons and trading stamps. Mind boggling.

She finished and it was quiet (thank God Jeffrey was out of the house), and Harry's eyes were misty in the jowly face, and for a long time he said nothing, and then inaudibly muttered over and over, "Son of a bitch...son of a bitch..." And she wondered did she do the right thing, burdening an intimate with knowledge of a past, fearfully withheld till now and which she had always vowed to take to her grave? If someone asks for the time you don't overwhelm them with the how and where the watch was made. Then he reached across the kitchen table and cupped her hand in his and said brusquely, "You stupid broad. Bottled up all these years. Who do you think you've been living with, some lox?"

"I should have known," she said gratefully and smiled wanly and blew her nose.

"This thing about insanity. Maybe it is and maybe it ain't, but it's sure the hell too late to worry about now. And I wouldn't say anything to the kids. Not just yet. Thing right now, all you dames are in pretty deep. I think you ought to get together with Hannah and Freda before you make any more moves. Get in touch with Tayback. If there's an angle that shyster would know it."

"No," she replied stoically, "He'd try to talk me out of going in to confess."

"Confess?" Harry cocked his head in disbelief. "Is that what you said? Confess?"

"I can't just stand by without doing anything to help Elsa and Sophie."

"How is that going to help?"

"Let the law figure out who did it."

"They'll throw the book at you, at all of you, that's what the law will do. You've done enough, you've paid your dues."

"Harry——"

"No, for God's sake!" Harry's voice rose. "One dame goes off a rock and all go. I'm asking you not to do it. No!"

"I have to do it."

"Crap you *have* to do it," Harry said sharply.

"Keep your voice down," Gertrude admonished.

"Damn it. Don't tell me to keep my voice down," Harry spoke angrily. "Every time I say something you don't like to hear you say keep my voice down. Well, damn it, I feel something too. If you'd have told me sooner, I could've gone after Gehbert myself or got some of the boys out at the yard to—to——"

"All right, all right," Gertrude snapped, her voice quaking, feeling her head throb above the right eye.

"All right then. No more foolishness."

Gertrude bristled and lashed back, betrayed by Harry's outburst. "Don't tell me what I can do or not do!"

"That's exactly what I'm telling you."

"Don't yell——"

"I'll God damn yell all I God damn want to!" he roared. "Now that's the end of it!"

"The hell it is!"

"The hell it ain't!"

"Why, you, you—" Gertrude sputtered, the throb increasing, bearing down upon the eye, glowering fiercely, the situation escalating out of control. "You lousy bull——"

"You shut up!"

"Don't tell me to shut up!"

"Shut up!"

"You shut up!"

"Shut up, shut up, shut up!"

"God damn you!"

Stunned by the sudden turnaround, rendered inarticulate by rage, the words choked in her throat. The throbbing above the eye became more intense causing it to blink shamelessly. She abruptly reached for the silver-plated cigarette lighter resting on the coffee table, scooped it up, clenched it tightly, and raised her arm to throw——

"You *crazy* or something?" Harry was aghast.

The word exploded. Gertrude regarded him with a stricken look and her arm collapsed. The cigarette lighter thudded to the floor and cushioned in the deep pile of the rug. No sooner had Harry uttered the unfortunate word than he could have bitten his tongue, but he was too deep into his own rage to immediately retract.

He turned and went into the dining room to a sideboard and withdrew a bottle of scotch, removed the cap, upended the bottle and took a long swig. Inwardly berating himself for his short fuse and fully contrite now, he returned to her.

Gertrude had not moved. Her eyes were misty but, damn it, she would not weep and did not look at him. In the thick gloom he silently retrieved the fallen lighter and restored it to the coffee table. Then he faced her, and as if the past five minutes had not transpired at all, calmly said:

"On second thought I don't know if talking to Freda and Hannah will do any good. What you've all cooked up so far is for the birds," adding wryly, "Fucking Mah-Jong game is a killer."

Gertrude did not acknowledge, staring balefully into space.

"I'm sorry," Harry murmured. "I shouldn't have said what I did."

She relented slightly. "I have a headache."

Harry went into the kitchen and moments later returned with a half-filled tumbler of water and two pills, and extended them in the manner of a peace offering, accompanying the gesture with a Bassett hound look. She took them both, still not looking at him, and plopped the pills into her mouth and sipped.

"Feel better?"

She nodded.

Encouraged, Harry said, "Christ, Gertie! You threw a pile at me. It's something out of Grand Guignol. Learning all that about you after living with you all these years." And slightly awed, "You really killed with your bare hands?"

Painfully, Gertrude nodded.

Harry puckered his lips in admiration. "You're some dame." Shook his head. "This whole thing has me off balance," and said again, "I'm sorry."

Gertrude finally looked at him and replied, barely audible and without bitterness, "I understand."

Relieved, Harry said, "Okay. I'm okay now. I said don't do what you want to do, but apparently that won't stop you?"

"No."

"There's the kids, you know."

"I know."

"That wouldn't stop you either?"

"No."

"They'll survive," Harry said flatly. "I guess whatever happens couldn't be worse than what you've already been through."

"I can only do it because of what I have been through."

Harry nodded and shrugged. "Well, okay." And continued, "You know," he sighed, "you'll drive me crazy."

Gertrude smiled at the reference, feeling the sudden lift of a tumorous weight dissipating the genetic spectre, and said quietly, "Harry, you have a terrible temper."

"I know," he said sheepishly.

"You drink too much and you're getting fat."

He frowned, "I know."

"You know something else?"

"What now?"

"You're a great guy, Harry."

"Sure," he grinned. "Just ask the dame I've been screwing for humpteen years."

"I already have."

Dino Ferrara had a distinct feeling of deja vu. He was listening to the confession of the third woman. She did not vary in detail and disavowed the participation of the others in the execution. Jonas Whyte, he knew, would go through the roof with this one, he was already up his ash-panelled walls with the second, a mind's eye picture that evoked an inner chuckle. But he said sternly:

"Mrs. Simon. Do you expect me to believe that three women come in with the same confession, insisting that only she committed the felony and excludes the others?"

"I speak only for myself, Mr. Ferrara."

Remarkable, thought Ferrara, another chip in the old canard, that only those who speak the truth look directly at you.

As Gertrude spoke, insisting that only she had done the villain in, something gnawed at Ferrara, nurtured by her facsimile recounting of the murder, something the medical examiner's report had noted. An additional fact beyond the poison, he'd have to check back on it—something, it seemed now, the three women had not revealed. Was it deliberate oversight, and if so, to what point, because not to mention it called attention to it—for *had* it been mentioned, there would not now be the increasing significance of its omission.

31

Freda was furious. It was the afternoon of Gertrude's confession. Hannah had arrived as originally planned the evening before. Along with Gertrude they were to consider how to cope with the ramifications of Sophie's unsanctioned act. But Gertrude was conspicuously absent. She had disregarded the appointment and as Sophie had, the day before, unilaterally confessed that morning. Tucked to the previous confessions, it was extensively reported by the media.

"Stupid! Stupid!" Freda fumed. "Time would have been on Elsa's side."

"Water under the bridge," said Hannah. "Leon insists that we talk to a lawyer."

Freda paced in agitation. "It may come to that, but not yet. You and I have to decide what we'll do, what's best for all uf us."

"Freda," Hannah said, feeling a remarkable calm, "I'm going to confess too."

"My God," Freda threw her arms up. "What is this? A disease? Can't you see what you're doing? How obvious all this is shaping?"

"I may be naive and confused about what will happen. I just don't want to think about that. But I just can't stand by and not do anything but read the papers or listen to the radio and watch TV knowing we're in—I'm in—just as deep as they are."

"Those stupid cunts haven't said anything about us or the

223

Mah-Jong game so let's keep our heads."

"Well, *this* stupid cunt won't say anything about the game either," Hannah retorted. "Or about you."

"Great! How am I supposed to feel about that? Four down, one to go?"

"Don't holler."

"Hannah," Freda said evenly, "Jesus, no. If we're in conspiracy trouble let the DA make the case. Let's not help him any more than he has been already."

"I'll be careful."

"Please. Don't go in."

"I have to. I honest to God have to. Leon's in my corner, and that will help me to brave it out."

"And a good man's hard to find," Freda said sarcastically. "Don't act out of any bullshit guilt."

Hannah bristled. "Your opinion."

"Damn right," Freda snapped. "And I just can't resist an I-told-you-so."

"In what way?"

"If you fucked-up over-aged martyrs would have let me be the one to do it in the first place, what's happening now wouldn't be happening. You'd all be spared."

"I'm very fond of you, Freda. That goes without saying," Hannah said unexpectedly. "What you say is very touching, very noble——"

Freda looked askance at her.

"May I quote one Freda Friedkin?"

Freda rolled her eyes.

"Bullshit."

Detective Milliken presented himself at the '38 Club, flashed his ID, and asked Esther Wexler if she was familiar with the Grossman case.

"You mean Wilhelm Gehbert," she replied, her voice tinged with contempt.

"You know Elsa Spahn, Sophie Langbein and Hannah Epstein?"

She hesitated slightly. "What about them?"

"They are members of this organization?"

"They participate."

"Did they confirm Gross—Gehbert's identity through this organization?"

"I don't know."

"Did they?"

Esther shrugged, spreading her hands, palms out. Milliken tugged at his nose, as if it were prelude to a deep thought. "Mrs. Wexler. I understand your reluctance to cooperate. We can subpoena your records." His voice softened sympathetically. "I'd like not to do that." And he returned the gesture.

"They could have," she relented. "There are other avenues of inquiry."

"Was it one, or two, or all three who made the inquiry?"

"I don't remember."

"Don't remember," he repeated. "Mind if I smoke?"

Esther half-smiled and was tempted to say, "I don't care if you burn." Instead tilted her head noncommittally. Milliken lit up and inhaled deeply. "I should quit," he said irrelevantly with a little boy smile designed to reduce the formidability of his bulk. Size worked well in most situations, but Esther Wexler appeared coolly unintimidated.

"Would you say they knew each other well?"

"I would say many members know other members."

"You are a social organization." Milliken indicated the large bulletin board on the wall beside her desk, on which were listed events, fliers in bold scrawly mimeograph, a past dance, a future bazaar, a bridge tournament now in progress.

"These days, mostly. In the early days, primarily placement and reparations. There would be committees formed."

"There would be committees formed to bring these affairs off, right?"

"The members cooperate."

"The three women could have been on a committee."

"They could have."

"Which ones?"

"I can't recall. We have a wide range of activities, mostly for fund raising. Dinners, dances, bridge, poker, pan, bingo."

"They're good players?"

"They're social."

"Any specific game?"

"Really, Mr. Milliken," Esther said with mild asperity. "I wouldn't know if they liked bingo any better than Mah-Jong."

Milliken reacted instinctively to a glimmer. "Bingo takes a crowd. Mah-Jong takes what—four—five players?"

Esther attempted to retrieve gracefully. "I'm not a player."

"It would take a covey. Did *they* play Mah-Jong?"

"Really, Mr. Milliken——"

"You mentioned Mah-Jong."

"I mentioned other games."

"But specifically Mah-Jong. If three played, there would have to be one more player—maybe two more."

"All right. One more, two more. Any combination of five out of dozens of players."

"True. You have a list of such players?"

"I don't think so. Our last Mah-Jong tournament was years ago."

"I see...Care to add anything?"

"I don't know that I have anything to offer."

"If you think of anything, I can be reached at this number." He extended a card but she did not reach for it. He placed it before her, and tugged again on his nose through an awkward pause. Finally he said, "Well, thank you," and started for the door.

"Mr. Milliken."

He turned hopefully. There was a lilt in her voice, a promise. "Yes?"

"It was long overdue. I'm glad the son of a bitch is dead."

The information Milliken had gleaned, little enough concerning a possible Mah-Jong grouping, was passed on to Ferrara. He would have dismissed it as meaningless to further the conspiracy theory, but it kindled anew when a fourth woman came in the same afternoon and insisted that hers was the only true confession.

It was early dark when Hannah completed her statement. After it was taped and written down and duly witnessed, Ferrara again asked if she wished, in view of her stubborn insistence not to have counsel present, smiling at the irony of her remark that she did not trust lawyers, to add or delete. She would stand on it.

Ferrara had reviewed the three prior confessions and the medical examiner's report, and this fourth had not mentioned *the* detail as the others had not. This unstated lack, oversight or collective calculation, loomed larger now, significant only by omission, but he could only speculate as to its importance.

He quietly asked, "Who is the fifth woman?"

It was a long shot question and Hannah's eyes went wide, obviously startled, but she said nothing. Ferrara pressed easily. "There *is* another woman involved, is there not?"

"I don't know what you're talking about."

"Mrs. Simon. You are the fourth confession in one week. Each of you does not deny knowing the others but cannot or will not recall who spoke to whom, and where or when what was said. Despite remarkable similarity of detail, each totally absolves the others of the felony."

Hannah examined her fingernails in silence.

"The four of you," Ferrara continued, "have the same concentration camp experience in common. Birkenau. You are all members of the Thirty-eight Club." He did not expect confirmation and said flatly, "And all undoubtedly excellent Mah-Jong players."

Hannah stiffened. "How do you know that?"

"Four can play but the game is more interesting with five. Am I correct?"

"Yes."

"Have you played with Mrs. Spahn, Langbein or Epstein?"

"Mr. Ferrara," Hannah said quietly. "You have my statement."

Within the hour the media proclaimed that a search was on for a fifth "mystery" woman possibly implicated in the death of Grossman/Gehbert.

The mystery lasted less than twenty-four hours.

Vicki sat at her grandmother's knees, legs curled under yoga style, enrapt, as Freda spoke softly with controlled emotion of the past, tracing her life to the present, culminating in murder. She had been too long reticent in revealing it to Vicki, who had always been curious. That she, Freda, shared with many of those who survived, a residual guilt of the victim, somehow inviting the crime and doubly guilty for outliving those who had not survived. That the imbedded pain was self-consciously personal and not to burden those who refused to hear or could not bear to be reminded of it. That time had layered other inhumanities upon inhumanity and that was the way of the world. No. She wanted Vicki to know not only because she was the dearest thing on earth to her, not because she sought approbation for what was done, but for Vicki's generation and unborn ones to know of the Holocaust. The dusty bin of history must not be its final resting place.

She wanted her to know, despite what she would hear and read, that she and only she, Freda Friedkin, was responsible for Wilhelm Gehbert's death. Her conscience was clear despite breaking a vow of silence not to reveal exactly what had transpired. She did not spare herself; the painful recall of ravished girlhood and events leading to the present, including the loathsome involvement with Gehbert; her duplicity in palming the lot and the poisoning and the multiple confessions gone awry.

When she finished, Vicki rose and her eyes were moist. She kissed her grandmother full on the lips and said huskily, "Grandma. I think you're the bravest person I'll ever know."

Now Freda sat before Ferrara and repeated the familiar confession. By now he knew it virtually verbatim. She admitted to weekly Mah-Jong sessions but did not mention the drawing of the lots. Insisted that there had not been discussion about Gehbert *before* his death that she could recall. But *after*, why yes, she definitely recalled regaling the players with his execution. If their indivudual confessions were strikingly similar to one another, it had to be because they were emotionally digestive and strongly retentive of the details. Good friends all, each had selflessly sought not only to effect the release of an innocent man but to shield her. She and only she was the one, only and true culprit.

He suddenly realized that the room had become silent. She sat demurely, her hands cupped in her lap, her face benign as if she had just finished reciting the Lord's Prayer. Earlier, when she had come to the commission of the crime, he'd reacted sharply to the elusive jigsaw aspect but said nothing. The mystery was cleared, and now he knew the truth and wondered why he was disturbed by it.

For a man who listened well, he had difficulty listening at all. From the moment of her appearance he had been unable to focus his thoughts, darting quicksilver into alien paths, and...

As she spoke..."But then it does not go as I expect. He is strong as an ox and suspects what I have done..."

...he felt...cherished a woman for thirty-two years...her passing had left a void, and he was not foolish enough to think that at his age...

"Finally he knows. Not who I am but what I am. I taunt him by shoving my wrist into his face so that he finally sees my number..."

...that lightning could strike twice...

"...but I miscalculated on the poison and its effect. And he attacks me..."

...Lightning? My God, that's for kids, the June-moon set. I'm an old man...

"...we struggle and I fear for my life until I beat him off with my shoe..."

...well, fifty-eight. Not young but then not decrepit either...

"...It is a high heel and I hit him with it above the ear. My left shoe and it was to his left side..."

The statement caught him by surprise, and he wasn't sure that he'd heard correctly. She regarded him quizzically, thinking perhaps she was speaking too rapidly and emphasized, "A three-inch heel. I don't often wear them. Women my age usually have difficulty with them. Varicose veins," she confided.

He nodded vaguely...knowing it now...but it did not alter reverie...

"...Then he collapses on the sofa, and I press a pillow to his face..."

....Father to three grown sons, grandfather to five, be still My Foolish Heart from the song of the same name. This woman is more concerned for varicose than mayhem, she is confessing to *murder!*

"...I push down with all my weight. My arms ache, I think they will snap...but finally..."

...so unlike Marie. And yet...

"...he dies..."

An essence. Yes, essence. What does that mean, an essence? Hell, if I know...

"...I wipe clean whatever it is I may have touched in the six or seven times I have visited him..."

...haven't felt like this...

"...curio cabinet..."

...years...

"...miniature Venus statues..."

...must be going bananas...

"...I arrive at seven-fifteen and leave at eight-twenty..."

...Jesus, he hadn't felt this way since his first matings with Marie...and what he was thinking now—blasphemous, a disservice to her memory...tried to squelch fantasy with a fierce concentration upon what she was saying, but it bobbed to the fore like a moth magnetized to light; tried not to look at her, listening, her voice trailing off, subdued and throaty...

She was finished, and when he looked directly at her she returned his stare unflinchingly. He looked away, absently brushing away an imaginary cobweb to clear his head, shocked by his inability to control what he felt, deeply stirred by juices long thought atrophied. But he had been circumspect.

The phone stabbed shrilly, and he was grateful for the interruption. There was an uncharacteristic elation in Jonas Whyte's voice. "Dino! Do you have the latest confession?"

"Finished this minute."

"Good. We're going to have a case."

Ferrara puzzled. "I haven't checked it against the others yet."

"Of course. But I think we're buttoned. We have a witness."

34

The five women were herded into the room with the one-way mirror. It was their first time together since meeting in Elsa's home to plan Renner's release. Belying inner turmoils, they regarded each other with the dispassion of strangers, as if they were any five middle-aged women collected at random for a shopping survey.

Peering through the mirror was Ferrara, Jonas Whyte, Milliken and Chevares, and the witness, Ramiros Ramos. A public defender was present to make sure the procedure was conducted fairly.

Ramiros was short, dark and staunch, a busboy at Papa Grossman's, now shut. Ramiros could not believe, would never believe that Papa Grossman had been the evil incarnate as disclosed in the press. Nazism was as remote to him as the Crusades. Grossman (never Gehbert) had treated him kindly, and he was saddened by his murder. It was only just that the miscreant be brought to justice. Ramiros had not always felt thus. He had been an illegal with the barrio's innate fear and distrust of Anglo authority, which even now, since married to Inez, native-born and a waitress he'd wooed and won between table hoppings and clearings, was not entirely dispelled.

Largely unschooled, still disbelieving that the voluptuous Inez had not only favored him with her heart but had conferred countryhood upon him, he would have been inclined to listen to her, wiser than he in the ways of his adopted country, not to get involved no matter how deep their affection for Papa Grossman and shocked at his violent end.

Papa Grossman had given both a week's pay for a wedding present. His murder, she insisted, was a gringo matter and he would not have come forward if not for Chevares. Chevares had questioned the employees, and what do you know, they were both from the same province, Hidalgo, from neighboring villages, and Chevares thought it not unlikely that they might even be distantly related. He skillfully withdrew from Ramiros that he'd noticed the woman for two days, including the day of the murder, loitering on the premises. His attention was drawn to the license plate of her car, RAM 051, a combination of digits and letters that with a slight stretch of the imagination spelled out his name. The woman did not come into the restaurant but stayed in the car or paced nervously. He would not have recalled her at all save for the plate, for there was always a woman about Papa and he supposed she was one of his dalliances. It was certainly none of his business, and he admired Papa for the macho he displayed at an advanced age. Despite Inez's objection not to identify the woman, Chevares had prevailed upon the loyalty to his late employer to do so.

Jonas Whyte exhibited a restrained buoyancy—take five confessions—point the finger at *one*—bingo! Ferrara, on the other hand, was perturbed. Four of the five women had confessed to the crime in exact cookie-cutter detail, overlooking the one vital detail, made vital by omission. One not mentioning it could be an oversight, four not mentioning it could be collusion or because they did *not* know the detail. But the fifth confession had included the variance, thus underscoring the omission by the four. Then why had the fifth mentioned it? He could see no gain to the four not to admit it or for the fifth to do so if the others had not, since it did not bear directly on Grossman/Gehbert's death. If all five had mentioned it, then it would merely have been an additional relegated part of the whole. Yet the fifth had glossed over it. He concluded that she had said it not knowing the others had not said it, that four out of the five women had not knowingly omitted it simply because they did not know this minor aspect existed.

In short, since only one had divulged it, he believed she had neglected to include it in the mass of detail when transmitting the how of the crime to the others. The four had delineated the poisoning and struggle that led to Grossman/Gehbert's death but not the specific of the high heel blow to his head as revealed in the medical examiner's report:

"... patterned abrasion from the heel clear enough to identify the object on the skin. No skull fracture. No hemorrhage inside the cranial structure." The woman's revelation was inconsequential to the final result. But mentioned only by the one out of five was sufficient to distinguish it from the others and mark her as the perpetrator.

So he knew with distressed certainty whom Ramiros Ramos would pick. The fifth confessor. Freda Friedkin. Within seconds of observation, Ramiros made his selection.

He unhesitatingly pointed to Gertrude.

Elsa was released and an accusation was brought against Gertrude Simon of a felony, to wit, a violation of Title 8, Chapter 1, Section 187 of the Penal Code. Pending were additional counts of felonies against Elsa Spahn, Sophie Langbein, Hannah Epstein and Freda Friedkin until Whyte could determine where the greater strength lay, as conspirators or accessories after the fact.

Behind the scenes, a cloud loomed between Ferrara and Whyte. The former had been privately reluctant to isolate Gertrude at this juncture, the witness notwithstanding. But he could not reveal his misgivings and obstruct his superior, who moved rapidly for the indictment, holding for a lesser count of manslaughter, while the latter was for the jury to decide the maximum penalty.

Freda, Elsa, Sophie and Hannah met in disarray at Freda's apartment.

"The stupid broad," Freda agitated.

"We blew it," said Hannah.

"Gertrude blew it," Freda insisted.

"She couldn't wait," Elsa attempted to soften. "Until it happened we were all certain through the fifth week that it wasn't going to happen."

"But to stupidly place herself at the restaurant and expose herself," Hannah wailed.

"Don't talk dirty," Elsa said with forced levity. It thudded leadenly. She shook her head. "I don't understand. She goes there with a gun and he winds up poisoned."

"We've got to pull together to help her," Hannah said with a sigh, "But so far we've mucked everything up."

"I have a brilliant idea," Freda said dourly, "One of us could go in and confess."

"I did it," said Elsa.

"No," Hannah said. "I did."

"I did," Sophie spoke. "Why don't we stop masturbating. Gertrude is in real trouble."

"Right," Freda said tartly. "We all know who did it," and added meaningfully, "I did."

"A roomful of echoes," Sophie said to no one in particular.

Elsa turned to her with sudden concern. "Sophie dear. Why don't you go to the hospital?"

"Not yet. I've got to help Gertrude."

"How does your not going help her?"

The others pounced upon her with loving concern to enter immediately. "Please, Sophie. We don't want to worry about you on that through what may yet happen," Elsa urged.

"Every day that you stay out endangers your life," Freda added. "Help us with at least one good tit."

Hannah frowned. "That's not anything to make bad jokes about."

"I'll go in," Sophie said, deeply touched. "I'll make arrangements when we leave here." The air was morbid and she said to divert, "Poor Harry. Has anyone talked to him?"

Freda went to the phone and dialed. On the other end Harry was a gibbering hulk, liquored, his speech slurry.

"Christ! I had no idea that she took the .38 from the yard and went looking for the bastard."

"Neither did we, Harry."

"You fucking crazy broads. Shoulda told me. I'da taken care of the prick myself. Gertie—she—she—" His voice broke.

"Harry——"

"Okay, okay. I'm sick. No, I'm okay. Poor Gertie. What she's been through." He brightened suddenly. "Listen. I got a call from Leonard Bowen."

The name was instantly recognized. Leonard Bowen was one of the handful of attorneys in the country who'd litigated themselves into celebrity status. They were showmen and talk show personalities who charged exhorbitant legal fees for their services. They would, however, waive the fee if the case was newsworthy and fight it for years if it had the potential for aggrandizement.

"He called from New York. Spoke to him this morning. Said he wanted to talk to you dames. I gave him your number and he said he'd call you four o'clock. What time's it now?"

"About that."

"F'Crissake, listen to the guy."

"Yes, Harry."

"Oh shit," he said with exasperation. "Someone's at the door. Prob'ly another lousy reporter."

"Harry——"

"Huh——?"

"We're sorry. We'll do whatever is necessary."

But the phone was left dangling, and she could hear muffled soundings, and then he was back. "Yeah. Reporter. Call me back after you talk to Bowen." And he hung up.

Freda relayed the conversation to the others, and Elsa said hopefully. "Leonard Bowen. He's the best. Gertrude would have a chance."

The phone rang. Hannah said, "That could be him," cautioned, "Please, Freda. Talk nice."

Freda frowned. "You're ranting," and picked up the phone. "Hello."

"This the residence of Freda Friedkin?" a raspy voice queried, Freda taken aback, for it was not the expected voice of a crisp secretary or the polished tones of a famous lawyer.

"Yes. Who——?"

"Listen, you Jew cunt. Who the hell do you think you and

your cunty friends are, knocking off a God-fearing, hunnerd percent American. All you leftover Jew bastards should oughta be cooked in ovens. Hitler was right——"

She recoiled and slammed the phone down, and immediately it rang again, but she made no move to it. The others exchanged puzzled glances.

"Obscene phone call."

The phone continued to shrill in the gloomy silence and then subsided.

"Oh God," moaned Elsa. "I suppose it's going to be like that from now on."

And then the phone rang again.

36

Ferrara stewed.

The wrong woman was charged. But he'd made no move to apprise Whyte as to who he believed the right one to be. He knew, as the case stood, he could make the best case for the people. They had supported him for thirty years, and it would be a violation of his personal code not to do so. Worse, he was withholding vital information to a possible miscarriage of justice.

More to the personal point, he could not understand why he was so drawn to the woman, especially since there had been no sign from her of any reciprocal feeling. It was unthinkable that there would be. Or that he could pursue it. He fervently hoped that through what contact there had been with her thus far and would yet be, that he had not and would not make a fool of himself. It was the stuff of soap opera. Not all of his varied experience as a prosecutor, loving husband, doting father and solid citizen had prepared him for the absurdly human frailty of attraction to a murderess.

He would remove himself from the case. And hope, as it was rumored, that Leonard Bowen would undertake for the defense. He disliked showboats, for Bowen was certain to attenuate it for media mileage. But Gertrude Simon would have the best defense in the country.

His churnings were interrupted by his secretary, who announced an unexpected visitor. Freda Friedkin.

241

She was ushered in and he reined himself, coolly decorous but curious as to her appearance and instructed his secretary to hold all calls.

Freda was apologetic. "Forgive me for barging in without notice, but I was afraid had I called that you would not see me. I'll try not to take up too much of your time."

"You should be represented by counsel, Mrs. Friedkin."

"I understand. But please hear me out. It's important."

"Is this anything that should be recorded?"

"I'd rather you didn't. If you think it will make a difference after you've heard me, I'll agree."

"Very well." He indicated a chair. She perched and took a deep breath.

"None of us told the full truth, Mr. Ferrara. The others, Gertrude, Elsa, Hannah, Sophie or myself. They told it insofar as they knew it. But what they knew is what *I* had told them." She spoke directly, her voice even, her eyes dwelling on his seamed face, a good face, she thought, of sturdy ethnic character, a face that invited confidence and exuded fair play. The truth was a last desperate ploy.

"We all planned to kill Wilhelm Gehbert but for various reasons ruled out actually doing it in concert. We drew lots to see which one of us would do it. Whatever means to accomplish it to be left to the individual chosen. The idea being any four out of the five would not know who that person was.

"Although the lots were drawn out of a dish, the others did not actually draw. Five lots were drawn but the marked one had not been placed in it. I had it. I palmed it. To this moment Gertrude and the others do not know this. I had designated myself to kill Gehbert because I felt, of all of us, a widow, and the only one without immediate family, that I had the least to lose in event of discovery. Which, sadly, has not turned out to be the case.

"Oh yes. We'd set an aribtrary time period for the killing to be done. Five weeks. One week for each of us. If it wasn't done by then—well—we felt we couldn't live forever with the idea that one of us, and that meant all of us, was incapable of killing no matter how we felt—and for our own sanities—if that was the way it would turn out—to forget it.

"So the confessions you have heard are essentially true. But we were shocked when Martin Renner was arrested. We could not stand by and do nothing hoping that by some miracle an innocent man would be let go. But that was not the case, so we decided to see who would go in to confess to effect his release. We agreed that whoever had done it would write out the details and mail copies to each of us, destroying the original letter, so that four would still not know who the fifth was. I did that. But this time I was excluded from the draw. Not because of suspicion that I might have done it but because I was the one to incontrovertibly offer proof of the dog bite and someone might have seen me either in the restaurant or going to his home and connect me to the killing. This time we—they, the girls—used tiles. Mah-Jong tiles. Do you know the game, Mr. Ferrara?"

"Only that it is very old and Oriental in origin."

"Yes. Well, that's not important. Elsa was chosen. We did not know that Gertrude had become impatient during the weeks of waiting for Gehbert to be killed and had, on her own, not telling anyone, gone to the restaurant to shoot him, working up her nerve for two days to do it. She might have, I suppose, on the second day. That was Tuesday—a day Gehbert did not go to the restaurant. He had a cold. That was the day I gave him chloral hydrate."

He sat unmoving as she did, searching his face for reaction, but there was none. She continued:

"I don't think anything is overlooked now. But if you have questions, I'm sure that I can answer in detail in a way Gertrude or the others cannot, for they simply wouldn't know." There was another pause, and then she said with finality. "Mr. Ferrara. I and only I killed Wilhelm Gehbert."

Ferrara rose from his chair, clasped his hands behind his back and looked out the window, unseeing. Then he turned to her, greeted by imploring eyes, her body straining forward, the knuckles of both hands tautly drawn clutching her purse upright in her lap.

"Mrs. Friedkin. How do I know you haven't made this up?"

"I am telling the truth."

"You were telling the truth before."

Tears welled and she reached into her purse for a handkerchief and dabbed at her eyes. He was startled by the break in her composure and fought to maintain his own. "I'm sorry," she sniffed.

"The others," he said, "could deny your story and repeat the process all over again."

"I have proof I was with Gehbert." Again she dipped into her purse and withdrew a tissue-wrapped object and carefully unfolded it to reveal the miniature Venus.

"When he resisted after the poison, the cabinet with many Venus miniatures fell. I put them all back. After wiping any fingerprints I might have left, I found this Venus on the floor. I was on my way out, in a hurry, as you can imagine, and did not want to reopen the cabinet, so without thinking I put it in my purse."

He glanced at it, nodded. She folded it back into her purse and waited like a little girl not knowing whether to expect commendation or a scolding from a stern parent.

"Who knows what you have just told me?"

"No one." Not quite true. Vicki did. A white lie.

"I see," Ferrara said thoughtfully and was not surprised to hear himself say, "I'll be in touch with you."

"But now you do know that Gertrude didn't do it," Freda beseeched, uncertain that she had accomplished what she had set out to do.

"I believe I know the facts," he returned evenly.

She rose and studied him keenly. Yes, a nice face, crisscrossed with living, wondered by his compactness if he had once been a prizefighter, immensely drawn to him, married no doubt, with a large family, her mind wandering, reading the dark eyes boring into her, something deeper—a sudden flight of erupted fancy that startled her to even think that—no, the circumstances were impossible——

She brought herself up abruptly and murmured, "Thank you," and left.

He stood there, her presence indelible in the faint smell of lingering cologne, haunting, tried to recall where he'd—realized with shock that it was similar to what Marie had infrequently used, knowing then he'd come to the decision that had been cohering ever since Ramiros Ramos had fingered Gertrude Simon.

37

In fact, Dino Ferrara made two decisions.

The first was the result of deliberation, of known and assembled facts, balanced against options, and the consequent outcome, allowing marginally for error. What Freda had revealed about the Venus, and then confirmed about the high heel, buttressed that decision. The second was uncharacteristic Ferrara. Emotional and impulsive.

He reached for the phone and dialed the guard on the floor and requested that he detain the woman who had signed in to see him. Then he darted out into the corridor to where a puzzled Freda was diplomatically halted by the guard from entering the elevator.

Her eyes widened as Ferrara came to her. With a barely perceptible tilt of his head to indicate a corner away from traffic, he placed a hand lightly to her elbow and led her to it. She turned to him and awaited explanation. For a brief moment he stood awkwardly before her, then becoming aware that his hand was still at her elbow, dropped it self-consciously to his side.

He longed to say: "Mrs. Friedkin. This is the wrong place and the wrong time and I may be the wrong guy with the wrong religion and the entire situation is cockeyed for me to say what I must and I may be a damn fool which is probably what you will think but I've got to get it out. You are a lovely and courageous woman. I know enough about you and I do not have to know more

247

because I know only that I do not want, whatever the outcome of the case, for you to depart my life as abruptly as you have entered into it. I am not prepossessing. I am not all things to all men, least of all, to myself. But I care very much for what will happen to you. I thought my life was over because two years ago I lost the most valued thing in it. But it would be no disservice to her memory to have found another to love. Forgive my replayed adolescence but I would like very much to moon-and-June with you. I have less miles before me than behind me, and I would like to walk them with you. I am a proven lover and husband although I no longer know how capable I can be in either department. If you have doubts about yourself we could find out together. Dare I hope that you can find room in your heart for me? If I embarrass you please be kind. I will not trouble you again. The loss will be mine but I thank you for rekindling the pleasure of fantasy. You have given me life again."

Instead, he stammered, "Uhm—Mrs. Friedkin——" and faltered, grinning stupidly, he knew, hands gesturing haplessly.

She discerned in the few seconds of eloquently communicated silence that what he felt was no less than what she dared to dream but could not encourage. It had been forlorn and beyond attainment, yet another price to pay in a star-crossed life. But the sheepish grin and his beseeching eyes and the strain of his body conveyed it. His thoughts were mate to her own. It would be now or never.

She searched for the words to put him at ease. And wondered why in hell she said as she was saying it, blurted, "Mr. Ferrara. I am a good cook."

He flooded with relief and beamed. "Thank you, Mrs. Friedkin."

"Freda."

"Dino."

The elevator opened and she entered and turned to look out at him. Before it closed, eyes caressed eyes.

Jonas Whyte was incredulous.

"Drop the case?"

"Yes."

The two men faced each other, coiled springs.

After Freda had left, Ferrara called Whyte, insisting it was urgent they meet. That was fine with Whyte. He was about to call Ferrara, he'd come to a determination on the women and wanted to review with him. Ferrara said he'd leave immediately and be in Whyte's office as soon as traffic allowed.

"Drop the case?" Whyte repeated and glowered.

Ferrara, on arrival, had taken the initiative. Before Whyte could outline the charges against the remaining women, he urged complete dismissal to include Gertrude Simon.

His presentation was succinct:

A) The five women did indeed enter into a conspiracy to murder.

B) Each to be tried singly will be time consuming and costly.

C) Wilhelm Gehbert, the son of a bitch, deserved to die.

D) No jury in their right minds will convict these five sacrificial ladies considering their motive in an act invited by the record and nature of the victim and the horror he had visited upon them.

E) If Whyte persists, he will resign.

He did not add, because it could not be stated, barely admitting to himself that, F) he had become enamored of Freda Friedkin, gutsy, fascinating dame.

Ferrara pointed to the front page of the evening paper he'd picked up in the lobby. The lead article read: WEDNESDAY NIGHT KILLERS TO BE CHARGED. The appellation was clear, of a journalistic mien that was adrenalin to circulation: PRESIDENT SHOT; MAN ON THE MOON; LONE EAGLE MAKES IT—intrigue immediately and vicariously conveyed upon eye impact; five little old ladies (none, regrettably, living in Pasadena and wearing tennis shoes) hatching a murder plot over an ancient game (with inscrutable Oriental overtones) to render an overdue justice upon a victim whose palpable villainy was proven out, was deliciously macabre.

Ferrara carefully pointed out that save for the fringe element of the American Nazi Party proclaiming Gehbert's murder to be a Communist-Zionist plot (as reported elsewhere in the article), no public outcry for retribution could be discerned. Also, it was rumored, three high-priced and prestigious attorneys, including Leonard Bowen, had volunteered to defend the women without fee in the spirit of justice.

Whyte perused the article. When he set it aside, his lips were bloodless, said tautly, "We're not trying the case in the media."

"Difficult to ignore," Ferrara said gently.

"Murder isn't therapy. We can't be swayed from duty."

Ferrara winced slightly.

"Certainly you don't condone it?"

"No," Ferrara replied. "But in thirty years of law enforcement I think I've earned an indulgence. I can't go by the book on this one."

"If each law enforcement officer in the department felt that way, pick and choose, we'd break down. Chaos. Anarchy."

"Understood. But it's something I feel in deep conscience. Also," Ferrara hesitated, then said carefully, "I would have to resign."

Whyte did not immediately respond, his eyes holding to

Ferrara like flints of granite. "It can be reassigned, but I don't like being countermanded," he said, his voice even but challenging.

Ferrara reacted easily, anticipating the response, regretful that it was the fact, forcing his hand to the reluctant plateau. "You will have my resignation in the morning."

Whyte regarded him darkly. "I consider that unnecessarily drastic and melodramatic to make the point."

"Nevertheless." Then Ferrara said levelly, "It would leave me free to defend them."

Whyte's mouth dropped at the bombshell Ferrara would have preferred not to use, noting the cords of Jonas's neck bulging over his collar. An eternity of seconds passed through which both men teetered. Whyte shut his eyes and tugged at the corners to clear them of nonexistent specks, opened them and said directly, "Switch sides? Unheard of!"

Ferrara shrugged.

"It's unethical."

"Debatable."

"The Bar Association would have to take a dim view of the switch. You can be brought up before it."

"I know the small print. There is nothing to cover the situation."

"Nonsense. It's never been done before."

"Precisely."

They were poised like two gladiators, measuring each other. The one, young, socially and politically ambitious, patrician and slender, immaculate in a custom suit even at the end of an arduous day; the other older, bellied but compact, of street-fighter origin, harking back to Sicilian hill-fighters. By accidents of birth they were oil and water.

Thought Ferrara: Don't fight it, man. Digest it. He said, "If you oppose me on this—well, it *would* intrude upon the case. I can't imagine you would relish an in-house—" searched for an emphatic but ameliorating word, "diversion." The implication was clear as to the time, expense and ramifications to the case itself.

"Have you already spoken to the defendants?"

The question was as sudden as it was unexpected. So obvious as to be pathetic. Jonas Whyte, he knew, did not like him, now with more reason than ever, but he had no desire to extend the distasteful situation or to embarrass him; hoped, really, that the younger man's usual perspicacity would prevail. Dogged pursuit of the emotionally weighted case would be forlorn to what he knew to be his ambitions.

In response to the question, a half-mirthless smile playing the corners of his mouth, he said:

"I'm prepared to call a press conference to announce that I'm bowing out as prosecutor and would be free to undertake for the defense," carefully adding, "providing they'll have me, of course."

If Whyte was reeling, he gave no further sign, his composure returned. He irrelevantly shuffled some papers on his desk, looked up and finally said, "Let's sleep on it and meet in the morning."

That did not satisfy Ferrara. He had momentum. Then, too, possibly fearful of the reason morning light could bring to evening emotion, shook his head and made his final bid.

"Once I enter private practice I would not consider any aspect of public service again."

There. Said. Put on the line. Quid pro quo.

Whyte lit his first cigarette of the day, breaking a promise made to himself only the day before to quit. He did not tender one to Ferrara, whom he knew did not smoke.

"I'll call you later tonight."

"I'll be home," Ferrara said, and left.

Jonas Whyte seldom brought office matters to his wife, but in a surly mood, he revealed Ferrara's ultimatum. It had been veiled blackmail. No other word would do.

Carolyne Whyte, good and devoted wife, adopted his anger. She had been shaken by the revelation of Grossman's true identity, but still murder was murder, and with people afraid to venture into the streets after dark, virtually nighttime prisoners in their own homes because entrusted public officials and judges were cynical and reluctant to prosecute hippies and homosexuals and rapists and pornographers and the Mafia and coddling criminals in a damnably permissive society, was it any wonder that there was such lack of respect and breakdown in law and order—how dare a subordinate challenge his superior—that Ferrara was a devious man who sought to embarrass her husband before the election because she knew, just knew he wanted to be district attorney—whoever heard of such a thing to make the switch from prosecutor to defense attorney—isn't that against the law? and if it isn't, it certainly should be, by God—the American Bar Association should disbar him forever, the very idea—but what could you expect of the stupid public and the tide of sympathy against their own interest—they didn't deserve her husband's dedication to stem crime—lawbreakers running rampant in the streets. Why only yesterday it was told to her that a dark-skinned family, Mexican or Puerto Rican or one of those, anyway, actually made an offer on the old Haggett house on the next block and the real estate agents are no better—anything for a buck—where will this country end up? It's terrible, all the newspapers and movies and television and radio, especially movies and television show so much violence—such hypocrites—decrying crime, actually fostered it—all the bleeding hearts and the ACLU should all go to Russia and live and see how they would like it there—can you in your wildest thoughts imagine five women with a thirty-year grudge, even longer, taking matters into their own hands and killing?—absolutely disgusting—

By the time she'd sputtered out, exhausted, Jonas had finished his martini and cooled in inverse ratio to her rage. He'd been sucked into emotion, a mistake he'd vowed never to make. Stubbornness is not strength and a wise man knows the difference. It was now apparent that this was not the case, with its weird twistings and turnings, to pursue in an election year.

When you looked at it, really looked at it, with the public basically sympathetic to the women and a capable man like Ferrara the department could ill afford to lose, let alone care to face as an adversary, the thing to do was evaluate. He respected his own pragmatism and could rationalize that the whole of it was a Rubicon he could bridge with salvaged dignity. Retreat is not necessarily defeat, and a clever man could actually turn it to advantage. A major objective had been achieved. Ferrara was not interested in his office.

Quietly, he crossed to the study, closed the door and went to the phone and dialed. Three rings and Ferrara answered. With feigned grace Jonas said that he'd reviewed the entire case. If Ferrara would reconsider, he would abandon it for lack of evidence. With an amenity to match, Ferrara declared he would be delighted to continue to serve under him.

After he hung up, Jonas, chagrined, thought the day will come when I'll hang that guinea bastard.

Gertrude was released. Charges against the "Wednesday Night Killers" were withdrawn. Sophie had a mastectomy.

Her left breast was removed. The right breast remained intact, found to be devoid of malignancy. The doctor warned that she should restrict activity, no undue body movement. She could adjust to lessened household chores for the healing period but dearly felt the loss of Mah-Jong play.

Max was visibly affected by her surgery. Other than two trips to the hospital when she gave birth, he had never known her to be ill. So much a Gibraltar fixture that when hospitalized, her absence created a vacuum. Father, son and daughter floundered in the kitchen. They were more crippled than she. Among them they could not boil water. Sophie returned to newfound appreciation, husband and siblings realizing they had always been in the presence of a taken-for-granted superior person, unselfishly catering to them. They vowed to change.

Max delayed an out-of-town sales trip and hovered. His resurgent tenderness was ludicrously touching. She insisted he leave, for they could ill afford to let the bills mount. She hoped that if there could never be a deep love between them, that at least a mutual respect, however belated, and born of crisis, would bind the rest of their days. Her son and daughter displayed a relentless affection; so much so, that she urged them out of the house. Despite the loss of a breast, she did not consider herself to be an invalid, and had rebounded from earlier abject self-pity to a reappraisal of her own worth.

More than anything else she wanted to get back to an evening of Mah-Jong to resume the loving banter of fellowship, so dear to her psyche. A month of Wednesdays had been forfeited since their last game. Had the sequence not been interrupted, the coming Wednesday would also be her turn to hostess. Despite the doctor's dictum, she insisted the women gather again. She could not participate, but a four-handed game would serve the greater need.

Freda, Elsa, Hannah and Gertrude were apprehensive. Collective affliction had sapped them. Each had endured trauma and pondered the degree it would influence the balance of their lives. Particularly as far as recapturing the spirit brought to an institutional evening which had entered its third decade of play, and maintaining enough zest to overcome the remembrance of murder. In the aftermath, they were not remorseful, only sad that it had to happen.

Unsure of what they actually felt about resuming the game, they nonetheless deferred to Sophie's insistence. She evoked the old saw: If you're thrown from a horse, get back on or you'll shy forever. Each, however, was adamant in relieving her of the hostess function and divided the usual snacks repast to furnish the evening.

Now they were grouped around the scarred bridge table, ringed by metal chairs, staring fixedly at the tiles heaped in its center. Then looked dumbly at each other but made no move to organize hands. Soft music emanated ritually from a nearby radio, but still no one stirred. As if the once-cherished tiles were now an alien mound of nettles.

Then, in silent anguish, Gertrude's eyes teared. She involuntarily shuddered, and despite effort not to yield, began to weep. Then Elsa followed and in contagion, Hannah, Sophie and Freda yielded, and the air was rent by their sobbing.

Gertrude brought herself under control after a cathartic trip to the john. "I don't know," she murmured. "I don't know."

"Oh, God damn!" Sophie exploded, about to cry again.

Freda withdrew a letter from her purse. "I have a letter," she announced. "From Rio de Janiero."

"I'm sorry," Gertrude said and blew her nose.

"All the way from Brazil," Freda added.

"Is it important?" Elsa finally acknowledged her.

"I think it is," Freda replied quietly. "It's addressed to me, but it's to all of us."

"Read it," said Hannah.

Freda turned off the radio and in the ensuing hush read the following:

> Mrs. Freda Friedkin
> 6553 Colgate Avenue
> Apartment 2B
> Los Angeles, California 90048
> U.S.A.

My dear Mrs. Friedkin:

My name is Leopold Waldis. You do not know me as such. But our lives have been inextricably linked. Through you I have fulfilled mine and I am eternally grateful. It is unlikely that I shall ever be able to repay you. It is another injustice added to what you have already borne.

Passion may lead me astray but I will try to be succinct.

In 1940 I am eight years old when I witness the death of my father by Wilhelm Gehbert. My father ran a medical clinic in Katowice, Poland. Gehbert was then his assistant. He joins Hermann Goring's Haupltruehand-stelle Ost-HTO, a confiscation agency to strip occupied territories. He used this to take over the clinic. My father resisted. Gehbert ordered his dog to attack him. Perhaps the dog was a more astute judge of character than was my father. Instead, he turns on his master, inflicting a deep shoulder wound. The dog is shot. My father is ordered to treat the wound. It is sad that he does not exacerbate it.

Humanity would have been better served had he been less competent and ethically scrupulous even to the end. Then he is shot. I try to beat Gehbert with my puny fists. I too expect to be shot. But Gehbert has another use for me. I am to be spared on condition that my mother submit to him. Before she is dispatched to a concentration camp she manages to have me smuggled out of the country. That beautiful woman is never heard from again. I emigrate to the United States, grow up, become educated and a citizen. After the war Gehbert is captured and tried. I am too young to embark upon the vengeance I swear will be mine after he serves a pitifully meagre sentence for his crimes. I do not marry for I cannot expect anyone to share the dark purpose to which I am dedicated. I live by my wits. I accumulate money in illicit enterprises to finance my mission. I am not ashamed of this. The means serve the end.

I contribute to Simon Wiesenthal. I am in Vienna when your inquiry on Wilhelm Gehbert crosses his desk. Weisenthal pursues SS Officers. Also Gehbert has served a sentence and Wiesenthal operates officially. He can do nothing.

For over twenty years I chase a ghost across half the world: Paris, Tel-Aviv, London, Oslo. Now he is in Los Angeles. I go there. I am now Martin Renner. I observe you. I observe him. Repeatedly you visit him and I am puzzled. But then I ascertain what you are attempting and are ill-equipped to do. Finally I will act. I break into his home. But you arrive unexpectedly. I hide in a position to see without being seen. You proceed with a knock-out drink. It is not effective and he struggles with you. It is all I can do not to intervene but I will if he overcomes you. But you manage to break free before I have to step in. Then you smother his face with a pillow. You leave thinking you have killed him. I check him. He appears dead but he is not. The evil are strong and they do not die easy. The softness of the couch absorbed your strength and your "mickey" was insufficient. I am denied the deliciousness I have savored in fantasy when I will finally confront him and which has sustained me. It has already taken too long and I cannot rule out that you may return or someone else will come. By now he revives but it is an easy matter to subdue him and press the pillow to his face. The job is done. I leave.

But capricious fate! A dog bite leads to Wilhelm Gehbert, a dog is Martin Renner's undoing. Barely out on the road a dog suddenly looms in my headlights. I swerve to avoid hitting it, topple into a ditch, break three ribs and am rendered unconscious. I am imprisoned within the car.

The rest is a matter of record. A young couple, seeking their dog, see the wreck and call the police. They arrive, revive me, pry me free, insist upon taking me to an emergency hospital. I comply so as not to arouse suspicion.

The couple tell the police of Gehbert. They stop to investigate. I am left alone in the vehicle. Despite pain and weakness I would run off but the Rosses hover. They are solicitous but impede and inadvertently keep me until the police return. They have discovered the body. I am transient and cannot satisfactorily explain my presence in the semi-isolated area at that time of night. Since the accident happened but a few hundred yards from the murder scene at the approximate time of the killing I am apprehended.

I am alone and I taste ashes. To the end it appears that Gehbert triumphs. I can do nothing but feign amnesia. Then God bless you, five lovely ladies intervene and I am released. Within twenty-four hours I am out of the country.

I could not write sooner. It was necessary to make certain that I arrive safely here and to complete arrangements to be reasonably secure and unextraditeable. I do not doubt that Gehbert has friends. As the hunted is hunted so is the hunter. I will be wary.

Earlier I said that I cannot repay you. I am wrong. I want you to know the truth and not carry the burden of guilt for even such as Wilhelm Gehbert. I have no such qualms. Also you must know this. If we do not hate for ourselves who will hate for us? There is justification for this: Leviticus 19-16: Exodus 2-11-12: Exodus 21-23-24 and the Talmud, Petrachot 58: "If one comes to slay you, rise up early and slay him first."

A new hope sustains me. After Armaggeddon we will meet with our loved ones in a better place.

You may, if you think it wise, show this letter to Dino Ferrara. He strikes me as a decent, understanding sort. I would like to believe that even in the United States there is a justice.

> Dahm Y'Israel Nokeam
> (The Blood of Israel
> will take Vengeance)
> LEOPOLD WALDIS

P.S. Gehbert's fly was open. I thought at least the last to see him would think he was a dirty old man who played with himself.

When Freda finished she creased the letter and returned it to her purse. For a long moment the women sat, unmoving and without comment. Then Elsa asked:

"Are you going to show it to Ferrara?"

"Yes," Freda said softly, with a signifigance beyond the content of the letter, the specific texture of her reply eluding them.

Hannah suddenly stretched both arms out and placed her hands on the tiles. Gertrude followed suit. Then Elsa, then Freda, finally Sophie with her right hand. For a long moment, they sat, moist-eyed, hands touching, and forming a circle. They looked from one to the other, silent, their hearts full.

Then the stillness in the room was broken as the tiles were mixed.

Temple Israel

Minneapolis, Minnesota

In Honor of the Bar Mitzvah of
JACOB BRYAN BLUMENTHAL

by

His Parents

November 18, 1978